THE VULTURE LORD
A ZOTHAR ATHRABIS NOVEL

Other great stories from Warhammer Age of Sigmar

• GOTREK GURNISSON •
Darius Hinks

GHOULSLAYER
GITSLAYER
SOULSLAYER

DOMINION
A novel by Darius Hinks

THE HOLLOW KING
A Cado Ezechiar novel by John French

THE ARKANAUT'S OATH
A Drekki Flynt novel by Guy Haley

HALLOWED GROUND
A novel by Richard Strachan

GROMBRINDAL: CHRONICLES OF THE WANDERER
An anthology by David Guymer

A DYNASTY OF MONSTERS
A novel by David Annandale

CURSED CITY
A novel by C L Werner

REALM-LORDS
A novel by Dale Lucas

THE END OF ENLIGHTENMENT
A novel by Richard Strachan

HARROWDEEP
Various authors
An anthology of novellas

BEASTGRAVE
A novel by C L Werner

THUNDERSTRIKE & OTHER STORIES
Various authors
An anthology of short stories

WARHAMMER
AGE OF SIGMAR

THE
VULTURE LORD
A ZOTHAR ATHRABIS NOVEL

RICHARD STRACHAN

BLACK LIBRARY

A BLACK LIBRARY PUBLICATION

First published in 2022.
This edition published in Great Britain in 2023 by
Black Library, Games Workshop Ltd., Willow Road,
Nottingham, NG7 2WS, UK.

Represented by: Games Workshop Limited – Irish branch,
Unit 3, Lower Liffey Street, Dublin 1,
D01 K199, Ireland.

10 9 8 7 6 5 4 3 2 1

Produced by Games Workshop in Nottingham.
Cover illustration by Dan Watson.

The Vulture Lord © Copyright Games Workshop Limited 2023. The Vulture Lord, GW, Games Workshop, Black Library, Warhammer, Warhammer Age of Sigmar, Stormcast Eternals, and all associated logos, illustrations, images, names, creatures, races, vehicles, locations, weapons, characters, and the distinctive likenesses thereof, are either ® or TM, and/or © Games Workshop Limited, variably registered around the world.
All Rights Reserved.

A CIP record for this book is available from the British Library.

ISBN 13: 978-1-80026-261-4

No part of this publication may be reproduced, stored in a retrieval system, or transmitted in any form or by any means, electronic, mechanical, photocopying, recording or otherwise, without the prior permission of the publishers.

This is a work of fiction. All the characters and events portrayed in this book are fictional, and any resemblance to real people or incidents is purely coincidental.

See Black Library on the internet at

blacklibrary.com

Find out more about Games Workshop
and the worlds of Warhammer at

games-workshop.com

Printed and bound by CPI Group (UK) Ltd, Croydon, CR0 4YY

The Mortal Realms have been despoiled. Ravaged by the followers of the Chaos Gods, they stand on the brink of utter destruction.

The fortress-cities of Sigmar are islands of light in a sea of darkness. Constantly besieged, their walls are assailed by maniacal hordes and monstrous beasts. The bones of good men are littered thick outside the gates. These bulwarks of Order are embattled within as well as without, for the lure of Chaos beguiles the citizens with promises of power.

Still the champions of Order fight on. At the break of dawn, the Crusader's Bell rings and a new expedition departs. Storm-forged knights march shoulder to shoulder with resolute militia, stoic duardin and slender aelves. Bedecked in the splendour of war, the Dawnbringer Crusades venture out to found civilisations anew. These grim pioneers take with them the fires of hope. Yet they go forth into a hellish wasteland.

Out in the wilds, hardy colonists restore order to a crumbling world. Haunted eyes scan the horizon for tyrannical reavers as they build upon the bones of ancient empires, eking out a meagre existence from cursed soil and ice-cold seas. By their valour, the fate of the Mortal Realms will be decided.

The ravening terrors that prey upon these settlers take a thousand forms. Cannibal barbarians and deranged murderers crawl from hidden lairs. Martial hosts clad in black steel march from skull-strewn castles. The savage hordes of Destruction batter the frontier towns until no stone stands atop another. In the dead of night come howling throngs of the undead, hungry to feast upon the living.

Against such foes, courage is the truest defence and the most effective weapon. It is something that Sigmar's chosen do not lack. But they are not always strong enough to prevail, and even in victory, each new battle saps their souls a little more.

This is the time of turmoil. This is the era of war.

This is the Age of Sigmar.

PROLOGUE

It feels like such a long time ago now, and yet it was only ten years. But these things are always relative; it is, after all, half my life.

In the days that followed I often wondered what would have happened if I had not led Selene to the cave; if I hadn't shown her what I knew to be true, and if I hadn't let that truth inspire me in the way it did. What would have become of her and what would have become of me? Would the events set in motion that day have flowed in a different and less obstructed line? Would we have lived normal and accustomed lives, going about our daily business, living and growing old and dying in the normal run of things? Would we have grown old together?

It is pointless to ask.

There are some who are content to let fate guide their actions and explain their failures, but I have never been one of them. Despite everything, even now, at some point I know I made a choice and everything that followed was a result of that choice. In the end, whether it was the right one or the wrong one is not for me to say. I only made it, and once a thing has happened, it could not have happened in any other way. Your only choice then is to accept the consequences no matter what they are. Long or short, that is the only real lesson life holds for anyone.

PART ONE

THE TOWER OF THE MOON

1

The cave was high above the bluff, an easy climb for me. It was one I had made a few times already, but Selene was wary of the fall. The sea cracked against the rocks below us. Specks of foam flew up like sparks from an anvil, bright in the morning sun. The sea beyond the shore was the sluggish grey water of Shyish, but up here against the Obsidian Coast it had a dark and sullen fury. The sky above was uncluttered, a soft and dazzling teal, and last night's moon was only a pale ghost against the wastes of blue. It was a warm day, heavy and humid. It is rare that it gets so warm in Shyish. I took it for a good omen.

'Don't be afraid,' I told her. I could see the shadowed mouth of the cave about thirty feet above us. 'Just put your hands and your feet where I do and take it slowly.'

I reached for a handhold on the smooth, black stone, the edge of the basalt cutting into my fingers, but not sharp enough to draw blood. The bundle was heavy against my back, the light tunic tight against my shoulders, but I swung out from the bluff onto the cliff face and scrabbled my feet to a lip of rock.

'Don't rely on the gravewort roots to take your weight,' I called to her. 'They won't. And whatever you do, don't look down.'

'I wouldn't dare...' she said.

I glanced back at her, standing there amongst the salt grass, the balmy wind catching at her flaxen hair. Selene was two months older than me. She would turn eleven at the end of the season, but already I had six inches on her and I was light and rangy with it. If the climb was going to be easy for me, then for her it would be more of a struggle. I knew she would rather have fallen to her death than admit defeat, though. Especially against me. We had been best friends our whole lives, but it's often the success of a friend that stings more than the triumph of an enemy.

She scraped her hair behind her ears, nodded once, lips compressed to a thin hard line. She had that look in her eye, wild and tenacious, that I recognised well. I knew she wouldn't back down now. As I climbed, turning my attention to the overlapping planes of basalt in front of me, the purple froth of the gravewort flowers bursting from the stone, I began to worry that I'd made a mistake and she wouldn't be able to manage. But then I could hear her breathing below me, slow and regular, grunting as she reached up and pulled. I could hear the pebbles trickling from the rock and falling towards the sea as she pressed her feet to each ledge. Together, inch by inch, we crawled up the face of the cliff in the sultry air, up to where the black mouth of the cave gaped open to admit us.

There was a shelf of salt grass in front of the cave, a shallow half circle no more than three feet across. We rested there for a moment while we caught our breath, examining the little scrapes and cuts we'd picked up from the sharp stone of the cliff face. The seawater bubbled and churned far beneath us. Beyond the bluff, about a mile distant where the coastline bulged out into the water, I could see the three high tiers of Lament, the levels of the city stacked one atop the other: the glaze of white marble, the dusty avenues of the lower quarter, the glint of light catching on the colonnades of the Regent's Palace at the very top. I could see the Tower of the Moon in the centre of the agora, black as pitch, seeming to absorb the light that streamed onto the city from the cloudless sky. High above the Tower, lifting from its crenellated brim like smuts and ashes rising from a column of smoke, I could see the vultures drift and settle. The reach of their black wings, like unfurled sails. The harsh sound of their morbid cries.

Beside me, Selene glanced warily at the mouth of the cave, shivering in the cool air. The entrance was no taller than we were and about ten feet across from side to side. Not a single beam of light reached into it.

'What if it's an entrance to the Underworlds?' she said. She sat and drew her knees to her chest, wrapping her arms around them, her face as drawn as if a tide of gheists was already pouring from the stone. 'The Underworlds are sacred – it's forbidden to trespass into them.'

'Well, it wasn't an entrance to the Underworlds yesterday,' I said, laughing. 'Or the week before that, so for now I think we're safe. Come on, I'll show you.'

I cuffed her shoulder, hauled myself to my feet. My legs still wobbled after the climb, and I stretched the knots from them.

'Aren't you worried about the race?' she said as I helped her up. 'There's only a couple of hours to go, you're going to be too tired to compete. Dardus is going to leave you in the dust.'

'No, he won't,' I said.

This wasn't bravado. I had run the race in my head a hundred times already. I *knew* I was going to win. I couldn't imagine it otherwise.

'Well, don't you seem sure of yourself,' Selene said, with a raised eyebrow. 'He's a lot bigger than you. And stronger.'

'But much slower,' I said. 'And he doesn't want it as much as me.'

Selene frowned. She glanced back over her shoulder and looked towards Lament. They would be gathering soon, I knew. Lining the agora with an honour guard of citizens, waiting for the king to cross the desert… I could see the gaudy flags and pennants raised against the propylon at the entrance to the city, the pavements strewn with black petals. My mother would be leaving our house soon, heading down towards the city gates with all the other elders of the council.

'And why do you want it so much?' she said.

I felt cold suddenly. The air in the cave reached out a clammy hand and caressed my shoulder, and it made me shiver. I looked into the darkness and felt for the bundle across my back, the rags and the flask of oil, the wooden stick. Quickly I unwrapped it all.

'Let me show you,' I said.

I lit the torch and led her into the darkness.

As soon as we were over the threshold the sound of the ocean fell away into a low and placid mutter. The shadows danced back from the torchlight and threw themselves against the walls, cringing from the flame. I could feel Selene following behind me, holding her breath. I could almost hear the hammer of her heart, and after a moment her cold fingers caught my bare arm and squeezed.

'It's all right,' I said. I took her hand. 'There's nothing to be frightened of.'

The cave contracted after a dozen feet into a narrower tunnel, only two or three feet wide. You could see where the walls had been knapped back, the ridged extrusions of calcite like the creases in a throat as it descended into the cliff. The stone glistened and sparkled with minerals, but it was perfectly dry.

'This is where they hid,' I said, my voice a whisper. 'When Zothar's armies came and punished the Jackal Kings. A thousand years ago, Selene, the last royal family took refuge in this cave. And then, at last, they all threw themselves down onto the rocks rather than surrender...'

Selene shuddered and I laughed, although there was little mirth in it.

'Your grandfather wouldn't approve, I bet,' I said, jabbing her softly with my elbow. 'Sigmarites always want to die in some heroic last stand, I've heard. Dying with a prayer on their lips...'

'He's not a Sigmarite!' Selene hissed.

'Yes, he is. Why else has he got that pendant around his neck?'

I'd seen it once when we were helping the old man clear his yard. He had his shirt off against the sun, the golden hammer hanging from a length of cord, nestling in the wiry grey hair on his chest. I hadn't said anything, although I was impressed at how bold he was for wearing it, and boldness always makes a grand impression on a young boy. He was the only one I knew who worshipped anyone other than King Zothar. I often wondered what Selene felt about Sigmar, although I could never muster the courage to ask. A person's gods are best left alone, I've always thought. The stuff of souls is a complicated business and we each look for meaning in different ways.

We came to the end of the tunnel, into a narrow chamber where the walls crested to a high point far above us. The air was warmer here, the cold edge smoothed away by a whispering breeze that curled in from some hidden aperture onto the headland. I raised the torch and showed Selene what I had found. I was rewarded with a gasp. Her eyes sparkled in the light of the torch, and I felt the touch of pride that it had been me who had shown it to her.

'I think this is what they did,' I said, 'before they threw themselves from the cliffs. They told the whole story. They wanted us to remember it. They didn't think that we'd ever forget.'

On the walls in front of us, sketched in black charcoal and ochre dust, was the story of King Zothar and the death of Neophron, his son. It was the tale of the vengeance Zothar had taken on Lament.

The drawings flowed like water, from scene to scene, starting from the left and ringing the cave in one unbroken line. I held the torch up high and traced them with my finger, spelling them out for Selene, although she knew the rudiments of the story as well as I did. Everyone in Lament knew the story; it was part of who we were. Here then was King Zothar crossing from the lost city of Theres, deep in the desert. Here were the Games of Lament, held every ten years, and here was Neophron competing for the honour of his city.

'Look,' I said. I pointed to the Tower of the Moon and the figure of Neophron falling to his death. 'This is where he dies... He would have won if his hand hadn't slipped at the top. He was almost there...'

My hand lingered on the fated boy, the sorrow so perfectly sketched onto his face by that forgotten artist a millennium ago. Falling, falling back into the empty air, hands grasping for the stone that had betrayed him, and the whole city standing below to watch...

Selene took the torch from my hand and crossed to the other side of the chamber, running her fingers underneath the images of Zothar's journey to the Underworlds, where he demanded of the powers that dwelled there that Neophron's soul be returned to him. Even now, after having gazed on it half a dozen times already, I couldn't look at this picture too closely. Whoever had drawn it all those centuries ago had been too awed or horrified to render it with any precision, and it stood there in front of King Zothar as no more than a blurred shadow, the suggestion of deep, malicious eyes, a skeletal grin. It was a figure from a nightmare. Once again, I wondered at King Zothar's courage, or the depths of his grief. Surely nothing less would have compelled him on such a journey.

'This is wonderful,' Selene said after a moment. She gazed up at the pictures, and it might just have been the torchlight, but I almost thought she had a tear in her eye. 'Who would have thought all this was here… You should tell someone. You should tell your mother, she can let the other elders know.'

'Why?' I said. I felt a surge of resentment at the suggestion. I didn't want anyone else to know, although at the time I couldn't have said why. I had shared it with Selene because she was my best friend, but if no one else had been bold enough to climb up here in all the years since then why should they deserve to know about it too? This was our secret, I thought. I looked again at the picture of Neophron, his doomed climb up the Tower of the Moon. As gestural as the drawing might have been, I still recognised something of myself in him. It was the one image my eye was drawn to most, no matter where in the cave I stood.

'It's our heritage,' Selene said. 'This is where it all started.'

She paused beside me, both of us gazing on the picture of Zothar's son. In the flames of the torch the image danced and flickered, and for a moment the light gave movement to the form. It was as if he was falling anew, tumbling endlessly from the Tower and plunging forever towards his death on the unforgiving flagstones below.

'I wonder why they did it?' she said. 'Why paint it on the walls like this, up here where no one would ever see it.'

'I don't know,' I said. 'Maybe…'

'What?'

'Maybe it wasn't for anyone else. Maybe it was just for them.'

'But then why do it if they were just going to die?'

She looked to the cave mouth at the other end of the narrow passage; the low half-moon of the open air, blazing in that darkness. I knew she was imagining the twin monarchs of Lament's last kings, their names now lost to all memory. Choosing to die, throwing themselves from the lip of the cave onto the rocks below.

'So they could leave something of themselves behind,' I said. 'A reason, an explanation.'

The oily rags dripped and burned, the flames guttering around them. The pictures on the cave walls were dropping back into the shadows.

'Who were they, do you think? The Jackal Kings?' she asked.

'Nobody knows,' I told her. 'Tyrants, monsters… their names are gone forever. King Zothar saw to that.'

'We should be getting back,' Selene said after a moment. 'You don't want to be late, or they'll just start without you.'

'I won't be.'

She took my hand suddenly and when I looked at her I saw that she had been crying. Her eyes were red and tears had tracked a gleaming line down her cheeks.

'Don't win,' she whispered. 'Don't do your best, please, Lycus.'

'I have to,' I told her. I looked away; embarrassed or ashamed, I couldn't say. I thought of Neophron falling from the Tower. That wouldn't be me. I would reach the top, and I would win. I *knew* it. 'Someone has to, and it may as well be me.'

She nodded, turned away, raised the back of her wrist to her eyes and wiped them dry. When she turned back, she gave me a faint smile, although it was the kind of smile a mother might give to a sick child; commiserating and sympathetic, and masking her true fear.

'Come on then,' I said, heading back into the narrow passage. I tried to make my voice sound cheerful and unconcerned. 'This will be a day to remember, won't it? The day Lycus won the Games!'

2

There is something chastening about the sick, Astraea thought, as she carried away the thin gruel of his vomit. They lie on the very edge of mortality, just a breath away from being no more than bones and memories. A sack of faltering skin and the spirit trapped inside it...

She passed through the narrow doorway that led into the sun-struck rectangle of the back yard and tipped the bowl into the drain. There was a bucket of water by the pump in the corner of the yard, a wooden ladle beside it. She cleaned out the bowl and stood there on the step for a moment, looking out over the baked, whitewashed clay of the wall towards the lower tiers of the city. She could see the flags hanging from the windows above the Grand Avenue, the petals scattered on the roads, the hanging baskets in the agora. A breath of sea-wind drew in from the coast and lifted the fringes of the pennants. If she squinted, she could almost see the plumes of purple dust rising from the desert a dozen miles away. The sunlight fell like a hammer on Lament, stoking a cool, clear glow from the white marble of the city. Mansions, manses and the pediments of humbler dwellings all shone under the sun's attention.

A faint haze of dust arose from the streets as the people began to gather. Astraea could see crowds forming on the other side of the plaza, where the dais had been raised. Everywhere, the rising twist of smoke from cook fires and ovens, the smell in the air of baking bread and roasted meat, of herbs and spices saved over the long decade for just this day. A ring of spectators surrounded the Tower of the Moon on the eastern side of the agora, the tall finger of black stone pointing crookedly at the azure sky. The vultures lit and settled on it, planing smoothly into the air, and wheeling around to take roost again. She could hear them calling, their grumbling croak, almost as if they knew…

A sliver of ice passed through her. It was nearly time.

She could hear Cleon coughing in his room behind her, on the cooler side of the manse. Astraea knocked the drops of water from the bowl against the doorframe, watched them spatter on the parched ground and instantly fade. It would be even hotter by noon. Who had ever known a hotter day than this in Shyish? It was unprecedented.

Cleon, her husband, seemed even more diminished than when she'd left him a few moments before. He lay there on the bed under a thin cotton sheet, as narrow and brittle as a bundle of sticks. She could see the outline of his skull, the cheeks sunken, the hollows of his eyes as dark as a hole in the ground. His skin was like wax, grey and glassy, his hands as twisted as tree roots. The dry-lung was heavy in him. His mouth was open as he gasped for air and she could see his black, receding gums. The room was wide and uncluttered, fresh with the scent of the sea from its coast-facing window, but still it stank with the smell of his breath. There would be no shifting the disease, nothing that pharmacy or prayer could accomplish. Only time would ease him of his suffering now.

Astraea crossed the room and opened the window another inch. She replaced the bowl by his bedside and leaned in to kiss his burning forehead. His hair was lank and the pillow was damp beneath him.

'Kalista will be in later to look in on you,' she said. 'I have to go, it's almost time...'

A spasm of pain shot through him, fastening his eyes. He nodded, sucked in a sip of air. When the pain had passed, he opened his eyes and stared up at her.

'I wish I could see it,' he wheezed. 'See the king again and his honour guard... See Lycus running in the Contest...'

She squeezed his hand. 'I'll tell you all about it, I promise,' she whispered. She smoothed his hair back, felt the tears prickle against her eyes. 'You'll be proud of our son, I know it.'

Cleon tried to laugh, but it broke apart into a hacking cough. Quickly Astraea brought the bowl to his chin and held it there as he dribbled up a string of bloody spit. There was a film of grease against his skin. She wanted to scream, wanted to dash the bowl to pieces against the marble floor. Wanted to take Cleon's throat between her hands and choke the life away, for all that she loved him. More than anything, she wanted to take Lycus and run, run for as long as their legs could bear them, until the desert had hidden them both away. It was an honour, she knew, the greatest Lament could offer.

As an elder of the city her heart would burst with pride to see him win the race. As a mother, she knew it would kill her.

She brought Cleon's hand to her mouth and kissed it.

'I'll tell you everything,' she said, 'when I get back.'

'Duty calls...' Cleon smiled.

'Always. Now rest, my darling.' She offered him the consoling lie. 'Rest and get better.'

She took her diadem wreath from the stand in the hall and passed into the baking streets, affixing it to her lacquered hair with a length of purple ribbon. The wreath, with its woven strands of acacia and willow, its garland of grave-beams and Hysh-flowers, felt heavy on her crown. She was dressed in a peplos of banded purple silk, a russet cloak thrown over one shoulder, the other bare. Her sandalled feet scuffed lightly on the marble pavement. As an elder of Lament, the ordinary citizens that she passed paid her respectful obeisance. Astraea inclined her head at each in turn, acknowledging the formalities even as she felt the dread spike and flutter in her stomach. She moved onto the thoroughfare that curved down towards the agora, passing from the cooler streets in the higher tier of the city, with their lines of shading trees, their high stone walls and sheltered squares. She glanced back over her shoulder. At the very apex of the city, high above her, she could see the Regent's Palace; a long, rectilinear precinct ringed by the high pillars of a gleaming portico, the entablatures carved with scenes from Lament's ancient and near-forgotten past. The palace roof was a high, wide dome of shining marble, gilded at its crown with panels of tarnished gold. It was visible from every part of the city, from miles outside it, the shining symbol of old Lament's power and influence.

It had once been the court of the Jackal Kings, she knew, but no kings had lived there now for a thousand years. The palace was empty, waiting for the regent to take up his position. Waiting for Neophron to come again, and to reign in King Zothar's stead…

The crowds began to thicken the closer she came to the agora, the open square at the centre of the city with its decorative ponds and marble benches, the rectangles of sculpted grass, the twisted beams of its coppiced woe trees. People jostled her as they passed, grown men and women hurrying to get a good position in front of the dais that had been set up against the plaza's northern side. Astraea's hands plucked nervously at each other as she walked. She scanned the crowds for a sight of Lycus' black hair, his rangy dart and swagger, but she couldn't see him. There were other children there, some climbing the woe trees to get a better look, the older youths betting with limpet shells and marbles on the outcome of the Contest. She couldn't see the boys and girls who would be running in the race, but she knew they were sequestered until the very last moment. Twenty of them, hidden in the lower chamber of the Tower of the Moon until King Zothar had arrived to see them begin. The heats had been running all week, and each day brought a new dread as Lycus had fought his way to the top. But what could she say? The honour of the family, the honour of Lament, was stronger than a mother's love.

She glanced to the northern gates at the other end of the Grand Avenue, which stretched in a straight line from Antigonas Road on the southern flank of the marketplace to the edge of the city. The avenue was bordered on each side by the elegant and lucid formality of Lament's public buildings – libraries and temples, council halls and granaries. The fluted columns were pale as milk and the white stone roofs beat back the sun. Each building was bedecked in flags and garlands, and the black petals were thick on the ground beneath them. She could see the risen dust from the king's procession breaking like a thundercloud in the desert. If she concentrated, she could almost hear the jangling clatter of their horses and weapons. They could only be a mile distant now.

She stood there and wrung her hands. The light was as hard as steel, unrelenting. What was this heat, this light? As if the city must be skewered by it, on this day of all days.

'Not long now then,' a voice said beside her. She turned to see

Haephastin, another elder on the council, writhing as he adjusted his formal gown. He scratched his head underneath the wreath and wiped the sweat from his brow. He was an older man, in his forties, burly and squat. His face was thick with the ease of comfortable living, but when he turned to Astraea, she could see the fear behind the sparkle in his brown eyes. 'Our lord and master arrives, and the Decennial Games begin once more… I confess, I can barely remember the last one, I had so much to drink that day. Damn this gown!' he said. He stretched his arm and twisted.

Astraea smiled. 'You look more like a sack of thorn-pears than ever, Haephastin.'

'This is not my natural habitat,' he growled. He adjusted the wreath as it slipped down his forehead. 'I enjoy my garden, my wines and my library. The formalities of the council can be delightful under normal circumstances, but this…'

'This is not a normal circumstance,' Astraea said.

'Indeed not.'

Haephastin glanced over his shoulder and took her elbow as he led her towards the dais. He spoke in low tones as they crossed the marble square, gently pressing their way through the bodies. She could see the other elders of the council assembling on the dais already, clustering around the two gilded thrones that had been erected in the centre of it: Melissta with her streaming auburn hair; Kaitellin leaning on his cane and stroking the fine strands of his wispy white beard. Baeothis strutted from one end to the other, his arms folded and his clean-shaven jaw thrust out, trying to give the impression of command, but Astraea knew he would be as nervous as the rest of them. Only Kaitellin remained of the council from the last Games, his popularity with the Failed guaranteeing him support.

'Ten years always seems an age away the day after, but before you know it, here it comes round again,' Haephastin said. 'We must gird ourselves, Astraea.' He looked at her keenly. 'No matter what happens.'

'I know,' she said. 'I am prepared.'

'Good, good,' he said. 'King Zothar protects...'

'King Zothar protects.'

There were servants passing through the crowds bearing trays of cool beer, jugs of wine, freshly squeezed thorn-pear juice. Haephastin swerved and snatched up a glass in one easy motion, knocking it back and smacking his lips.

'It's just a shame Cleon can't be here to see it all,' he said. 'How is he anyway? Dry-lung, I know, can be...'

'He is doing as well as can be expected,' Astraea said. She thought of her husband, burning on his cot, the bones of him thrusting through the skin, the stinking, fibrous matter he coughed up every morning. 'He is as comfortable as he can be.'

'Well, you have my sympathies, and my prayers,' Haephastin said. He threw the glass aside and it shattered on the flagstones. 'Zothar have mercy, maybe he will recover.'

'Perhaps,' she said. 'Perhaps...'

They had reached the dais and Haephastin offered her his hand as he took the wooden steps onto the stage. She could hear the sound of Zothar's army clearly now, the tread of his soldiers, the regular beat of his cavalry. A murmur threaded through the crowd, a ripple of electricity like a lightning-flash. Astraea glanced around – and then suddenly she could see her son, Lycus, sprinting through the crowds, weaving and dodging, his little friend Selene at his side as he headed for the Tower.

'Lycus!' she cried. She waved Haephastin onto the dais ahead of her and hurried over to the children. She grabbed her son's shoulders, turned him to her. 'Where on earth have you been, you should have been with the others an hour ago!'

He grinned at her, his chest heaving, green eyes flashing in the bright sunlight. His tunic was dark with sweat, and his black hair was wringing wet. There were scratches on his bare arms and legs, a streak of dirt on his face. Astraea licked her thumb and wiped it away as Lycus writhed with shame.

'Mother!' he wailed. 'Get off, I'm not a child!'

Selene laughed, but she looked chastened at Astraea's scowl.

'Forgive me, elder,' the girl said. She looked at her feet. 'It was my fault. I didn't realise the time. Go, Lycus, I'll watch from the highest tree I can find!'

Selene scurried off, disappearing into the press of bodies swarming across the square. Lycus watched her go, and with her seemed to go a touch of his bravado. He looked like a boy again. A scared little boy.

Astraea crouched beside him and hugged him close. The moment fluttered above her, her dread taking flight on black wings, as black as the vultures that lazily soared from the Tower. She felt the heat of his body beside her, this body she had brought into being and nurtured all the years of his young life. Her throat was thick, and she could not trust her voice.

'It's all right, Mother,' he said quietly. 'I'm going to win, I know it.'

'Don't!' she whispered. She held him at arm's length, her eyes boring into his. She saw him through a film of tears. 'Please, Lycus, I'm begging you. You know how ill your father is, it will kill him, it'll… There will be no shame in coming last…'

'Yes, there will!' he said fiercely. 'To be one of the Failed will bring shame on us all! Father will be proud of me, and so will you. So will everyone.'

He slipped away and ran towards the Tower, looking back at her with something like regret. *He looks so young*, she thought. *He is just a child.*

There was a blare of trumpets near the gates, a clash of drums and a ragged gasp that moved like a wave across the crowd. The hammering tread of marching troops, the jangle of spurs and sheathed swords. Astraea stood and wiped her eyes dry. She straightened her gown, adjusted the spread of her cloak and took the stairs up onto the dais. She stood with Haephastin and the others, beside the empty thrones.

'Here we go…' Haephastin whispered at her side.

'Zothar watch over us,' Melissta breathed. She looked straight ahead. Astraea could see her trembling.

'For the honour of Lament,' Baeothis said. He stood at attention, his arms rigid at his sides, his shoulders back.

Astraea thought she was going to be sick. Fear thumped in her stomach, surging up into her throat. It prickled against her skin. She remembered the last Games, ten years ago, and the Games before that. Like a dream, they stretched out before her. For a thousand years, Lament had been giving its sons and daughters to the Games.

The crowd around the dais fell back, a space opening between them like a parted sea. Drums beat discordantly, the players faltering in their rhythm. There was a cry from somewhere over on the avenue – involuntary, terrified. Astraea looked towards the Tower of the Moon far off on her left, soaring there at the corner of the marketplace a hundred yards away. The vultures climbed, spiralling, agitated, from its crown. The wind shifted and she could smell the rotting flesh. Then it shifted again, and she could smell the deep desert – old bones, thorny scrub, the dry and everlasting sands. The Lord of Athrabis had arrived. The Lord of Lament.

Kaitellin stepped forward and spoke into the silence as the Bonereapers crossed the agora. Though an old man now, his voice still carried far across the crowd.

'All hail!' he cried. 'Hail, King Zothar!'

He rode at the head of his honour guard, two columns of spearmen five abreast and a hundred long, and between them cantered a troop of cavalry on barded steeds. On either side of him rode his flag-bearers, their black pennants marked with the rune of Athrabis, his city kingdom in the heart of the desert and far from the Obsidian Coast.

King Zothar himself was mounted on a steed that was near eighteen hands high. It had the same shape as a warhorse, the same proud bearing, the sense of speed and power, but its skeletal frame was a mixture of bone amalgamated from any number of different creatures. It had two barbed tusks and the flaring eye sockets made it look as if the skull had come from some monstrous, predatory bird. There were human skulls packed and clustered in the hollow spaces between its ribs and thighs. Its breast was shielded by overlapping plates of dark nadirite, at the centre of which was a red jewel that fumed with a molten glow.

The king's eyes glared yellow beneath the bone crest of his helmet, his skeletal face stark and forbidding, the colour of old ivory. A cloak of rich, arterial red hung from his pauldrons. His armour seemed to shine with a dull, purple iridescence and a great curved scimitar was sheathed at his hip. Majesty and threat radiated from him. Astraea had to clutch her hands together to stop them from shaking.

Behind him on his left strode his Soulmason, an ancient skeletal figure wearing a tall, conical headdress encrusted with dark jewels. He was sitting cross-legged, hunched over on a strange walking throne that was nearly as tall as King Zothar's steed. Its birdlike, clawed feet picked carefully across the marble flagstones. On the right of the king rode another figure; a young man who wore the same armour and crested helm as his liege, but who was entirely human.

Astraea met this young man's pale blue eyes as the procession drew near. He gave her a thin, dreamlike smile, his expression glazed and distant, as if he were watching all this through a haze of smoke. She thought at first that he was amused by the procession, by the gathered crowds who had come out to greet the Bonereapers, but then she could see the tightness in his jaw, the tension in his neck. He was terrified.

She found that she could not remember his name, not his real name. She recalled him at the Contest ten years ago, when the Games had last been run. Now here he was, returned to Lament, at the very end of his journey. He had been Neophron for a decade, since he was a boy. Soon, he would need that name no more.

King Zothar held up his skeletal hand and the two columns of Ossiarch troops came to a crunching halt. They presented arms, locking their spears to their shoulders, their gleaming shields held at their sides. One column marched quickly across the frontage of the dais and set up position on the far side, the other mirroring them on the western edge: two peerless blocks of infantry at motionless attention. The king's cavalry, a troop of perhaps twenty riders, dismounted and led their steeds towards the rear of the plaza.

The walking throne slowly knelt and the Soulmason shuffled from the seat, stretching and supporting himself on his staff. At the tip of the staff was a glowing green jewel, smouldering with a sickly inner light. A ragged purple cloak fell to the bones of his feet. He looked over at the dais, a few yards away, at the gathered elders standing there not daring to meet his eye. Astraea felt the Soulmason's gaze slither over her, and it was broken only when King Zothar slipped from the saddle and approached. Astraea risked a glimpse at him. He clacked slowly across the marble flagstones towards the dais, one hand resting on the pommel of his scimitar. The Soulmason followed in his wake, the young man sliding from his skeletal steed and following him, still with that detached expression on his face.

As the king approached, Astraea could see that his cheekbone was cracked and flaking, the line of his radius and ulna on his left arm strangely fused. He was at least a foot taller even than Baeothis, broad and powerful, and the yellow eyes burned in their sockets like blazing suns. His gaze bored into each of them in turn. Astraea found that she could not look away. She kept thinking that the skull-like visage was just a mourning mask, such as any of the bereaved would wear in Lament; that it could be plucked away, and a human face would look back at her from beneath it. But no; it was what it was. It was the skull of a dead man, and it grinned without mirth.

There was absolute silence, across the entire city. No one dared speak. All stood in reverent quiet, awed to be part of this moment. A god was walking amongst them.

Slowly Zothar mounted the stairs to the stage. Astraea lowered her eyes. She could smell him, the dusty scent of old libraries and dead wood, the faint spice of the desert wind. She could feel the slats of wood bend beneath his weight. He passed by each of the elders in turn, pausing for a moment and staring at them as if trying to bring their names back to mind.

Melissta collapsed, she was so overcome. She flung herself at his feet and wailed, the great tresses of her auburn hair spilling across the dais like rusty blood. Baeothis helped her up, but Astraea could see that he was equally moved. His hands shook, and his jaw was slack. He looked like an ox dragged into the slaughterhouse, dazed even before the terminal blow.

King Zothar took the gilded throne. The young man, Neophron, sat in the smaller throne beside him. The Soulmason stood leaning on his staff behind them both.

Kaitellin shuffled over and cleared his throat.

'Your grace,' he quavered. 'The honour done to us today is–'

'Kaitellin, is it not?'

The king's voice was like the grinding of the stones on the shore, like the cold wind coursing the midnight sands. He stared at the assembled crowd, running his gaze from side to side until it came to rest on the black spire of the Tower.

'Yes, my liege,' Kaitellin said.

He shuffled closer. Zothar leant forwards in the throne.

'Bring them out,' he said.

3

Beams of light fell through the cracks in the stone above us, striking the dry straw that covered the floor. You could see motes of dust rising and falling in them, glinting like silver and gold. They didn't seem to move at an ordinary speed, drifting as if they were outside time and all its conditions. I felt suspended in that light, poised on the edge of motion, waiting for a breath of air to move me.

Other than those beams of light, it was dark in the chamber. It was a circular space at the bottom of the Tower, about twenty feet across. A spiral staircase curled around the inner walls, leading up to the first floor thirty feet above. There were ten floors altogether in the Tower of the Moon and then the open platforms at the top. Three hundred feet, I calculated. Give or take. And at the end of the Contest, I would have to climb every one of them from the outside.

There were twenty of us waiting in the chamber. Ten boys and ten girls, all who had won through the heats over the last week.

Sprinting, the long jump, boxing, athletics, swimming. Each of us had won something or had excelled enough to be put forward to the next round. Now here we all were, breathing raggedly in the dusky light, listening to the sounds of the crowds outside, to the marching tread of King Zothar's troops as the voices fell silent and the Ossiarch Bonereapers came. You could feel the silence like a weather front, sultry and dark, moving swiftly from the horizon until it smothered you.

I looked up at the ceiling above us, watching the way the light cut through from the upper windows, aslant. Like white fire, fuming with dust.

'Can you smell it?' Dardus said beside me. He had wrapped his arms around his chest. Despite the heat he was shivering. He tried to disguise it by shifting his weight from foot to foot, as if he were limbering up for the race. He was looking up too.

'Yes,' I said. 'I can smell it.'

The faint, sweet scent that crept into your lungs and lodged there, immovable. Sickly, rank, the smell of the dead. The bones from the last twelve months would have been collected already for the tithe, but there would still be bodies up there not yet picked clean. Sky buried, laid out for the vultures three hundred feet above us. The Tower was tall enough so that, outside in the city, the smell rarely reached you. Sometimes though, when the wind changed, or when the day was still enough and the sun was hot enough, the smell trickled down into the streets. Sometimes, the vultures let loose a scrap of flesh and it spilled down into the marketplace. Then one of the priests would emerge from the Tower and hurriedly pick it up, secreting it in his leather bag and taking it all the way back up to the top again. Only the priests were allowed onto the platform, where the bodies were laid out and the bones were gathered. I had tried to imagine what it looked like many times, with the corpses rotting in the sun and the vultures scavenging them. I was glad that I was not a priest.

Dardus stood a head taller than me, and he was nearly twice as wide. He was much stronger than me and quicker than he looked too. He had a fringe of blonde hair falling forward into his bright blue eyes, which he shifted with a flick of his head. Although we were the same age, nearly eleven, you could already see the man in him; tough and brawny, and no doubt even quicker to throw his weight around than he was now. Nonetheless, we were friends. He was perhaps more Selene's friend than mine, but we had shared the same tutor in the district school, and although his family was lower than mine, he still lived on the second tier. There was old wealth in his family, on his mother's side, from one of the bonded merchant families, but as far as I knew that money was nearly spent.

I would have to beat Dardus to win the Contest, which I was sure I could do, but I tried not to think about what me winning would mean for him. He would become one of the Failed. Afterwards, only the lower tier of the city would be open to him. He would spend the rest of his life with no voting rights, no rights for anything but the most menial employment. That was the risk we all took, getting this far. That and death. Such was the Contest.

'So,' he said to me now, as the hush descended outside. 'You still think you're in with a chance at this?'

He knocked me lightly with his elbow and grinned. I staggered back, tried to make the jab seem more powerful than it actually was. The grin looked more like a grimace, as if he were going to vomit.

'Maybe,' I said. 'I did well in the swimming and the long jump. Sprinting too.'

'Sprinting means nothing,' Dardus scorned. 'This is a distance race, never forget it. Stamina's what counts. And will. The will to go on.'

I looked up again, tried to picture the Tower from the outside.

'And climbing,' I said. 'Don't forget climbing.'

One of the other boys, Pelleus his name was, turned and spewed into the straw. I was surprised; he was older than us, nearly sixteen. Dardus and I were the youngest here, the rest were nearly men and women. Age doesn't matter in the Games though, only ability. A child had as much chance as a youth, although anyone over eighteen was not eligible. Again, such was the Contest.

Pelleus was comforted by his friend Ellena, a willowy girl who kept her hair cropped close, and who I had seen make a leap of nearly fifteen feet in the long jump the day before. He slapped her hand away and turned on us, scowling.

'Just the damn thorn-pears I ate earlier,' he muttered. 'Should have stuck to goat's milk.'

'It's not too late to fall out,' Dardus said. He even sounded sincere. Pelleus was tall and strong, taller than Dardus certainly, and already you could see the beard growing in on his jaw. And yet it did look like he wanted to drop out. His face was pale, his lips drawn and bloodless. To forfeit was unthinkable at this stage. You would lose everything. Better to die than lose, so the saying went. Honour was all, and we took our honour very seriously indeed.

'Don't play smart with me, boy!' Pelleus snarled. 'They shouldn't let children run anyway, you don't know what you're getting into.' He jabbed a finger at me. 'I bet you don't even remember the last Games.'

'I'm not a child,' I said. 'I'm nearly eleven.' This drew a hollow laugh from the others.

'A babe in arms,' Ellena snorted.

'And don't think just because your mother is an elder that you get any special treatment,' Pelleus warned me. He drew the belt of his tunic tight, stooped to adjust the strap of his sandals. I looked down at my own bare feet, dusty in the straw. 'All are equal in the Contest, remember that.'

'And all are equal who fail,' I said.

Pelleus snarled and made to seize me, but then we heard the quavering wail of Kaitellin as he welcomed the king. The drums stopped and not a breath of air was heard. All of us fell silent at once, frozen there in the humid dark, with the smell of death filtering down to us from the top of the Tower. Dardus met my eye and swallowed. I could smell the sour stink of Pelleus' vomit, and it made me want to spew myself.

For a moment, for just the barest moment of time, I wondered what I had done.

There was the tread of feet, the shuffle of leather sandals outside the ironoak door. Then it was swung wide open, and the priest said: 'It's time.'

How to explain the Contest to those who have never taken part in it and who never will?

The Games themselves, that week of athleticism, triumph, and failure, are one thing. The whole city gathers to watch those who have put their name forward, convinced they can beat their peers and gain a place in the final twenty. It is a carnival, a theatre, a week that is partly a celebration and partly the most solemn religious festival. Prayers are given up to King Zothar, and as the bones of the dead are gathered for the tithe the grieving relatives come out in their mourning dress to give thanks that their loved ones are being gifted to him. The Games are the city at its best, when Lament's cool, white marble streets become a gaudier spread of flowers and decoration, and the people allow themselves a more reckless appreciation of life. The three tiers of the city are united in celebration.

The Contest is different though. It is what the Games have led towards – it is what the last decade has led towards, and there is no greater or more sacred moment in Lament's calendar.

He or she who wins the Contest becomes more than just the city's champion. They become the prince of Athrabis. They become King Zothar's son, filled with the restless soul of long-dead Neophron.

The route of the race led through the agora and down the Grand Avenue to the city gate, and then looped around the walls of Lament into the craggy hills behind it. There were goat tracks choked with thorn-pear trees, treacherous drops to either side into the sharp gullies and ravines that crossed the hills, and the threat of boulders haring down from the higher slopes to crush your body into paste. There were bone-gryphs in those hills, it was said… And yet this wasn't the most dangerous part of the route. After leaving the hills, the runners had to cross the short plain to the curve of the Obsidian Coast and then swim a mile of open water to the promontory where Lament's fishermen moored their boats. Flense-fish swam those waters, and the sluggish tide hid a deadly undertow. From the promontory, any runners who still survived had to make their way back to the city for the most difficult part of the challenge: the Tower of the Moon, the smooth black stone, and the long climb to the top.

'You could still drop out,' Dardus whispered to me as we stretched and calmed our minds on the starting line. 'I mean… you're the youngest here.'

I could see that he meant it, that he was not just trying to dismiss a rival from the race. His face was flushed. Sweat was gathering on his upper lip. I turned and saw Pelleus twisting a crack from his neck, hooking his sandalled feet behind his back, pulling the muscles of his thighs taut. The others all prepared in their own way. I saw Cantus mouthing a silent prayer, wily Daeana with her scarred face gazing at the ghost of the moon high above the Tower, young Tethes looking frantically for his mother.

Twenty of us. How many would be left, I wondered, at the end?

'*You* could, you mean,' I said to Dardus. I tried to smile. 'Why would I drop out and shame my family? I'm going to win.'

I had seen it, I wanted to say. In the caves above the bluff, I had seen myself in Neophron's face, climbing the Tower and reaching the very top. I would not fall.

Something flashed across Dardus' face then. It was not anger or hatred, but something almost like disgust. He was offended that I thought I could win. That I thought he could ever lose.

'We'll see,' he said. He set his jaw and crouched to the starting line. 'I'll be sure to toss you a coin when you're cleaning out the latrines in the lower tier...'

For the first time I looked over at the dais, fifty yards away from us on the right-hand side. The raised platform, the thrones, my mother standing there with the other elders. I couldn't see her face. I saw Neophron sitting there on the smaller throne, his hands gripping the armrests, his face unreadable beneath the flared bones of his helmet. His armour shone like jet, smoky and severe in the harsh sunlight. What did he remember of this day, a decade ago? What had he felt as he prepared to run?

I looked at the king and shuddered. The drums began to beat. I set myself to the line that had been painted across the marble flagstones and I tried to concentrate. The drums rattled and snapped, building to a mad crescendo, crashing out into silence – and then, clear as a bell, Kaitellin called for us to start.

As soon as I started running, my mind felt clear. All the fears and anxieties fell away. I was just a body in motion, cleaving through the warm air and the cluttered streets. The agora disappeared behind me, and I barely heard the crying of the crowd. The Grand Avenue slipped by and was soon a memory, and then I was out in the open air beyond the city, through the gates into the grey scrubland on the edge of the desert, with the wide sky like a starched sheet above me.

My bare feet kicked up plumes of dust as I settled into an easy rhythm. For the first hour I thought of nothing but the feel of the ground underfoot, the pressure of the breeze as it flowed around me. I kept the high city walls on my left, the sloped battlements of white stone, each crenellation packed with the people who had scrambled up to watch us run. I ignored the others, didn't care that Dardus and Pelleus were so far ahead of me.

I was in the centre of the pack as it spread out and began the long hike into the looming hills, the jagged range of black volcanic stone. I scrambled up the steep goat tracks, grasped at the roots of the thorny scrub that overspilled onto the paths to pull myself higher. The air began to clear, and a cool breeze lanced in from the distant sea. I glanced back and saw Lament laid out before me on the edge of the plain, at the feet of the tumbling hills. I felt I was seeing it in the round for the first time. Suddenly, it seemed so small. A grid of pale streets, the two higher tiers rising one above the other, the Regent's Palace at the very top, with its sloped marble roof and elegant portico, its empty, ornamental grounds. Beyond it, the Obsidian Coast was bare of life. A few fishing huts, a road that led to unknown distant prospects in the north. The endless spread of the desert to the west, the grey sands tinged purple and masked by a rising haze of dust, and then the sea to the east – boundless, eternal, flowing to the very edge of the realm…

From up in the hills, for the first time, I had a sense of the world as something bigger than I had ever realised. Our great city was merely a small corner of a vaster whole.

Ellena was the first to die. She slipped on the loose shale as the goat track began its perilous descent, falling heavily to the cusp of the escarpment and throwing out a hand that met nothing but the open air. I saw her drop over the edge as I scurried down the path behind her, watched with numb detachment as her head cracked against the rocks a hundred feet down and split apart. Pelleus looked back once and hurried on. He did not stop and neither did I.

Later, I heard that two stragglers at the back were taken by the bone-gryphs as they reached the peak of the hills, where the scrub is thickest and provides the best cover. Whatever truly happened to them, they never left the hillside, and they were never seen again.

I ran on, leaving the hills behind me, cutting still with the same easy pace across the dun grassland that led to the coast. I could feel the salt spray on my face, fresh and invigorating. Pelleus was still in front, Dardus not far behind him, two or three others whose names I didn't know. Then, a few strides ahead of me, I saw Tethes buckle and collapse, his face grey. He coughed blood, fell onto his back, his chest heaving. I skipped lightly over him and carried on, risking a quick glance back to see where the others were. Daeana was putting on speed about twenty yards back, her long legs hacking the dry grass, the declining hills behind her like an eruption of frozen smoke. She squinted in the sunlight, a ragged snarl on her face. She was peaking too early, I thought. I was content to let her pass me as we headed for the shore, the sloughing sea beyond it.

I say 'content', as if these were feelings I could have articulated. In truth, I couldn't form a coherent thought as I ran. I had no strategy, no tactics, other than a simple intuition. I knew how to run this race, that was all. It was as if I had run it before.

The shoreline at the first promontory came up to meet us, a narrow shelf plunging into the bucking sea. The water was grey and greasy, heaving back and forth and sending up pillars of foam where it slopped against the rocks. Off to the left, the shore curved back into a wide natural bay, before sloping out again into the second promontory a mile away. On a calm day you could swim this in thirty minutes, but when the sea was this wild it was going to take far longer – if, indeed, you could make it at all.

Pelleus and Dardus dived in without pause, cutting into the water like knives. I saw Daeana plunge in feet first and come up screaming at the cold, her face a mask of shock. An older youth – Kaston, I think his name was – came tearing up behind me and threw himself into the water like a boulder dropped from a mountain top, his arms clutched around his knees. The waves surged over him, and I didn't see him come up. By then it was too late for me to care because the water was on me too. I waded in, felt the pebbled black beach suddenly fall away beneath my feet – and then I was deep in the freezing mouth of the ocean and all the breath had been plucked from my lungs.

I struck out, my mind lost in a fog of cold. Arm over arm, head to the side, gasping in air. The waves pulled and pushed me, flinging me sometimes far out towards the open water and sometimes hard up against the rocks at the shore. I would push myself away, try to move with the tide, always feeling for the dread seduction of the undertow beneath me. Everything else I forced from my mind.

I saw Daeana disappear beneath the waves, her eyes slack and half-dead with exhaustion. A raised hand, fingers splayed, then nothing. I swam on, arm over arm, head to the side, sucking in air. Dardus was perhaps thirty feet ahead of me, Pelleus a few feet beyond, but I was actually catching up with them. Through salt-lashed eyes I could see the narrow finger of the second promontory, the calmer waters of the fishing harbour beyond it. I didn't dare look behind to see who was following.

We were perhaps only another five minutes from the promontory when the flense-fish took Pelleus. I saw its tough, leathery hide as it reared out of the water just behind him, the triple-rack of needle teeth, its flaccid black eyes. The twin dorsal fins looked sharp as sword blades, and it was the silence of it more than anything that almost made my heart stop with fear. Pelleus, sensing something was wrong, looked over his shoulder and screamed. The fish lunged and bit, and in moments the grey waters foamed red. It shook its snout, rending a chunk out of his ribcage, and the noise Pelleus made as he died chilled me deeper than the cold water ever could.

Dardus thrashed and screamed, in a blind panic, striking out for the shore even though the promontory was closer.

'Stop!' I yelled. I spat water, tried to calm myself, swapped to a breaststroke and gently kicked out. I felt panic beginning to smother me too, but somehow I made my voice clear. 'Dardus, if you make any more noise, it will kill you. Easy strokes,' I said, as calm as a parent soothing a feverish child. 'Easy strokes, gentle and easy and soft. Just listen to me, Dardus. Just listen to my voice.'

I reined him in from the edge of madness. He turned in the water, sobbing, copied my motions. We passed through a foaming slick of blood, saw Pelleus' bobbing carcass as the flense-fish came in for a second bite. I could hear its jaws working, champing the meat and bone. I prayed with every ounce of my soul to King Zothar that the fish be turned away. Be content with what you have, I thought. Leave us alone, in the name of all that's holy.

Somehow, we made it through that last stretch of water. Although I saw another two sets of fins gliding effortlessly past us, the flense-fish were drawn by what remained of Pelleus and left us be. I cringed with every slow kick of my legs though, expecting at any moment the sharp tug and the searing pain as the fish bit into me. I had never been as scared in my life as I was on that awful swim. When I felt the first rising shelf of sand beneath my feet, I thought I was going to weep with relief.

We dragged ourselves from the water, shivering on the black sand, as pale as tubers. Dardus' lips were blue, and his eyes were sunken hollows. He lay there on his back, sucking in air, while I sat and stared out to sea, shuddering. I saw two or three others crossing the bay, faint dots bobbing in the waves. I wondered at the bravery it took, to make that crossing after you had already seen one of your fellows torn apart like that. Such was the Contest…

I stood up, stretched, slapped my arms against my chest and dragged off my wet tunic.

'What are you doing?' Dardus groaned.

'What do you think?' I said. 'The race is still on.'

I started to run and heard him scramble to his feet.

We stayed side by side for that last stretch, feet slogging through the grey dust, until the walls of Lament came back into view. The sun had retreated, and a cool, fragrant breeze was blowing in from beyond the city. The water soon dried on us.

The sky was threaded with dark cirrus, like spiderwebs. I could see the rows of people standing on the walls as they waited for us to return. How many of them were parents looking desperately for a glimpse of their children? My mother would still be on the dais, I knew, with King Zothar and Neophron. Despite her strange outburst as I had headed to the Tower earlier, she would not be swayed from her duty.

We stumbled through the gates of the city, crushing the black petals underfoot, the twin carved swords of the marble propylon soaring thirty feet above our heads, marking the entrance from the gate into the city proper. The Grand Avenue stretched away before us, straight as a lance, but I was barely aware of it. Red spots were dancing in front of my eyes and my breath rattled and tore in my chest. The white marble pillars in front of the city library, the domed chamber of the granaries, the treasury hall with its blazing pale porticos – all of it looked to me like no more than the disordered bones of some colossal gargant, scattered to the grey earth of the Obsidian Coast. The people who lined the avenue, cheering and howling with encouragement, clapping and wailing and rending their clothes, were just a smear of light and colour. The only thing that gripped my sight was the jet pillar of the Tower of the Moon, spearing up towards the brooding skies.

Both of us, our feet unshod, left bloody footprints along the avenue as we ran. Dardus, digging deeper than I would have thought him capable, put on a short burst of speed to reach the edge of the plaza before me. I glanced once at the dais, saw the king sitting motionless as a sculpture on his throne, saw Neophron with his face as blank as a mourning mask. My mother had her hands raised to her mouth. I thought she might be weeping. But then I looked away and the Tower of the Moon was before me.

In all my preparations, I had given the most thought to how to climb this structure. There would be no easy handholds, I knew, as on the cliffs above the bluff. But although the Tower looked as smooth as polished marble from a distance, up close there were old gaps between the cyclopean stones. The Tower was old, the oldest thing in the city – before the first stones of Lament were laid, the Tower was there waiting. In Shyish, care of the dead always takes precedence.

I flung myself at it and scrabbled for a handhold, prising my fingers into a narrow gap. My toes, dry now from the dust of plain, found an easy friction and pushed me up. Then it was just a question of keeping one arm braced while the other snaked up for another purchase, my feet finding the gaps my fingers had already explored. Before I knew it, I was reaching for the arrow-slit window of the first floor.

I was aware of Dardus beside me suddenly. Sweat poured in a stream down his face. His eyes looked like they were going to burst from their sockets and his hair was plastered to his forehead.

He swung himself up and used his longer reach to grab for the edge of the windowsill at the same moment I did. I felt his fingers slide over mine, felt the weight of him as he let go with his other hand, crushing my grip. The sharp basalt edge of the sill cut into my fingers.

'Let go!' I cried.

I didn't mean to do it. It was like drawing your fingers back from a fire, the involuntary movement to avoid pain. I snatched away my hand, but Dardus' hand was still on top of it. Whereas I still had a firm grip on the other end of the windowsill, Dardus had thrown all his weight onto that hold. Now he was clutching nothing but the air.

I heard him gasp, saw the shock bloom across his face as he dropped. Thirty feet to the flagstones below, a height hard enough to kill. He clutched at the stones, ripping his fingernails, turned, landed with a dull thump. I saw him splayed out on the flagstones with his leg bent back at a strange angle. At first, he didn't move, but then I saw him struggle, heard his high-pitched scream, saw the crowd rushing towards him. I could even see at the other end of the marketplace a few more runners who had made it this far. Honour compelled them. Honour, or the dread of becoming one of the Failed.

I thought of Neophron falling from this very summit, a thousand years ago. After that, there was nothing to do but climb.

4

She saw her son standing there, flanked now by Baeothis and Haephastin. The two men held Lycus tightly by the upper arms, the formal pose to demonstrate that the boy was now deep inside the ritual and there would be no going back. But she did not think he would run. Through the fear and exhaustion she saw in his face, there was a flash of steel as well. He had been victorious. Against everything, he had come first. He was the youngest winner for as long as anyone could remember.

The crowds stood in awed silence behind them. Every step and every bench was covered with people, and the branches of every tree were clustered with children who had climbed up for a better look. The shutters on the low, single-storey houses on Antigonas Road had been thrown open. People leaned out on their windowsills or had clambered up onto the flat roofs to watch. All the merriment of the heats before the Contest had faded away. There was not a sound in the whole city.

As she stood there on the dais, at the side of King Zothar's throne, Astraea looked at her son. He was fifty yards away, but it may as well have been the other side of Shyish for all she could do for him now. He had been cleaned up, his bleeding feet bound and shod in leather sandals. He wore a new tunic, a brocaded wrap of Ghyranian silk. The square still seemed to ring with Dardus' cries as he was borne away to the healers, his leg shattered. He had been lucky to live, although as Astraea looked at the other survivors of the race, that bare half dozen who had made it to the base of the Tower, she wondered if Dardus would have preferred death in the end. The other runners sat despondently on the flagstones, their heads in their hands, some weeping, others so shattered by their loss that they looked stunned. They would now become members of the Failed, shunned and banished to Lament's lowest tier, with no other prospects for them but the menial work that kept the city running. They would cart the nightsoil to the botanical gardens. They would sweep the streets, clean the gutters, maintain the wells, and all they could look forward to was the distant moment ten years hence when another cohort would join them, the residue of the next Games. All who failed in the heats; all who survived the Contest and yet did not win. Such was the custom King Zothar had instituted. Blessed were they to have it.

The drums began as the tithe was brought out, a hard and regular rhythm that pulsed across the square. Astraea shifted her weight from foot to foot. Her head was pounding in the heat and the drums seemed to beat to the same rhythm as her heart. There were dark clouds moving towards the city. The breeze carried with it a sharp hint of the cold sea.

A dozen priests, dressed in the long purple robes of their order, came bearing the ironoak chests of the tithe. Their faces were just shadows under their hoods. For days they had gathered all the bones of those who had died over the last year, everything that had been picked clean by the vultures on the platforms at the very top of the Tower of the Moon. The tithe was an annual event. In a normal year it would be collected by a delegation from Athrabis, a tithemaster and a troop of Mortek Guard, who would carry it back all the long miles to King Zothar's fortress in the desert. This year was different; it was the year of the Games, and so the tithe would be presented to King Zothar personally. It was counted a great blessing to die in the year of the Games and a curse to die the day after. Astraea found herself thinking of Cleon. For the briefest moment she wished his body did not cleave so stubbornly to life.

Six of the king's Mortek Guard dropped their shields and spears and marched across the flagstones from the front of the dais. Their helms were lustreless in the growing gloom and the sound of their skeletal feet on the marble was flat and without presence. They hefted the boxes to their shoulders and marched back to the dais, where they placed them before the king. The lids were opened, the stacked bone presented. Astraea glimpsed shards of gnawed ribcage, a broken skull still fringed with gristle and hair. If Zothar made any kind of gesture, she didn't see it, but the lids were closed, and the chests were taken away.

Neophron leaned forward on his throne and wiped a line of sweat from his lip. He gripped his knees to stop his hands from shaking and his breath came panting from an open mouth. He couldn't be more than twenty-five now, Astraea thought. Fifteen when he had won the Contest. She could remember him as a youth, scrambling as easily as a goat up the sheer incline of the Tower, the vultures scattering in a flurry as he reached the top. Did he see this moment at the time, she wondered? Or, as with any young person, did a decade seem impossibly distant to him then?

Suddenly, the Soulmason rapped the dais with the pommel of his staff. All eyes turned towards him. Three times he struck the stage, and at the fourth stroke King Zothar stood.

The red cloak streamed back from his shoulders. The sword hung easily at his hip. His armour glowed, flawless and unmarked, and the jewels on his breastplate and helmet burned like embers. He gazed slowly from side to side, a frozen death's-head glare. Under the command of that will, the whole crowd sank down to their knees. Some covered their faces, so cowed by their master that they could not bear to look on him. Astraea knelt with them, her head lowered. Under her brow, she could see Lycus still standing on the other side of the square, even though Baeothis and Haephastin knelt too. Did he know to remain standing? Had he been told? Or had he intuited it; that in this moment alone, there was something like parity between him and the king?

She swallowed hard and pressed her hand to her chest, trying to still the violent beating of her heart.

'Subjects of Lament,' the king spoke. Again, his voice carried like some natural force; like the boiling sea, like the thunder that muttered in the clouds when the cold seasons came to the coast. 'One thousand years ago,' he said, without passion, 'our cities competed in these Games – for honour, for victory, for the approval of our ancestors. Theres and Lament, locked forever in rivalry. Until one day that changed everything.'

Slowly, he raised his skeletal arm and pointed at the Tower of the Moon. As if commanded to follow his direction, Astraea gazed at it, and it was like she was seeing it for the first time. It almost repelled the eye; a cylinder of glassy black stone, pitted and cracked in places, ancient, reaching up three hundred feet into the air. It was the structure around which the city had been made, the earliest artefact of their distant ancestors in the storied Age of Myth.

'From there is where my son fell, a thousand years ago,' King Zothar rasped. 'Neophron, the scion of my house, the hope of my name. He was the best of us, and he died on the cusp of a triumph that would have gained him nothing more than a fond memory and a fading victory wreath.

'But I would not accept so meaningless a death. Not for someone so vital, so... alive. I journeyed deep into the Underworlds of Shyish, without fear, without concern for my own life, and I bargained with powers in the earth that are more terrifying than any of you can possibly imagine. I demanded my son's soul... and I was given it. And yet, no bargain can be made with such powers without a commensurate sacrifice... Service is demanded for such a gift. And so, I gathered my armies and made my conquests, and became as you see me now. I raised myself above you, fit to worship.'

He stared at the crowd, as if daring them to disagree. The moment stretched and there were scattered groans and prayers shouted from amongst the people. King Zothar clutched the hilt of his sword. Astraea almost thought that he was going to tear it free and strike.

'Neophron's soul was returned to me, but with certain conditions. It is ever a restless thing. It can fill no human vessel for longer than a ten-year span. It must be... released and allowed to find new harbour. It must find a worthy refuge from the best amongst you. In payment and in worship. For I am a god above you, and all gods demand their tribute. Such is the Contest...'

He beckoned Neophron forwards. As if in a dream, Astraea watched the young man stand and remove his helm, his thick, dark locks tumbling to his shoulders. He smiled as if remembering the face of a loved one or the happier days of carefree youth. When he stepped forwards and stood beside the king, Astraea saw how glazed and detached he looked. She wondered if he were drugged or drunk. Or did he step to this willingly, obedient to the last, in final tribute to the being that had been his father for the last decade?

'Neophron has been my faithful heir, these ten years past,' King

Zothar announced. 'He has stood by my side in far Athrabis, and he has learned all that the heir of Athrabis needs to know. He was a worthy son to me, and he will be a worthy son again.'

The young man turned slightly, still smiling. He looked at Astraea and swallowed, a faint line between his eyes. Green eyes, she saw. Like Lycus' green eyes.

Aetius, that had been his name, she thought. *From the third tier. His mother was a weaver.*

She remembered him running, still swift, across the agora at the end of the Contest. His dusty feet, his lopsided, exhausted smile. As if all he had to do was keep running and then the whole of Shyish would be his for the taking…

'Bring the boy forward,' Zothar said.

On command, Baeothis and Haephastin stood from where they had been kneeling, Gently, they led Lycus forward. His hands were in fists at his side, his chin raised, his black hair hanging in his eyes. King Zothar, with Neophron at his side, stepped down the wooden stairs from the dais and approached Astraea's son. Shuffling behind them, leaning on his staff, came the Soulmason, his ragged cloak drawn about his shoulders as if the cold was something he could feel.

Astraea saw Neophron step forward. He embraced Lycus, holding his head to his chest. He leaned down and spoke something in the boy's ear, and Lycus looked at him with… what, she thought? Fear? It wasn't that. It wasn't sadness or regret, sorrow or respect. It was as if Lycus had come across his own reflection unexpectedly. He cast a neutral gaze over a face he knew better than any other.

Please, she begged, although who she was begging, she could not say. *Please, let this pass from him!*

King Zothar drew his sword. Neophron – the young man, who had been known as Aetius, whose mother was a weaver and who lived all his young years in the third tier of the city until the day of the Contest – raised a hand to his father's shoulder and bowed his head. He looked happy, Astraea thought. He looked content.

Zothar drew back the blade and swung.

There was a scream in the crowd. A woman pushed through and fell to the ground, tearing at her face, ripping her clothes, and beating at the flagstones. She cried as if her soul had been torn from her. Aetius' mother, Astraea realised. Neophron's mother.

The vultures rose from the pinnacle of the Tower, scenting blood, wheeling high above the square. The clouds came in then, across the bone-white city, dragging their shadows with them. A chill wind from the depths of the desert. The sun seemed chased away.

Like a jackal creeping up to scavenge a kill, a tall, spindly creature emerged from the body of King Zothar's troops. Yellow teeth stretched in a monstrous grin across a narrow skull, tendrils of bone wavering from the back of his head like the weeds of some deep-sea plant. His eyes were emerald points of fire, dancing excitedly in the empty sockets. His teal robes were so long that they hid his feet and made it seem as if he were floating. The Boneshaper drew near, made obeisance to King Zothar, and then began to weave his magics.

Someone had bundled the mother away. Her faint cries echoed sadly from the streets in the distance. It was a blessing, Astraea knew. She shouldn't have to see what came next.

The Boneshaper slowly began to move his hands in the air above the young man's body, pulling and twisting. There was a sound like tearing parchment, a wet, slopping wrench. Blood sprayed in a fine mist, atomising in the cooler air. The corpse jerked and writhed on the ground, as though the Boneshaper held it in place through the power of his will alone. He tore the bones from the body one by one, amalgamating them into some fluttering, amorphous shape that dripped and spun lazily beside him, spattering blood onto the dusty flagstones at his feet. Astraea, the bile surging in her throat, clasped her hands together and prayed.

'King Zothar, bless us and watch over us,' she whispered. Her mouth was dry. The drumbeat of her headache hammered at her temple. 'Take this man as our tribute to you, Lord of Athrabis, Lord of Lament, Lord of Lost Theres. Bless us and keep us, Lord of All.'

Zothar stood forwards, his arms raised. A line of blood dripped leisurely from his blade. The Boneshaper took the mass of bone and began to pluck strands from it, ropes of osseous matter that he spun in the air like spiderweb. Then, casting and flicking his hands, the air buckling with the spark of amethyst and violet, he wove this mass into the body of his king. Astraea saw the cracked cheekbone knit back together; saw the fused bones of his forearm crack apart and strengthen. Everywhere, the worn skeleton of the king was refreshed and restored, his stature growing as the bones of his dead son were woven into him. From every corner of the city, it seemed, from open windows and rooftops and from the tops of the trees, the people of the city watched the sacred mystery in awe and reverence. The immortal king was renewed.

'Zothar... *Zothar...*' came the hushed whispers, the mumbled prayers. Tears were shed, faces were covered.

Astraea could not look at the remains of the body. Two priests scuttled over to bear it away to the Tower, with all due reverence, leaving a sheet of blood against the stone. The armour would be taken and stored, with all the other sets, in the Regent's Palace.

'Make your judgement, Se'bak,' Zothar commanded. They both stood before the boy now. The king held his blade ready as the Soulmason limped forward.

On the dais, Astraea stood, to a sharp look from Kaitellin. The old man gave an almost imperceptible shake of his head and tugged nervously on his beard, but Astraea ignored him. As if hypnotised, she stumbled from the stage and followed the king and the Soulmason across the agora.

The jewel on Se'bak's staff began to glow. He held it above Lycus' head, raised the bones of his left hand and gently rested them against the boy's chest. Lycus shuddered, as if ice-cold water had been dashed across his face. An age seemed to pass. The Soulmason was motionless, the dull red glow of his eyes guttering in his skull. Astraea felt like a reed whipping in a storm, like a strand of wire stretched so taut it sang. Zothar's back was to her, his sword in hand and the blade still dripping with his son's blood.

Se'bak lowered his hand. He turned to his lord and master. Lycus was pale, his eyes darting from the terror of the king before him, to his mother a few feet behind. Astraea wrung her hands and bared her teeth.

'The vessel is filled,' Se'bak said. 'There can be no doubt. Your son lives again, my liege. Green eyes too, for what that's worth...'

She screamed, as Aetius' mother had screamed. She flung herself at King Zothar's feet and beat the ground in despair.

'Please, lord!' she cried. 'By all the mercy you hold, grant not this blessing to my son, I beg you!'

Rough hands grabbed her and drew her away; the Hekatos of the Mortek Guard, the captain of Zothar's army.

'Give the word, my liege,' he croaked, 'and her life is yours.'

Astraea felt the sword blade against her throat, the cold nadirite biting into her skin. Zothar deigned to look at her then. She felt as if her soul were being flayed away by the power of that gaze. The yellow eyes were as pitiless as the sun.

'Please, my lord!' Lycus said. He stepped forward, shaking. He knelt and bowed his head. 'My king... I would beg only one boon of you, that you let her live. Please... my father.'

There was no weight to the decision in the king's mind that Astraea could see. No conflict between policy and desire, not even the simple capriciousness of a god when confronted by his worshippers. It was not mercy that made King Zothar order her release. It was simple indifference.

Astraea crumpled to the ground. Zothar sheathed his sword and stood before Lycus, staring down at the boy.

'Neophron,' he said. 'Once more you return to me.' He reached out, but then drew his hand away.

'Now prepare yourself,' he said. 'Say your farewells. The journey to Athrabis is long and you will not see these people until the Games come round again.'

5

Night was falling as the delegation left Lament, but I knew the Bonereapers would fear no darkness. King Zothar rode at the head of the column and the people cheered him out, some scattering black petals at the feet of his steed, others throwing garlands at his soldiers. And yet there had been something strained and false about those cheers, I thought, more an expression of relief than gratitude. In every face I met as I rode amongst them, perched on Neophron's undead steed, I saw a smothered dread and a buried gladness that the Games were over, and the king was leaving.

We took the northern road as it mirrored the line of the coast for a mile or two, and then cut away to the west, towards the desert. I glanced back to see the flat roofs and tall columns of Lament disappear in the darkness behind us, the three levels of the city like flat white stones stacked atop each other. I wondered if I would ever see my home again. I didn't think of the Games to come, even after everything I had seen that day. They were ten years away – a lifetime to me – and with the peerless optimism of youth, I was sure that somehow my fate would be different. Neophron had died in the shade of the Tower from which he had fallen a millennium past. When my time came, I had no doubt, I wouldn't die under the blade of the king. How could I? I had won the Contest. I was special.

The desert soon opened to us as we rode on, a flat and featureless spread of sand that was stained a faint purple colour from the light of the lunar orb as it swelled above us. 'Nagash's Eye', as it was known in Lament, although who or what Nagash might be was something I had never considered. Legends say that the souls of those who die in the Contest are gathered together on the surface of the Eye and that they look down on and protect their loved ones in Lament below. It is a great honour to die in the Games; less so to take part and fail. I thought of Dardus suddenly, his scream rising from the flagstones as he lay there with his leg twisted under him. It would have been better if the fall had killed him. I tried not to think of the trials ahead of him once his leg had healed. He would be removed to the third tier, given lodgings by the gates or in the tangled, grimy streets near where the drains decanted into the sea. His life would be shackled now to a broom to sweep the streets, a bucket to cart the nightsoil. I felt sorry for him. I hoped Selene would look out for him and that even if Dardus blamed me for what had happened, she was more forgiving. Our eyes had met when the Soulmason had acknowledged me. I picked her out of all the children who smothered the woe trees, hanging there like fruit from their branches. Her eyes, the film of water across them, the drawn horror in her face. I hoped I didn't look as scared as I had felt.

I was riding close to the rear of the column. Ahead were the twin lines of the king's honour guard, his Mortek troops marching in flawless precision, each led by a proud Hekatos with a wide-crested helmet and an ornamental spear. Between them rode the king's cavalry, twenty riders on their skeletal warhorses, their shields and spears fastened to their saddles. Two riders carried the flags of Athrabis, the pennants hanging limp as we crossed the airless land.

I found that my gaze was always dragged back to the figure of the king as he led us onwards across the desert. From this position, all I could see was the sweep of his scarlet cloak, the jostling skulls inside the ribcage of his steed, the bone-crest of his helmet. And yet my eyes were drawn to him as if to a storm in the distance, a natural phenomenon that humbled me in its scale and power. I had seen the bones of Neophron torn from his corpse and woven into the body of the king, had seen him refreshed by the sacrifice into something more powerful still. I couldn't allow myself to think of it, but I knew that one day my bones would form a part of King Zothar too. In some way, I too would rule.

This deep in the desert, the sands began to flow into dunes and barrows like the contours of a frozen sea. Here and there we passed the disgorged spars of ancient buildings – ruined temples from the Age of Myth, perhaps, forgotten settlements long since buried by the drifting sand. Far away I could see streaks of green light, spectral flashes on the horizon that were accompanied by faint, drifting screams. I rose in my saddle slightly, straining to see what they were.

'Gheists,' said a creaking voice at my side.

The Soulmason had ridden up beside me, slumped in the seat of his strange walking throne. The two legs, like the claws of a gigantic bird, scratched and picked at the sand. His cloak was a tattered purple thing around his shoulders and the jewel on his staff was now dull and opaque. The gemstones on his headdress glimmered with the moon's light. In the depths of his skull, two red embers burned.

'Spirits of the dead?'

My voice sounded ludicrously childish compared to the Soulmason's ancient croak. I wondered how old he really was. How many years had it been since he had last been a mortal creature, like me?

'Spirits that are too tormented to be of any further use to Nagash. They are cast into the wastes of Shyish, there to wail their distress into the wilderness.'

The Soulmason chuckled, a ragged click of his jaw, as if he found something amusing about this.

'Nagash,' I said. I looked up at the black sky, the lunar orb pulsing with an aethereal white flame. 'Like the moon? In Lament, we call it Nagash's Eye?'

The Soulmason chuckled again, tapping the pommel of his staff against the side of his throne.

'Nagash is All, my child,' he said. 'This is but one of the many things you will learn as King Zothar's son. The realm is wider than you realise and your little corner of it is but a fragment. An important fragment, true, and somewhere of immense importance to our liege, but a fragment all the same. There will be much for you to learn, as Neophron.'

'Is that to be my name now, lord?' I asked.

'There is no need to refer to me as "lord", child. I am Se'bak, Soulmason of the Legion of Athrabis, and I have served the king too long to care overmuch about titles and honorifics. Se'bak will do.'

He turned in the throne, swaying slightly to its odd rhythm, and looked at me. I found I could meet those eyes, red and blazing as they were. If there was not kindness as such in them, there was certainly something closer to tolerance or simple respect. Strange as it may seem, I warmed to Se'bak then. He had taken the time to speak to a scared boy, in a way that did not make me feel I was being mocked or patronised.

'It is indeed what you must be called now,' he said. 'Do not forget, you are now Neophron, as was and as will be again. You must answer only to that name and put aside whatever name you had before.'

'Yes, Se'bak,' I said.

I thought back to the moment a few hours before, when Neophron had embraced me after the Contest. There had been a smell of dust and old bones about him, a musty scent of libraries and archives and ancient storerooms. He held me to his chest, and I could feel his heart thumping savagely behind his ribs.

'Do not be afraid,' he had whispered to me. He had bent down and looked me in the eye. 'This moment is foreordained, and it could not happen any other way. King Zothar will come to mean more to you than you can possibly imagine, and like me you will go to this willingly. I promise.'

There had been such sadness in his smile that I doubted him. As his steed carried me slowly across the burnished wastes, streaked with silver and amethyst from the rising moon, I wondered again at his words. *It could not happen any other way...* Was that not what I had thought myself, since the moment I entered the heats? When I discovered the caves and saw those ancient sketches of Neophron's death as he fell from the Tower, did I not see myself in his despairing face, as if the line of my fate had long been written down, undeviating?

And yet it was true that I felt no different. As Neophron's head had come tumbling from his shoulders, dragging with it a ribbon of blood, I felt the ice of fear wash cleanly across me, but nothing else. Was his soul in me now, lurking somewhere in my sinews, staring silently through my eyes? I shuddered. I flexed my fingers on the reins of the steed beneath me, that weird collection of bones and skulls. Were these still my fingers? Or were they now his?

'My lord,' I said, before correcting myself. 'Se'bak... may I ask you something?'

'At all times you may have that freedom,' Se'bak said. 'I am to be your tutor and train you as the heir to Athrabis and Lament. Ask, and to the best of my abilities I shall answer.'

'When you inspected me after King Zothar... when Neophron died, you said that "the vessel is filled", and that the king's son lived again.'

'I did.'

'But I feel... How can his soul be in me now and yet I can't feel it? I am still myself. At least... I think I am.'

'You are,' Se'bak said, 'and you are not. The masonry of souls is a complex mystery, child, and even after all these years I find there is still much for me to learn, with all my centuries of experience. But look around you now and tell me what you see? Who marches with you?'

I did as he commanded, taking in my surroundings. Not the desert spaces that we moved through, the drifts and dunes and the outcrops of cracked obsidian that were scattered across the sand, but the troops that escorted us on our way. The Mortek Guard tirelessly marching, obedient to their lord's least whim. The undead cavalry on their barded warhorses, their helmeted skulls always scanning the horizon for threat. The king himself, brooding and dark, riding with a subdued power that kept all of us in his thrall.

'King Zothar's troops,' I said. 'The Legion of Athrabis.'

Se'bak cackled again. He waved out his bony hand to indicate the twin columns of Mortek Guard.

'This is far from the Legion of Athrabis, my boy. Under his command, the king has thousands upon thousands of soldiers and cavalry. He has war machines beyond compare, and Boneshapers and Soulreapers and Harvesters... No, what you see here, my child, in this small delegation, are souls. Simple souls, yoked to a single purpose. It is the task of the Mortisan Order to find the best aspects in the souls of those we conquer and use those aspects to animate our forces. In these, our simplest troops, this soul-stuff is only so much blended fuel to cleave them to their purpose, so they can wield a spear and obey a command. For myself though, and certainly for the king, we have carried our souls unaugmented from the day of our deaths to the very present. And they are great souls indeed.'

'I don't understand,' I said.

'I do not expect you to understand,' Se'bak said, not unkindly. 'Suffice it to say, it is possible for two souls to be blended in one vessel, and for one to be dominant at the expense of the other. You may never think as Neophron or bring to mind his memories, but he will be there inside you all the same. I have seen him in you,' he said. 'Make no mistake, you are now the refuge for his sundered soul.' He glanced quickly at me. 'For the next ten years, in any case...'

I nodded, although I still did not feel the truth of it. Perhaps that would come in time, I thought.

I lost myself for a while in such speculation, as the column marched and rode across the desert. It was only after another hour that I realised how tired I was. I had not rested since that morning, before I had climbed the cliffs with Selene. The Contest had nearly shattered me. I began to sway in the saddle. It felt like we had been riding all night, although the skies were still rich with darkness and the pale moon still flickered above us. Morning seemed far off, if it would ever come. The dry, dusty scents of the desert began to make me drowsy. I realised how much I missed the smell of the sea, which was ever-present in Lament. I wondered if I would ever get used to its absence.

'Hold, child,' Se'bak said. I felt his hand reaching out to steady me, the cold touch of bone on my bare skin. 'Athrabis is near, and you shall have rest when we reach it. Ah,' he sighed. He pointed to the west, where the moon was at last beginning its long decline.

'There, Neophron… see its spires and pinnacles. See the walls of the necropolis, the dread fortress of King Zothar…'

I looked, my eyes less attuned than the Soulmason's to the darkness that surrounded us, but after a moment I could see something glowing on the horizon. We drew closer. As the necropolis began to cohere from the shrouding night, I knew that I would never forget the terrifying majesty of that vision.

Even in darkness it gleamed with a deep and sultry light; an eerie, spectral green that seemed to have no source but the black obsidian and the sculpted bone that framed it. Three high towers rose from the barbican, one directly above the gate, the other two flanking it on either side. Their spires were as sharp as spear points, and they were pitted with arrowslit windows. The crenellations of the battlements alone would have dwarfed the gates of Lament. The walls stretched away into the night like the spread wings of some colossal bird, black as pitch, and the vast portcullis, at least fifty feet tall, slowly began to rise at our approach. There was a wide avenue a hundred yards across, stretching from the desert sands towards the gatehouse. It was made of what I took at first to be pale marble, but then realised was polished bone. I could see the cracks and sutures in it, like the lines between the fused plates of a human skull.

My fatigue fell away as we approached the silent city. It lurked in my muscles still, but my mind was alert, and I felt a strange sense of familiarity as we drew near. I looked to the sentries high on the walls above us as we headed for the gate, the skeletal Mortek Guard with spears and shields standing at attention, and knew that I had seen them before. When we passed through the barbican and beyond the outer walls, I was sure that I recognised the blunt magnitude of the castle keep at the far end of the avenue, a squat tower a mile distant, with a line of merlons at its summit that were as jagged as a row of teeth. Were these Neophron's memories, then, rising in me at these familiar sights? I had an image of my soul as a body of dark water, Neophron's thoughts and impressions rising like flense-fish from the depths. I could not take the measure of them yet, but I knew now that they were there.

'Welcome, once more,' Se'bak said at my side, 'to Athrabis.'

The scale of it was overwhelming. As the avenue stretched away from us into the heart of the city, I looked to the buildings on either side; huge, soaring black structures adorned with baroque decorations; gurning, cadaverous gargoyles; twisted columns like fused spinal cords; buttresses as long and wide as the Grand Avenue in Lament; gigantic, obsidian skulls that overhung the streets as if peering down on the tiny figures that walked along them. Radial streets disappeared into the green darkness on either side. Pointed archways rose above us, decorated with runes and hieroglyphs. Basilicas and temples, grand libraries and auditoria flanked the street, at the head of monumental staircases that in their scale and surface area must have been larger than the entire agora back home. All of it was carved in the same black stone as the Tower of the Moon, the polished obsidian that seemed to absorb all light, or in vast lengths of fused bone blackened with age and twisted into weird, unnerving configurations.

My head reeled as we followed the avenue into the heart of Athrabis, the clatter of hooves ringing back as dull as a cracked bell from the walls around us. Everywhere I looked, the streets were empty. Apart from the sentries on the walls above the gate, I had seen no companies of troops patrolling the roads, no messengers or emissaries flitting from the buildings, no lieutenants awaiting the king's return. If I hadn't known otherwise, I would have assumed that Athrabis was just another lost city abandoned in the wastes of Shyish, its citizens fled or spirited away to some dark fate and its streets a refuge for no more than the vultures and the bone-crows. I shuddered to think that I might now be the only living thing here.

We came to a halt on the edge of a vast ornamental square, each corner marked by tall, decorative obelisks of ferrous stone. There were four sunken gardens arranged in a grid in the middle of the square, but they held no plants or flowers, only humped barrows of black sand, sparkling with amethyst. The Mortek Guard marched on, carrying the ironoak chests of the bone tithe, the sound of their marching feet eventually fading away into the cold silence of the city's depths. Se'bak still rode beside me on his walking throne. He held his hand up and bid me attend, as King Zothar turned his steed and faced us.

How to explain the impression he made on me then? In Lament, I had been shaken to the core by him, and yet I had felt the thread of some connection between us as Neophron had died and I had been summoned to him as his son. Here though, with the yellow lights of his eyes burning in the sockets of his skull, with the tall nadirite helmet casting a shadow across his brow, with all the dread grandeur and majesty of Athrabis behind him, I felt I would collapse under that gaze. I was only a child after all. In the same way I had felt madness pluck at me when the flense-fish rose in the bay that morning, I felt it creep closer now. I was far away from everything I had ever known, plunged into a world that was dark and frightening – a world of gods and monsters, of great kings and greater sorrows. No one would have blamed me for weeping then, but somehow, I managed to compose myself. I thought of Selene taking my hand in the caves that morning, asking me not to win. I thought of my mother doing the same, in the moments before the Contest. But I had won all the same, and that had to be worth something.

It could not happen any other way, Neophron had told me – before his father had hacked his head from his shoulders.

'You will rest now,' King Zothar said to me. There was no emotion in his voice, nothing at all. 'Se'bak will show you to your quarters. Food will be provided for you and in the morning it will begin.'

'What will, my liege?' I said. My voice sounded feeble in this overwhelming space, like the squeak of a mouse.

'Your new life,' he said. 'Your life as my son.'

He pulled the reins and turned his steed away. Flanked by his cavalry, he rode on across the square.

Se'bak led me into one of the side streets that stretched away from the square, a cobbled passage with a ribcage vault high above it. There were aetherlamps strung along this passageway, casting down their faint green glow. Again, I had the feeling that I had been here before. I knew that before we reached the end of this passage we would turn off to the left and pass through a tall, arched gateway into a small, cobbled forecourt. There would be a door panelled in viridescent nacre, and beyond that door would be a series of dusty rooms and chambers, with stale sheets on the bed, where a pale light would fall through the high, narrow windows.

'Here is where I leave you, Neophron,' he said. He made a short bow in the seat of his throne. 'These will be your chambers in Athrabis, although no part of the city is closed off to you. As King Zothar's heir, you will see all of it in turn. You will find food and clothing to your tastes within. I will see you in the morning, when your training will commence.'

He bowed again and withdrew, the walking throne crossing the courtyard and clacking down the passageway back into the city streets.

I slipped from the saddle of Neophron's steed, drawing it by the reins to a holding post beside the door. It did not want for food or water and so I gave it no more mind as I explored the rooms of my new chambers.

The air inside was cold. Each room was bare of ornament. The walls had at one point been painted with a drab whitewash, but the paint was peeling from the stone now and there was a layer of dust on the simple wooden furniture. In the bedroom I found a cot with plain sheets thrown back from it. I wondered if this was where Neophron had slept last night, before he woke to his last day on earth. There was a wardrobe in the corner of the room containing an array of simple tunics, cloaks, and sandals in various sizes, some of them so old the leather was beginning to crumble.

I ate a frugal meal in the cold kitchen, sitting at a low table on a horsehair bolster. There were bottles of zephyrwine caked in dust, a pitcher of water, fresh bread, and dried thorn-pears. When I had finished, feeling as if I was following the strange sequences of a dream, I undressed and lay on the bed, drawing the sheets across me.

I don't know how long I lay there before I fell asleep. It was the quiet that kept me awake, I think. The immense weight of a city that was utterly silent.

6

It was a place designed to bring comfort to the afflicted, but to Selene the healer's shop always made her feel nervous. The opaque jars of ointments and foul-smelling unguents, the reed baskets full of dried grave-toads and scarabs. Phials of iridescent venom sat on the shelves behind the dusty counter and there were strings of snakeskin hanging in papery strips from the walls. Stone geckos and fire-rats squabbled in glass tanks beneath the window. Desert birds pipped and chirruped from the cages hanging from the ceiling, oblivious to their eventual fate. Blinded, their tongues torn out, the birds would be slit open and their blood drizzled across the eyes of those afflicted by sand-blindness. There was a rank smell in the air of rich spices and peppery herbs, of powdered clay and fermented fruit. The light, as it fell through the dusty windows, made the high afternoons feel like dusk and Selene never left the shop without feeling drowsy and thick-headed. Most of all, it was the healer himself who made her feel uneasy. Part of the priestly order in Lament, he always seemed as if he would prefer his patients to die as quickly as possible so he could convey their bodies to the Tower and let the vultures feast.

The bronze bell clattered above the door as she entered, bearing a phial of grave-sand as payment. She tried to hold her breath against the smell, but the healer took so long to emerge from his storeroom at the back that she was forced to gulp down a lungful of the stench. She gagged, held her nose to the crook of her elbow, only snapping her arm down when the healer parted the beaded curtains and stepped behind his desk. He was a grim, cadaverous man, tall and bony, his hair shaved to his scalp and his eyes peering at her from their sunken sockets. Many of the priesthood starved themselves to affect this skeletal look, to bring them closer to what they saw as the ideal of King Zothar and his Ossiarch troops.

'Ah,' he said. 'Young Selene, here once more, I surmise, for her grandfather's medicine?'

'Yes, thank you,' she said. She held out the phial between forefinger and thumb, as far as possible so she wouldn't have to feel the healer's touch. He slipped the phial into his robes and rummaged under the counter until he found a small cedar box lacquered in onyx. The healer flipped open the lid to show Selene the contents; two dozen small amethyst-coloured pills.

'Make sure he takes these before meals in the evening,' he said, passing it over. 'And offer all the appropriate prayers to King Zothar.'

Selene took it from him. This time she couldn't avoid the cold, clammy feeling of his skin.

'Although, of course,' the healer added, 'you're well used to the rituals of his care by now, aren't you? How long has it been since the Games? Six months? If only he had died before then, he would have been blessed indeed, and his bones would have gone back with King Zothar himself to Athrabis...'

The healer stared at the window, as if gazing out on the streets and spires of the desert city, his hand against his chest and a faint smile on his sunken face.

'He's getting better,' Selene said, affronted. 'The medicine's working, he'll be back on his feet in no time.'

'Of course he will,' the healer said, coming back to himself. He raised an eyebrow, as if they were both sharing a private joke. 'Although I must warn you that old age is an illness few of us mere mortals manage to overcome.'

She left the healer's shop with her head spinning, sucking in a lungful of the clear afternoon air as soon as she was outside. The shop was on the street of the apothecaries, by the western wall in the lowest tier. There were healers who plied their trade higher up in the city, but Selene's grandfather had always put his stock in the older folk remedies and didn't trust anyone who charged more than one phial of grave-sand to help the sick. Every month then she had to make the journey down to the western wall and brave those foul smells and sinister sights and risk the clammy touch of the healer's fingers against her palm as he took his payment.

The sun was falling in the west now and she hurried along the street to head home. Down in the apothecaries' quarter, the shops and houses were low wooden things, simple one- or two-storey shacks humbled by the white cyclopean stone of the city walls that ran along beside them. They seemed drab and frightening things to her, dark and shadowed. She couldn't imagine that some people actually had to live there.

The ground was layered in an inch of sand, blown in from off the desert, and her feet crunched through it as she paced the length of the road. Further ahead, she saw a street sweeper gathering the sand into drifts against the wall, stooping to sweep it up into an ash cart. He was old, his face gnarled with age and the elements, his grey hair hanging sparsely across his face. He glowered at her as she passed but Selene averted her eyes. He was one of the Failed, she knew. She wondered how long ago he had risked his fortune in the Games and lost. Thirty years? Forty? And now fate had dumped him here and had spun away from him, fickle as ever. All he had to look forward to was a life of this servitude; sweeping the streets, tormented by the city children, an object of scorn and approbation.

She felt sorry for him and paused a moment to look back down the street. He bent again to brush the sand into his dustpan, his leg trembling. An old injury from the Games, perhaps, still troubling him after all these years. Had he run in the Contest, even? Made it as far as the Tower and then watched as another gained the prize ahead of him?

She thought of Lycus suddenly, although she had tried not to think of him overmuch these last six months. Her heart had lurched in her chest when she saw him come haring across the agora at the end of the race, flinging himself onto the black stone of the Tower. Even then, she had prayed for him to stop. Let him drop down those first few inches and slump to the ground, and let Dardus win instead. Fall, as Dardus had fallen, and break his leg rather than gain what came next…

She had turned away when King Zothar sliced Neophron's head from his shoulders. She had felt the great wave of soul-struck awe ripple through the crowd, heard Lycus' mother scream like she had been stabbed, but she had not watched. When she told her grandfather later, confessing her transgression with the tears running down her face, he had hugged her close and told her he was proud of her.

'Give him that last dignity,' he had said. 'He died as no more than the vanity of a monster's grief, the least you can do is turn away.'

She remembered his words and they troubled her all over again.

Her grandfather had always troubled her; he was such a proud, headstrong man.

She came out from the bottom end of Antigonas Road into the wide, open space of the agora, the market and meeting place of the whole city, felt the fresh sea breeze from the coast cooling her skin. The woe trees rippled their branches and dropped their leaves onto the flagstones. Everywhere she looked there were people talking or trading in the market stalls, or just sitting on the benches passing the time. Old friends debated philosophy or the work of the council; young men and women, suitably chaperoned, eyed each other warily as they strolled between the sunken gardens. Children ran and played, losing themselves in games of dice and marbles. Members of the Failed drew water from the well and dragged their overflowing buckets to the water tanks that were dotted throughout the city. Priests intoned prayers and swung their censers and called the faithful to the city temples, there to give thanks to King Zothar. The agora was the heart of Lament, where all the city's public business was done. During the hours of light, before the Obsidian Coast was swallowed in the darkness of evening, this was where the people truly lived.

Selene skipped lightly across it, clutching the cedar box of her grandfather's medicine, dodging between the merchants and the street magicians, kicking at the piles of dead leaves beneath the woe trees. Her heart lifted after the gloom of the apothecaries' quarter, but she felt a touch of ice when she remembered where she was going. Still, she reassured herself, he might be an old man, but he was strong at heart. The healer was wrong. It was just a passing illness. Before long, her grandfather would be as strong and proud as he had always been.

On the other side of the agora there was a narrow lane that curved around and decanted into an enclosed courtyard behind the Street of Sorrow. The backs of the houses rose high on each side, the three-storey wooden tenements of the lower tier. Washing lines were strung out between them and from the kitchen windows you would always smell the warm and enticing scents of home cooking, hear the soft lullabies of mothers singing their children down for their afternoon naps. A lone tree grew from a marble planter there; some said it had grown from a seed brought from Hysh, in the ancient days before King Zothar had journeyed to the Underworlds to bring back his son. Whatever its provenance, Selene had always been drawn to it; she loved the lustrous silver bark, the way the branches thrust up towards the distant sky, the curled magenta leaves that deepened in the autumn to a rich and vibrant purple. She always made this detour on her way back from the healer's shop, to sit for a moment on the marble planter and bathe in its restoring shade.

She turned the corner at the end of the lane and paused as she noticed one of the Failed standing amongst the fallen leaves. He had his back to her and he was feinting and stabbing with a length of stick, duelling an imaginary opponent as if his life depended on it. His tousled blonde hair was dark with sweat, his plain brown tunic patched in places. He couldn't have been much older than her. Selene hid herself in a doorway for a moment and watched. He was a street sweeper, she saw, although his broom was propped up against the tree and the vigour of his swordplay had scattered any leaves he'd managed to gather right across the courtyard.

She was about to turn and go, to leave him to his play-acting, when she realised who it was.

'Dardus!' she said.

The boy whipped round, dropping the stick he had been using as a sword. His face was narrow and pinched. There was a smear of dirt against his cheek. He snatched up the broom and held it defensively in front of him, addressing himself immediately to the fallen leaves. He still limped, she saw, although the broken leg had long since healed.

'I'm sorry, miss,' he mumbled, scouring the cobblestones with his broom.

'Dardus, it's me,' Selene said. She stepped closer. So raw was the humiliation in his face as he looked up at her that she wished she'd just turned around and left him alone. She should never have said his name. You didn't speak to the Failed if you could help it.

'Selene,' he said. 'I haven't seen you since...'

She barrelled ahead, wanting to spare him any further upset.

'I was just coming back from the healer's,' she said brightly. She held up the cedar box. 'Grandfather's medicine.'

'He's still unwell?' Dardus said. Slowly he lowered himself to the edge of the planter, using the broom for support. 'I'm sorry to hear it. I always liked him. He's a fierce old man, but always kind.'

'He'll get better,' Selene said, confidently. 'I'm looking after him.'

'I thought you were living with Lycus' mother now,' he said. He grimaced, although whether from the pain in his leg or the sound of Lycus' name, she wasn't sure. After a pause, she walked across the courtyard and sat next to him.

'I just visit her when I can, to see how she's doing,' Selene said. 'She's been very upset, since... and with her husband so ill too.'

She thought of that quiet house now; the smell of sickness drifting through its corridors, the feeling of grief and anger like a tangible thing in the air. Astraea sitting silently by the door into the back yard, staring into that sunstruck space, chewing the dead skin around her fingernails. Her black hair as lank as seaweed, her eyes like shards of flint.

'Formed quite the bond then, the two of you?' Dardus said.

He picked a stray leaf from the edge of the planter and idly began to shred it between his fingers.

'I think she's sort of adopted me, since Lycus left... She misses him so much.' She looked at his face. 'So do I.'

Dardus snorted and cast the shredded leaf aside. He stretched out his leg and rubbed his knee.

'I can't say that I do,' he said.

'It wasn't his fault,' Selene told him. 'It was the risk you both took when you entered.'

Dardus sneered at her. 'You weren't there. You may have been watching from the trees, but you weren't there on the Tower when he threw me off.'

'I *saw*, Dardus,' she said softly. 'It was an accident, I'm sure it was.'

With a groan he levered himself to his feet again, leaning on the broom. He made a half-hearted swipe at the flagstones, scattering a few leaves to the corner of the courtyard.

'It was no accident. I had the handhold before he did, and he flung my hand aside. I'm telling you, Selene, that's how it was. And then I fell, and the ground took me, and I was left with nothing...'

He stooped and picked up the stick again, swishing it from side to side.

'I was faster than him, stronger, more fearless. You should have seen him crying when the flense-fish came out in the bay, he would have died then if not for me! If I'd met him in the fencing, during the heats,' he said, 'I would have taken his hand off and that would have been the end of it.'

'You don't mean that,' Selene said. 'He was your friend. You should be proud of him. He's the youngest winner of the Contest there's ever been, he's been raised to be the king's son, it's...'

'It should have been me!' Dardus cried. He turned on her, his face twisted with rage, flushed and angry. '*I* should have felt Neophron's spirit entering me, *I* should be sitting with the king as we speak! Not him! And what do I have instead?'

He threw the broom on the ground and slashed at the tree trunk with his stick. Leaves fell from the shivering branches. Selene recoiled. For a moment she thought he would turn on her and strike her down. Then, his anger spent, he dropped to his seat on the planter again and cast the stick aside.

'I've only seen my parents once since I fell from the Tower,' he said bitterly. 'When I was lying in the healer's tent, having my leg set. I think they hoped I had died. When they saw that I was still alive they knew the shame I'd brought on the family. You know,' he spat, 'if anyone saw me leave the third tier I would be taken to the priests and whipped. If I did it a second time I'd be exiled. That's what it is, Selene,' he said, 'to be one of the Failed. It isn't fair. None of it is. And all because Lycus stole the glory that should rightfully have been mine.'

He looked up then, staring over the rooftops to where the vultures planed in towards the Tower of the Moon, their harsh, discordant cries echoing across the rooftops as the afternoon began to fade.

'I wish I had died in the Contest,' he whispered.

She took his hand, clasping it in both of hers.

'I'm sorry, Dardus,' she said. 'I truly am. And none of it's fair, I know that. Everything, it's all…'

She looked for the words, but she couldn't find them. She could hear the cries and laughter of the marketplace, could smell the cooking from the windows in the courtyard behind her. Life, in all its simple glory, continued around her, but all she could hear was the crying of the vultures, the echo of a boy screaming on the flagstones as his leg broke under him. Was it the pain that made him scream, or the sudden knowledge of what his life would be like from that moment on?

'I'll come and see you again, Dardus,' she said, standing up. She clutched her grandfather's medicine in her hands. 'I promise. You might not be able to leave the third tier, but I can come down and see you whenever I want. And I shall. None of it's fair, but we can make it fair ourselves.'

She turned and ran, leaving Dardus and the courtyard behind her, the silver tree that some said grew from a seed brought all the way from Hysh, in the days when the people of Lament had never heard of King Zothar or his son.

Her grandfather was lying on the bolster in his simple whitewashed room. The plaster was peeling from the walls and there was a spreading patch of damp high up in the corner, but he saw no reason to fix it, not now.

'Why waste good money patching up an old place I'll soon see the back of, eh?' he would demand, and Selene would have no answer. Then he would grin, the roguish old-man's grin of someone who had long made their peace with the world and everything that was in it.

She thought he was asleep as she slipped into the room. His iron-grey hair was scraped back from his forehead and his drooping moustache almost covered his mouth. His skin was grey, the eyelids dark and his cheeks hollow. Grey stubble like iron filings was scattered across his jaw. The first few buttons of his shirt were undone against the early evening heat, and she could see the glint of his pendant. Selene paused to light the lamp on the bedside table, the wick fizzing in its pool of oil. When she looked again, she saw that he was awake.

'Been and gone already then?' he grumbled, struggling to sit up. He slapped away Selene's hand as she tried to help him. 'That healer didn't try to swindle you, did he? Damned priests, never trusted them an inch...'

'He didn't, Grandfather,' she said. She sat on the bed at his side and opened the lid of the medicine box.

'One phial of grave-sand,' he muttered, peering at the amethyst pills. 'They fleece you when you're still alive and then they pick the flesh from your bones when you're dead. Never mind the birds they use, *they're* the bloody vultures, Selene. Never forget that!'

With a sour look, he pinched one out of the box and crunched it between his teeth.

'Grandfather!' Selene protested. 'You're supposed to have that after meals! And wash it down with water.'

'Water?' he scoffed. 'Forty years a fisherman before it got too much for me, I've seen enough of water to last me a bloody lifetime. Here,' he said, 'help me up and bring me an ale. These damned pills taste fouler than I remembered.'

She struggled to lift him, letting him brace himself on her shoulder as he levered himself out of bed. He was still a big man, broad in the chest, his jaw firm and proud. Years of hard work along the Obsidian Coast had given him a constitution that could shrug off any illness, but old age had caught up with him at last. Time, the foe no man could outrun.

It was a small house, three square rooms with low plaster ceilings, a veranda at the front that faced onto a small kitchen garden thick with herbs and grave-flowers. The veranda looked down the slope of the Keening Way towards the distant northern gate. While her grandfather sat himself groaning on the bench, Selene poured him some ale from the jug in the kitchen and brought it out to him. He smacked his lips with relish as he drained half the cup.

'I never see why so many folk go for wine,' he sighed, 'when good ale is at hand.'

The night was drawing in across the city. The sun smouldered in the west, a ring of fire. Far Hysh was beginning its slow curve across the disc of the realm, a speck of white light looping through the cosmos. Selene sat beside her grandfather and looked up at the sky as it faded into purple. The pale stone of the city dwindled to a steady grey, dull and lifeless. She could see the lunar orb shining brighter as the sun declined, Nagash's Eye like a shard of polished bone high above the columns of Lament.

'Do the souls of those who fall in the Games really go up there?'

she asked. 'I saw my friend Dardus today and he wishes he'd died rather than survived and failed. I can't imagine him up there though, his soul looking down on us.'

Her grandfather turned to her, scowling. 'The young lad who fell from the Tower? A damned disgrace the way they're treated. They have the courage to run in the first place, they should be treated with more respect even if they don't make the distance.'

Selene felt the shiver of transgression and craned her neck to look over the veranda wall in case anyone was passing on the Keening Way.

'Not so loud!' she hissed. 'Anyone could be listening.'

'Let them listen, they might bloody learn something,' he huffed. He sipped at his ale, seemed deep in thought for a moment. 'I don't know about the souls in Nagash's Eye, but it seems poor recompense for death if you ask me.'

He glanced at her again. She could feel his reticence before he spoke. He held the ale cup in both hands, staring down into its depths as if expecting to find his words there.

'When your parents died I did right by their own beliefs. Your mother... Well, she took to your father's faith, and I respected that. A person's gods are their own business, right enough. I took them to the Tower when the dry-lung carried them away, brought you here to live with me. Never tried to force my own faith on you, neither.'

Selene was silent. They had never delved this far into the subject. She wanted to ask about the pendant, but she knew that he would have to come to this in his own time and in his own way. He could never be rushed in anything.

'When I was a young man,' he said quietly, 'I was fishing far out into the bay when a squall took me. Knocked my father, your great-grandfather, clean overboard. Never saw him again. The sea's cruel like that – it gives, but it takes a hard payment too. The storm dragged me so far out I thought I would never see shore again, but then the winds changed, and they threw me against the rocks far down the Obsidian Coast, further than I reckon most have ever been from Lament. When I woke up, I was in a merchant's tent, part of a caravan that was taking a day's rest before passing on to Thanator's Manse, they said. Quite a journey…'

'They were human?' Selene asked. She had never heard of there being other humans along the coast. As far as she knew, there were only the people of Lament and the Bonereapers of Athrabis.

'Human as you or me,' he said. 'Well, I learned a thing or two while I was recovering in that tent. They were decent folk, traders, and merchants all. They told me about the wider realm, about the gates that lead to the other realms. They taught me about one other thing too.'

'What?' Selene said, although she was sure she knew.

'They taught me about Sigmar. Gave me this.'

He pulled out the pendant from under his shirt – the golden hammer, lit with a burnished glow.

'Sigmar isn't like other gods,' he said. 'He's more powerful than them, for a start. He sits in High Azyr looking down on us all and he actually cares for those who follow him. He doesn't ask for sacrifices for his own pleasure or his own amusement. He asks folk to make sacrifices because it's the right thing to do. The strong give up more than the weak because they can. The powerful protect the lesser amongst us because they should. All this,' he said, waving his hand to indicate the city, the coast, the broad night sky, 'all this is just the way things are here. But it doesn't have to be like this forever. Remember that, Selene.'

'I will,' she said.

'Sigmar takes the best souls to him, to fight alongside him even when they die. He doesn't stash them away like prisoners in the moon or expect some weeping courtesy from them when he deigns to visit their city, like King Zothar.'

He reached over and clasped her hand, holding it tight. His expression was so fierce she could barely look at him. The pendant seemed to shine like white fire around his neck.

'Be one of those best souls,' he said, his voice shaking with all the force of a command. 'Be strong, be brave! And fight for those beneath you.'

'I shall, Grandfather, I promise!'

He started coughing then, thumping at his chest while his face flushed red. The ale cup spilled from his fingers and cracked on the ground. Selene helped him to his feet and back into the house, where he lay down once more on the bolster.

'See,' he said, managing a smile. 'So much for that damned healer, like all those priests. They're just bloody vultures, Selene, all of them. Never forget that either!'

7

His name was Khetera, and he was Hekatos of the legion's first phalanx; King Zothar's lieutenant, the second in command of his army when they marched to war. There was a black jewel above the runic boss of his shield that he would use to dazzle me whenever I advanced on him. He had a wide, lateral crest on his helmet that looked like the jawbone of a flense-fish, and his curved nadirite blade was unnotched no matter how many times he struck out at me. The lights of his eyes, sunk deep in the black sockets of his skull, flickered from yellow to green. The worn ivory of his teeth always seemed to be grinning. He hated me; of that I had no doubt. Six months I had been sparring with him and every time it was a wonder I limped back to my quarters with nothing more than a few cuts and bruises, or scrapes from hitting the tinder-dry, black earth of the parade ground every time he knocked me down.

'Advance,' he hissed now. The parade ground stretched around us, two acres of bare, beaten earth. He hunched over, his shield up, sword raised high and angled with the point towards me. Nervously I stamped forward, the blade heavy in my hand. I swung a backhand from high left to low right. Khetera pivoted and caught the blow on the edge of his shield, turned again and smacked the pommel of his sword into my forehead.

I saw white light, a searing red streak that blinded me. From somewhere behind me, I could hear Se'bak chuckling to himself. I was on the ground suddenly, my elbow skinned and blood dripping down my forearm. I wanted to cry. I always wanted to cry, but I managed to stop myself.

'Pathetic,' Khetera muttered. He turned away and stalked back to his position. His voice never seemed to rise above a sibilant whisper, but I could always hear what he said. 'A waste of bone, and a waste of my time. This child is barely whelped, and I am to make a soldier of him?'

'I bow as always to your military expertise, Khetera,' Se'bak said graciously, 'but it is our lord's wish. King Zothar has commanded you in this.'

'And I obey, without question.' He looked down at me. If a skull could be said to sneer, that's what Khetera did. 'On your feet, boy. Again. Advance.'

I looked to Se'bak. He was sitting in the gloom of the cloisters that ran around the outer circuit of the parade ground. He had left his throne behind and sat now on a chair that looked as if it had been constructed from a human pelvis and spinal column. His tattered robes were drawn around him. The jewels in his headdress sparkled as he turned his head towards me.

'You heard the Hekatos,' he said. 'On your feet, Neophron. The heir of Athrabis must be a soldier as well as a statesman, remember.'

I got up again and dusted myself down, picked up the blade from the dirt and warily held it at guard.

'I remember,' I said.

Indeed, it was impossible to forget. Se'bak's lessons had drilled such sentiments into me from morning to evening for six months. When I woke, even before I had eaten, I trained with the king's Deathriders for an hour, mastering the canter and the gallop of their armoured warhorses, the same strange steeds of blended bone I had ridden from Lament. After a hurried breakfast of the plain fare left for me in my rooms, I would spend hours in the Grand Library with Se'bak – a space of such overwhelming scale, with ribbed and vaulted ceilings that were at least two hundred feet high, shelves of scrolls and codices that seemed to stretch on for miles into the dust-fumed distance, that I would certainly have got lost there if Se'bak hadn't been on hand to guide me out again. I learned all anyone could possibly want to know about the flora and fauna of the Obsidian Coast, of the earliest settlers who had made the Coast their home in the ancient days of myth, of philosophy and politics and law.

The resources of the Grand Library were endless and yet even this vast space was but a small building in the city's wider scheme, tucked away off the central square where I had been brought half a year earlier. Armouries, barracks, the strange laboratories of Se'bak's Mortisan Order, mausoleums, and auditoria – Athrabis was built on a scale that was almost too big to comprehend. In the centre of the city the streets were a thousand feet across, the buildings looming above them like mountain ranges, jagged and bleak, the black stone lit with that endless, eldritch green light. Even at the high point of the day, it seemed as gloomy as dusk in the shade of those mighty structures. After my lessons in the library, I had to take the long walk through those cavernous streets, heading across the centre of the city to the barracks and the parade ground in the eastern quarter, where Khetera would knock me around until evening.

Truth to tell, I could not honestly say which was more tiring; the study with Se'bak, or the combat training with Khetera. Both left me feeling drained by the end of the day, in such a state that it was hard to keep hold of my memories of home. Lament seemed very far away and a long time ago. I tried to go to sleep at night thinking of my mother's face, but as every day drew in, it receded further and further away from me.

Khetera spent the next hour so vigorously demolishing my defence and so easily turning aside my attacks that I was ready to throw my sword on the ground at his feet and damn the consequences. What prevented me from doing so was the sight of King Zothar standing in the shadows on the other side of the cloisters, where the doors led into the barracks armoury. His yellow eyes burned in the gloom and his arms were folded across his breastplate as he watched. He wore his battle helm and I saw that his sword was sheathed on his hip; even the king did not go unarmed in Athrabis. War, it seemed, was always at hand, although who the king had cause to fight was a mystery to me.

It was the first time I had seen the king for many months. The sight of him, even a few dozen yards away, was so forceful I almost dropped my sword. Khetera, never slow to take an advantage, lunged in and knocked it from my hand, and then, as a final humiliation, used his shield to shove me sprawling back into the dust. He stood over me, sword raised, his cold, malevolent glare pinning me to the ground.

'You are little better than a dog in the street to me, boy,' he hissed in that papery voice. 'No more than a king's folly…'

He pulled the sword back. For a moment I thought he was going to strike. Then, his voice filling the wide empty space of the parade ground like an icy wind, King Zothar spoke.

'Enough.'

I got up. Instantly, Khetera fell to his knees. He planted his sword point in the dirt and rested his forehead against the crossbar. Se'bak stood from his chair and bowed deeply. Of us all, only I remained standing. Again, as I had when he approached me after the Contest, I knew instinctively that the formalities did not apply to me in quite the same way.

Zothar walked without urgency across the parade ground. I didn't know if I should pick up my sword and salute him, and so I stood there with my hands at my sides, trying not to shake as he approached.

Strange to say, but there was little about the other Bonereapers that disturbed me now, if indeed they ever had. Their skeletal form had always been idealised in Lament and the frescoes in the temples accustomed people to their image from an early age. To see a construct of bone walking and talking, exuding power and majesty, was a sight only seen in the city every ten years, at the end of the Games, but it was not unexpected. Se'bak, wrapped always in his moth-eaten robes, limping on his staff, was a daily presence in my life now. Even Khetera, much as I despised him, was a familiar figure to me. The sentries I saw patrolling the battlements or guarding the formal chambers of the city were merely the low troops of Zothar's army and I found nothing in them to repel me.

King Zothar was different though. It was not just his size or bearing, although he towered above me at well over six feet. But whereas Se'bak and Khetera could both be intimidating in their way, forceful and possessed of great arcane and martial strength, Zothar seemed far beyond such a natural response. I was overawed by him the same way I was overawed by Athrabis. It felt as if he was built on a similar scale, so alien and dominant that you felt like an insect beside him. The force of his will flowed around him like an aura, and when you were caught in its web it was hard not to feel repulsed. The soul cringed back from the exercise of something infinitely stranger and infinitely more dangerous.

'Return to your regiment, Khetera,' he said. The Hekatos immediately stood and saluted with his sword. Without another word he marched off across the parade ground. 'Se'bak,' Zothar said, 'return to your chambers. Neophron will resume his studies tomorrow.'

'Yes, my liege,' the Soulmason said. He looked at me askance, for the briefest moment, as he bowed, but then the moment had passed, and he shuffled away to his study and his laboratory.

I stood there in the centre of that empty space, feeling utterly alone. King Zothar beside me seemed as distant and impersonal as a mountain range or a piece of monumental architecture. He said nothing for a long moment, staring down at me, appraising. Then, turning away, he said:

'Follow.'

We crossed the parade ground and headed through the barracks, along lonely, ill-lit corridors of black onyx and carved bone. From the barracks we walked through narrow passages and empty roadways, like chasms carved between the buildings that soared above us. We crossed immense open spaces that were decorated with towering statues; skeletal horsemen rearing from jet-black plinths that were themselves at least twenty feet high. On we pressed through the city, walking for what felt like mile after mile, as the soft green light of the afternoon paled into a purple dusk. All the way, King Zothar said nothing. As I walked behind him, dogging his long stride, I was sure that he had forgotten I was even there.

Finally, as we passed into another huge public square, a vast rectangle of paved ground at least a mile across, lined by dead trees that grasped with their spindly black branches at the fading sky, I saw where we were headed. On the other side, rearing from the city the way a hidden peak rises from a mountain range, the Palace of Athrabis was waiting for us. The monumental staircase rose in a steep tier to the massive double doors, each carved from bone and studded with iron bosses. The architrave above the peak of the columns that ringed its frontage was at least a hundred feet above the level of the doors. The higher pinnacles, the flared battlements, the great spires and towers of its soaring height, were lost to me in a haze of mist. So great was the palace, I thought it must pierce the very clouds.

Sentries saluted us as we passed through the double doors, clattering their spears to their shields. If they thought it strange that I walked with the king, they gave no sign. We passed into a great hall with a floor of gleaming black marble, the ceiling vanishing into the shadows above us. The footsteps of the king clacked against the stone and echoed back to us, but in my leather sandals I made no sound as I followed him. Lamps shone dimly from iron sconces high on the pillars that flanked the hall. I was reminded sharply of the time I had led Selene into the caves above the bluff on the morning of the Contest. I tried to bring back her face, the shade of anxiety that had crossed it when she had asked me to fail.

It felt as if we walked through the palace for as long as we had walked through the city, but eventually we came to a chamber deep in the body of the building. Two more sentries drew the doors wide as we approached, closing them behind us. The floor of the chamber was the same polished black marble as the rest of the palace, but the walls were decorated with friezes showing great military victories; the king's Deathriders charging into a mass of fierce, fur-clad humans; the king himself, his steed rearing beneath him, as he pointed his sword towards more distant conquests. There was a circular table in the centre of the chamber that was twenty feet across, made of some dark, metallic crystal that seemed to flicker and shine with a dull red glow, like burnished oil. The walls of the chamber were lined on one side with towering bookcases, each shelf stuffed with dusty scrolls and stacks of vellum. There were weapons mounted on the other wall, of a style that I didn't recognise; strange, rough-hewn axes with leering glyphs on the pommel; barbed spears that glimmered with a sinuous, violet light. Trophies, I imagined. Relics of a lifetime given to war.

On the other side of the circular table, covering the far wall from floor to ceiling, was an immense bas-relief sculpture that had been carved from a sombre, green-flecked stone. King Zothar stalked across the chamber and stood in front of it. After a moment I realised that it was a map. I was still standing in the doorway, unsure of what I should do, when the king spoke. He did not turn to face me.

'Come closer,' he said. 'Stand by my side and tell me what you see.'

I did as he bade. I looked up at the map, the curve of the coastline, the contours of mountain ranges, the wide spread of the desert wastes.

'It is the Obsidian Coast,' I said. I looked for Lament, but I could not see it at first; then, as if noticing a speck that mars an otherwise clean sheet, I saw a tiny, jewelled pin in the bottom right-hand corner of the bas-relief. I recognised the line of the bay, the hills that rose behind the city. And then I looked properly, and I realised what I was truly gazing upon. How small Lament seemed, suddenly. How insignificant.

'This is your kingdom,' I said. 'This is the kingdom of Athrabis.'

'This is the kingdom of Zothar,' he said.

He pointed high on the western fringe of the map.

'Here is where Acharnae once stood, a proud city now ground to dust beneath the feet of my army. Here,' he said, sweeping his hand across a patch of desert towards the east, 'is where the Kingdom of the Painted Jewel once struck its borders, now cast to ruins by my will. In these seas once sailed the Reaver Fleet, an empire of orruk pirates and cut-throats that raided far and wide along the Obsidian Coast. Their ships now moulder at the bottom of the sea and their bones are fused into the palace walls that surround you.'

'I have never heard of these places,' I said, 'these peoples.'

'None have, but those with the memories to recall their destruction.'

He looked at me then, staring down with the pale fire of his eyes. He pointed at Lament.

'And here is where the Jackal Kings ruled for time out of mind, the twin monarchs of Lament, calling as tribute to their power the Games that were held in that city every ten years. The Games that are held there still. None now remember *their* names, that is certain. I have scoured them from all memory as payment for their insolence.'

'The Games... where Neophron died,' I said.

'Where you died, my son. From lost Theres we marched, in all our pomp and circumstance, crossing the desert to present ourselves to the Jackal Kings. Neophron was a bold young man, confident and quick, but he was not so strong as the others who competed. And yet he won through the heats, and he earned his right to run in the Contest. He climbed the Tower...'

'He fell,' I said softly. I felt the wind pluck at me, the stench of the dead rising from the platforms above. The grim chuckle of the vultures as they squabbled over the rotting flesh.

'He fell, and from that moment on I cursed Lament and the kings who ruled there. I made the journey few mortals have ever attempted. I confronted he who rules over the cities of the dead, he who is Monarch of the Underworlds, Master of Souls, the power in the earth of Shyish who none can gainsay.'

'Nagash...' I whispered. The words came back to me from Se'bak's mouth, as we rode across the desert. 'Nagash is All...'

'Nagash,' King Zothar said. 'He returned your soul, Neophron, and he asked of me conditions that I was only too willing to accept. Overlordship of the Obsidian Coast, in his name, as the head of his Ossiarch legion...'

Zothar held up his skeletal hand, turning it in the soft green light of the aetherlamps. He stared at it as if seeing it for the first time, or as if he had forgotten the bargain he had once made. He closed his fist and lowered it again, and when he spoke, I almost thought I could hear a soft trace of regret in his inhuman voice.

'Theres was… abandoned. One by one, I murdered my generals and had them returned to me as the undead warriors you see now. Se'bak, my soothsayer, gained power immeasurable over the souls of the dead. Khetera, the head of my army, became the head of my legion. And slowly, as we conquered our way across the coast, Athrabis took form. My city, my fortress. My necropolis.'

'And what of Lament, my lord?' I asked. 'It stands still, it…'

'It stands because I will it. The Jackal Kings are long since wiped from the memory of your people, but Lament is where Neophron's soul will ever return. After each ten-year span, it must be released to live again, to find new harbour, and every ten years the Games find for me a worthy vessel. Man or boy, woman or girl, it matters not. Neophron lives once more… for a little while at least. This is the tribute I demand, as payment for my loss.'

He stared a moment longer at the extent of his kingdom. My mind reeled with what he had told me. I thought of the paintings I had seen in the caves with Selene and some part of me latched on to them as an anchor, a way to stop myself from spinning away into horror and confusion. I thought not of the image painted there, of Neophron falling from the Tower, but the idea of those last kings hiding in the caves even as their city was conquered by Zothar. Monarchs, lords of all they had surveyed, reduced to shivering wretches waiting to die, scrawling the moment when everything changed on the walls of their refuge.

In the depths of my shock, I realised one other thing too, the implications of which did not occur to me until sometime later, when it was already too late to make a difference.

Zothar was not a god. Like all of us, he was the servant of

something greater, something more powerful. If the people of Lament were the slaves of Zothar, then Zothar and his legion were, in their way, the slaves of Nagash.

'Come,' he said now, drawing me aside. His red cloak billowed out behind him as he strode from the chamber. I hurried to keep up.

We passed through to the other side of the palace, walking its endless gloomy corridors until we came to another set of monumental double doors. As they swung open onto the streets of the city, I wondered if they too had been made from the bones of Zothar's enemies, in the centuries since he had wrested Neophron's soul from the Underworld. How much of Athrabis was the refuse of his victories, the bones torn from those who had opposed him and set to new purpose? We walked through a mausoleum, I realised, an ossuary of the conquered.

Beyond the palace gates, set in a steeped tier of rising steps, there was a long, low building, slate grey and without windows, with only one door allowing admittance. Unlike the forbidding doors that guarded the entrance to the palace, there was only one small iron gate set into the outer wall here. A lone Mortek Guard stood there as sentry, and he saluted as we approached. King Zothar stood with his fingers resting on the handle.

'The map can give you one impression of my kingdom, and Lament's place in it,' he said. 'But sometimes a more tangible example is required.'

He swung open the door and we stepped inside.

The only light came from the street outside, the faint tinge of the aetherlamps, the eldritch glow of the obsidian and the black bone. It was enough to see by, though, and what I saw was a hall that stretched off into the shadows and that was stacked from floor to ceiling with the tithes taken from Lament, over who knew how many years. There were skulls still bearing scraps of leathery skin;

ribcages; shoulder blades; the jumble of femurs and fibulas. There were bones from thousands and thousands of people, from the bent and brittle skeletons of the very old to the bones of the very young. Every dead body that had passed through the Tower of the Moon and been cleansed by the vultures had found its way here, gifted in the tithe as tribute to King Zothar.

'Do you understand?' Zothar said. He swept out his hand. 'Do you see?'

I looked at the stacked bone, stretching off endlessly into the distance. I didn't know what he wanted me to say.

'Athrabis has no need of Lament's tribute,' he said. He sounded almost sorrowful, as if he regretted the need to take it in the first place. 'My army is beyond counting, and in the wars I fight I can replenish any loss with the bones of those I destroy. Lament's dead is a drop in this ocean.'

'It means nothing,' I said.

I remembered the climb, the smell of the rotting bodies. My father would be placed there one day, in the Tower of the Moon. My mother, Selene. Everyone I knew.

Zothar turned on me, eyes blazing. His hand, as cold and hard as steel, gripped my shoulder. I cried out, but he did not relent.

'No!' he hissed. 'It means everything! The value is not in what we receive, but in what we are given! To Lament, all this is beyond price, the bones of their very dead. They give because it is demanded. It is a symbol, do you understand? A symbol of my rule, and in its way it makes them feel of the same value. If they realised how meaningless this really was to me, how little I needed it, then they could not continue and would fall into a hopeless lassitude from which they would never recover. But the symbol keeps them working, keeps them living, keeps them organising the Games that provide for me the *real* tribute.'

He released me, the hand lingering on my shoulder a moment

longer. He reached up and with those ancient shards of bone cupped my face.

'You, Neophron,' he said. '*You* are the tribute that I receive from Lament. You are worth more to me than the entirety of my kingdom. I would watch it all burn if only I could keep Lament in my grip and know that every decade you will return to me, and that I will regain what I should never have lost.'

8

The priests had been, and the body prepared. Wrapped in his death shroud Cleon was ready to feed the sky. The vultures would feast this day, and – praise the king – a year hence his bones would be added to the tithe.

Astraea stood in the colonnaded hall as the priests departed. Each made the gestures of respect to the other; Astraea because she was an elder of the council and the priests because they guarded the sacred mysteries and ushered the body to its final transformation. As was the custom though, she wore not the ceremonial trappings of an elder, but the mourning mask and the black woollen robes of the bereaved. When she followed the corpse in the procession to the Tower, she would no longer be seen as one of the leaders of Lament, but as no more and no less than someone blessed with a death in their family. She would have given something to the tithe and that would make her worthy of a respect beyond compare this day.

The mourning mask was of carved and painted wood, shaped

into the semblance of a skull. The straps bit into her skin as she stared out through the eye sockets. The priests crossed the threshold back into the streets of the city, their hoods covering their heads. Astraea stood at the door and watched them go, Lament spread out before her, a line of light breasting the morning clouds and casting a pale glow down onto the neat avenues and clustered houses of the second tier. At the gate, one of the priests paused and looked back.

'We will return at midday, my lady,' he said. His face was a dim patchwork under the shadow of his hood. 'For your husband.'

'Thank you,' she said. Her voice echoed inside the mask. The heavy woollen robes dragged at her shoulders and itched against her skin.

'Praise this day,' the priest said, nodding. 'Praise King Zothar for what we are about to give him.'

'Praise him,' Astraea said. It was not just the mask that made her voice sound flat in her ears.

When she had closed the door behind her she sat for a while by Cleon's body. It was bound and wrapped like a cocoon in white shrouds, silent and utterly still as it lay there on his bed. A smell lingered in the air even though the window was open. The stench of the dry-lung, voided bowels, the acrid tang of whatever sacred oils and unguents the priests had used to clean and prepare him.

She reached out a hand and laid it gently on the body. It was a miracle he had lasted this long. At the end, he had been no more than a husk. With every coughing fit he had hacked up another spongy fragment of his lungs, spitting it into a bowl with a mouthful of foamy blood and bile. Death had been a sweet release, she knew that. To die was to serve and to serve was to find a fulfilment that could not be found in any other way.

And yet... she thought. And yet...

She thought of her son. It had been his victory in the Contest that had kept Cleon going. He had been so proud, so flushed with reflected glory. It had seemed like a new lease of life for him, but in the end, it was only a way of prolonging the agony. A year past and the Contest still found new ways to cause her pain.

There was a tentative knock at the chamber door. Astraea turned to see Selene standing there, her hands respectfully clasped in front of her, her head bowed.

'My lady,' she said, in a thin, small voice. 'My respects to your husband, and my commiserations to you. Praise–'

'Yes,' Astraea said sharply, cutting her off. 'Praise indeed.'

'I'm sorry, my lady.'

Astraea unhooked the mask and let it drop into her lap. The air in the room seemed thin and the light seemed too bright all of a sudden, the smell more intense.

'No, Selene,' she said, 'I'm sorry.' She smiled at the girl. 'I accept your commiserations with all due gratitude. Now come,' she said, standing up. She looked down at the body. 'Let us sit through in the parlour until the priests return. Let us leave Cleon in peace until they come for him.'

She made two cups of tea with dried Hysh flowers that had been picked from the garden. Together they sat at the front of the house, the shutters on the window open and showing them the thoroughfare flanked by its shading trees as it curved down into the lower city. Voices reached them from the agora in the distance, laughter and argument and the tolling bells from the Tower. It was almost time.

'How is your grandfather?' she asked the girl.

'He's fine, my lady.'

'Astraea, please. There's no need for any formality between us, Selene. You were Lycus' best friend, and you've been such a…' Astraea felt her voice catch and raised the cup to hide it. 'You've been such a help to me since he's been gone. With Cleon, with… with everything.'

'Thank you… Astraea.' She lowered her eyes. When she spoke again her voice was as quiet as a whisper. 'He isn't really fine,' she said. 'He's very ill, and…' She glanced back towards the closed door of Cleon's room, where the body lay.

Astraea reached across and took her hand.

'Anything you need from me, you will have,' she said. 'You can live here, as long as you need to.'

'Thank you,' Selene mumbled.

'He's a strong and irascible old man, though,' Astraea said. 'I'm sure you'll have many years with him yet.'

'I hope so,' Selene said. The smile she offered her was wan and sad.

Astraea turned the conversation away.

'I saw you the other day in the agora, talking with Dardus,' she said. 'He was Lycus' friend as well, wasn't he? I remember him falling from the Tower, his leg…'

Selene's eyes were wide with fright. The tea sloshed over the lip of her cup as she started forward.

'I won't do it again!' she said. 'I promise!'

'Hush, child.' Astraea waved her down. 'I think it's a good thing. A brave thing, in its way. To think,' she said, 'it could so easily have been Lycus… And if it had been, I would have been comforted to think of a friend as steadfast as you, spending time with him, even though he had failed.'

'I wouldn't have thought an elder of the city would be so understanding,' Selene said. She sipped her tea, watched Astraea carefully over the rim of the cup.

'No,' Astraea admitted. 'And I'm sure others on the council would not agree, but… I don't know. Perhaps, since Lycus left, I find custom and tradition less of a comfort than I thought I would.'

They sat for a while in an easy silence, both of them drinking their Hysh flower tea and listening to the common bustle of the city beyond the window. Astraea thought about Lycus, and she thought about the Failed. Would it have been better if he was where Dardus was now? Shunned, made unworthy in the eyes of his family and his city? Could she have watched Lycus fall from the walls of the Tower with joy in her heart, knowing that the rest of his life would be misery and bitter failure, instead of a brief decade in the heart of Athrabis with the king? How much worse would it be to see him every day, dragging nightsoil from the latrines or filling buckets at the well, knowing it was forbidden to speak to him? Selene was still only a child and had licence of a sort, but it was expected that the citizens of Lament treated the Failed as they deserved. But then, how could she while away ten years without him, knowing that the next time she saw him would be at the time of the Games, when King Zothar would strike him down?

How can custom be so cruel, she wondered, when it is all we have?

They came for Cleon at midday. Astraea heard the scuff of the priests' sandals on the path, the tolling of the bell at the front door. She hid herself behind the mourning mask again and stood there to admit them. Selene stood nervously in the parlour, unsure what she should do.

'Would you accompany me?' Astraea asked her. 'It would be a comfort to me, child, in this time.'

'Of course,' Selene said. She took her hand. Together they followed the procession down the thoroughfare towards the Tower.

Six priests in purple robes carried Cleon's body, hoisting it onto their shoulders. At the bottom of the thoroughfare, where it decanted into the Grand Avenue, an honour guard was formed from the other members of the council. Melissta touched her hand to her forehead and bowed. Kaitellin, leaning on his staff, inclined his head in all solemnity. Baeothis stood proudly with his arms at his sides, as if the honour was somehow reflected on him as well.

'My greatest commiserations, Astraea, my dear,' Haephastin said. He took both her hands in his and raised them to his lips. His face looked pouchy and bloated, as if he had been drinking. 'Praise be this moment, and what King Zothar receives from us. You are blessed, truly,' he said, but Astraea could see the look in his eyes. Not doubt, exactly, but a sense of dull routine. This was just what was done on such occasions, and it meant little more to him than that.

How many here felt the same, Astraea wondered. Adrift in rituals they rarely considered and barely understood?

A bell pealed from the Tower. A crowd had gathered in the square, as was usual on such occasions; common folk pleased for the diversion in their day; the pious, mumbling prayers as another life was gifted to the tithe. The Tower loomed above them all, a shard of dark stone, repelling light.

The priests walked slowly to the door, bearing Cleon high on their shoulders. The bell rang its tolling sorrow and the whispers in the crowd fell to a respectful hush. Astraea felt the skull-face of the mourning mask pressing against her, almost suffocating. She longed to tear it from her face and dash it to the ground. The door opened, the ancient slab of ironoak swinging wide as the priests entered. And then, as Cleon disappeared into the shadows forever and the door slammed shut, the vultures sprang and chattered from the rooftop high above them; harsh cries and mocking laughter, a greedy excitement to the way they flapped their ragged wings and came soaring back.

Astraea felt the tears flowing down her face. She was glad of the mask then. She thought of Lycus a year now past, fitting his fingers to the gaps in the stone, clawing his way up one foot at a time.

She felt Selene's hand in hers, the press of her grip, comforting, consoling. She squeezed back.

The vultures settled on the battlements. They would be taking Cleon up the spiral stairs now, floor by floor, to the platform at the top. He would be stripped of his grave shrouds, exposed. A year from now, the next tithing, what was left of him would be added to the cedar chests.

She wanted to hate the birds, but they just acted according to their nature. Their function was pure, devoid of motive or purpose.

It is King Zothar, she thought. *He is the real vulture, scavenging at our dead. His mouth is stained with our blood. He is the Vulture Lord.*

'It's over,' Selene said sadly. She still held her hand.

'Yes,' Astraea said. She took off the mask and looked at the Tower. 'Take me home.'

9

It was a place of such devastating silence that the smallest sound could wake me; the changing of the guard on the battlements, the wind haring through the streets; the mournful, savage cry of a gheist out wandering the wastes beyond the city walls. I would lie there in the half-light, my lamp burning low on the bedside table, my chambers slumbering around me, and I would listen. It was comfort, of a sort. A reminder that other things moved through this lonely space, even if none of them were alive the way I was alive.

One morning, perhaps a year after I had first been taken to Athrabis, I woke early to the sound of marching feet, the rattle of weapons. This was no changing of the guard, I realised; it sounded like an army. Was the city under attack? From whom? Who was there in all the wilderness of the Obsidian Coast who would possibly threaten King Zothar's realm?

I snatched up my sword from the corner of the room and ran out into the courtyard. My steed, Neophron's steed, stood patiently under the weight of its armour by the hitching rail. I leapt into the saddle and guided it out onto the street, following the sounds of marching until I had threaded my way to the ornamental square in the centre of the city, where each corner was marked by those tall and sinister obelisks. I stood at the mouth of a narrow street that led into the square and looked on what I had never thought to see. There amongst the sunken gardens, ranked up between the barrows of black sand, was the Legion of Athrabis.

Words cannot do justice to the sight. I realised at once that the delegation Zothar had sent to mark the end of the Games in Lament was no more than the tip of a blade he held at his command. This was the weapon entire; rank upon rank of Mortek Guard standing at attention, spears shouldered. Troops of Deathrider cavalry stretched across the square as far as my eyes could see, spears tucked in stirrups or swords sheathed at their sides. Vast war machines of bone and coiled sinew, their crews clambering over them in preparation. Monstrous hunched creatures, twice as high as a man, with pulverising bludgeons in place of hands and what looked like the torsos of Mortek soldiers fused to their chests. Flags and pennants snapped and fluttered in the chill breeze. I could hear the Hekatoi barking orders to their regiments, as more and more troops poured in from the surrounding streets. The numbers of the legion must have been in the tens of thousands at the very least and they had spilled from every corner of Athrabis to form up in its centre. Every barracks and stable I had assumed was empty was merely filled with the patient dead as they awaited their orders.

I rode nearer, looking for the king. I could see Se'bak mounted on his throne, swaying with that queasy gait as he guided himself through the ranks. There was a sudden tug on the reins of my steed, and I nearly fell from the saddle. I looked down to see Khetera leering up at me, his sword in his hand, his tall nadirite helmet polished and gleaming.

'Get back to your playroom, boy,' he snarled. The bones of his jaw clacked with anger. 'Your place is not here.'

'Where are you going?' I demanded. 'Are we at war?'

Khetera laughed, a horrible, snickering sound.

'We are always at war, boy. One day perhaps the king will feel sentimental enough to include you, but not this day. Now go, before I drag you from the saddle and thrash you for your impudence.'

I reared back, my mount's hooves kicking in the air. Khetera lost his grip on the reins, but he stood square in the middle of the narrow street and would not move aside.

'I want to see King Zothar,' I said. I don't know what flash of madness made me draw my sword, but I did so. Khetera laughed again and held his own blade at guard.

'Come then,' he sneered. 'I have more pressing business this day, but ever can I spare a moment to humiliate you further...'

I could run him down, I thought. I pictured his skeletal frame trampled to pieces under the hooves of my steed or speared on its tusks and flung aside. I would stand over his broken bones with my sword in hand and hew his skull from his shoulders...

I looked up and saw, no more than twenty feet away, King Zothar on his warhorse. He stood on the edge of the square, at the head of the army he would shortly lead from its gates. The light seemed to buckle and flee from him, so dark was his presence there. Only the yellow eyes, staring, seeing all...

Khetera sheathed his sword and bowed, and then marched back to rejoin his regiment. Zothar said nothing. He merely sat there on his mount and considered me. For a moment it felt like the same indifferent consideration he had given my mother when he signalled for her to be spared after I had won the Contest. I felt the touch of fear, that I had overstepped a mark.

'You ride to war, my lord?' I said quickly. 'Please, let me come with you. Let me fight at your side.'

'There will be time for that,' Zothar said. 'For now, you will remain.'

'But, my lord…!'

'Do as I command,' he said.

He guided his warhorse to the square. He did not look back, as if having no doubt that his command would be obeyed.

The weeks that followed were some of the hardest I spent in Athrabis. After I watched the legion march in its endless serried ranks to the gates of the city, the dust rising above them like a fog as they disappeared into the desert wastes beyond, I returned to my chambers. I propped my sword up in the corner of my room and lay on the bed, but rest eluded me. Instead, I spent the day wandering the streets on foot, peering into deserted halls, exploring desolate temples and galleries. Most doors were open, but some were locked against me. In the palace, strolling through its echoing corridors, my sandalled feet making no sound on the polished marble floors, I headed to the chamber where Zothar had shown me the map of the Obsidian Coast. The doors were barred, however, and in the palace there was not a single soul who could open them for me.

I was utterly alone. If any guards remained inside the city, then I could not find them. The battlements were bare of troops, and the barracks and the parade grounds were empty. In the labyrinth of the library, I saw nothing but the bibliopomps – the skeletal, bird-like creatures that flitted between the shelves and carried scrolls and volumes in their beaks. Athrabis had been emptied of its army, marching out to fight who knew what foe and for what reason.

I felt abandoned. It was a strange and dislocating change after the last few months, when I had spent every day either in Se'bak's company as he tutored me in mathematics, languages, and history, or under the vicious tutelage of Khetera on the parade ground. Yet I did not miss either of them (and certainly not Khetera) as much as I missed King Zothar himself.

I had been spending more and more time with him of late. Often he would summon me from my chambers at odd hours, appearing in the courtyard on his steed and calling me to obscure rooms deep inside the palace, where he would show me scrolls detailing the history of lost Theres, or storerooms where some of the ancient artefacts of that forgotten city were kept safe – crumbling stelae showing the position of the celestial orbs, amulets that once belonged to a prominent merchant family, their names forgotten, or sherds of pottery from common household vessels. He would display these objects without any comment further than their basic description, as if expecting me to interpret them for him, or detail my impressions. Then, satisfied or otherwise, he would lock them away again and leave me to find my way back to my chambers while he strode off into the shadows of the palace.

At other times, he would call for me to join him at tense formal dinners, where I would sit at one end of a massive onyx table that was itself dwarfed by the dark, echoing hall in which it was placed, while he sat thirty feet away at the other end and spoke haltingly of his son, Neophron. I would pick at the food that was presented to me – grey meat of strange provenance, limp strands of root vegetables that I didn't recognise, a jug of tepid wine – while Zothar sat at an empty plate and watched me eat. The walls of the chamber were so far away they vanished into the shadows on either side. The vaulted ceiling could only be dimly perceived a hundred feet above us. Aetherlamps stuttered on tall sconces, freestanding at either end of the table. Every forkful that ascended to my mouth was covered with his rapt attention, the yellow eyes glowing in the darkness like those of some desert creature caught in the moonlight.

'You always had such a fierce appetite, Neophron,' he would say. 'It gave me great pleasure to watch you grow up strong and healthy.'

Often he spoke to me like this, addressing me as his son directly. At other times, as if conscious that I was but a temporary shell for his son's soul, he would refer to Neophron in the third person. I was 'you' or 'he' interchangeably and I couldn't determine what made the difference in his mind on any given day. Sometimes he would tell me stories of Neophron's youth, as if recounting memories that he expected me to share. And sometimes, in the faintest and most insubstantial way, I almost did remember them too. There was a tale of Neophron as a child, when he had decided to hide for the day in some obscure corner of the palace at Theres, causing uproar when the staff realised he was missing. As Zothar told me this, sitting at the opposite end of the immense dining table, I had the sharpest impression of the musty attic room where Neophron had secluded himself; the motes of dust spinning in the web of light as it fell from the lattice window, the shell of a dead scarab lying on the floorboards.

'Tell me, my lord, of your journey to bring back Neophron's soul,' I asked him once, raising my voice and calling down the length of the table. 'It sounds a thing of myth and legend, so extraordinary that I'm sure I would thrill to hear it.'

But Zothar fell silent. He gave an evasive answer and the conversation, such as it was, stuttered to a halt. We sat there in silence for the rest of the evening, while I tried to eat. He would not speak of such things, it seemed.

I began to feel almost sorry for him, if such a thing were possible. All these moments, these strange and uncomfortable occasions, were like he was trying to acquaint himself with someone after a long absence, trying to bridge the distance that time had placed between them. Had he done this with each of the winners of the

Contest over the centuries? Sat here in this draughty hall, in this trembling darkness, reminding them of the childhood memories that sat somewhere behind a transposed veil inside them? I could barely articulate it to myself at the time, but when I returned to my chambers after these interminable occasions were over, I felt the press of sympathy swelling in me. He did not care for me exactly, not for Lycus, son of Cleon and Astraea, but he had nursed his grief for so long that in his dealings with me was reflected an ancient and ever-nurtured love.

I had been there a year now, in the dim and sinister streets of Athrabis, alone apart from the ministrations of the Bonereapers who were set to watch over me and train my body and mind. I was utterly without family or friends, without anyone my own age, without even someone else capable of feeling the blood flowing in their veins. Is it any wonder then that when such love was tentatively displayed, I took it up with gratitude?

Three weeks later, the army returned from its campaign. I was in the library off the ornamental square one gloomy afternoon, in the grand cathedral of the city's knowledge, searching through the stacks and the dust-shrouded shelves for information on old Lament and the Jackal Kings. The sky was bruised and dark, streaked with purple clouds. The library was thick with shadows. Suddenly I could hear the tramp of marching feet, like thunder rumbling in the distance, the overwhelming howl of the city gates yawning wide. I ran to a tall, lead-lined window, where a tallow candle burned atop a human skull in a recessed niche beside it. The flame cast an eerie glow on the glass, showing me my own reflection. I was shocked at how thin and pale I looked, and how much older too. The long and brutal hours training with Khetera had evidently hardened me.

Down in the square, the obelisks were like dead trees shorn

of their branches. Flecks of icy rain struck the glass. I could see the front ranks of the Mortek Guard marching through the wide pathways, a stream of soldiers that seemed never-ending. Flanking them were the Deathriders, and when at last the Mortek Guard had passed, I saw those weird, hunched behemoths lumbering past, their hollow backs full to the brim with bloodstained bone.

I ran from the reading room and took the steps on the imperial staircase two at a time, bounding down into the cavernous hall and sprinting for the doors. I stood on the threshold, looking down into the square, which stretched away from me for half a mile. Near every square foot of it was filled with the king's legion. Some of the troops had clearly been in battle; shields were notched, and bones were fractured, but if they had taken significant casualties, it wasn't obvious by their numbers. I couldn't see Khetera anywhere, but I doubted I was lucky enough that such a vicious fighter would have fallen in combat.

I could see King Zothar and Se'bak in the distance, turning north and making for the palace with a cabal of Boneshapers at their side. Zothar seemed slumped in the saddle, only one hand on the reins. I was surprised to find myself worried that he had been injured. The Ossiarch Bonereapers were immune to pain, but I was concerned that he had taken an injury too severe to be repaired. If Zothar fell, then what would my position be in the kingdom of Athrabis?

I scurried down the colossal staircase into the square and followed, feet slapping on the wet stone. I knew my way to the palace by now and the only difficulty I had was in weaving my way through the vast crowds of Zothar's troops as they made their way back to barracks. I pushed through wet bone and cold steel, recoiling at the stench of blood from their weapons. Up close, I could see that the legion had been involved in some bitter fighting; slung onto the back of the massive Harvesters were stacks of bone that had clearly been taken from fallen Ossiarch troops.

Zothar and his entourage, mounted on their bone-construct war-horses, quickly outpaced me. I followed as best I could, reaching the palace a good ten minutes behind them and pushing my way through the half-open double doors. The hall glimmered with the soft emerald light of the aetherlamps. Shadows danced up the flanks of the stone pillars and there was a trail of bone dust scattered across the polished marble floor. I followed it towards the map room, Zothar's private study. I could hear low voices in the distance, muttered speech that I couldn't decipher. The door was open a crack, enough to let me peer through into the room. I could see Zothar sunk into an ornate, high-backed chair that looked as if it had been carved from the skull of some strange avian creature. Half his ribcage had been shattered and the jewel on his breastplate was fractured. The lights of his eyes were dim, like guttering candle flames. His helm and his sword were cast to the ground at his feet. Se'bak stood there beside him, muttering incantations. Phaetor, one of the Boneshapers, was weaving threads of osseous material from a stack of rendered bone beside him, spinning and coiling them in the air and then using them to reknit Zothar's injuries. I watched as the ribcage re-formed, as Se'bak prised the soul gem from Zothar's breastplate and replaced it with one that glowed with lustrous fire. I wondered how close to death he had come – to true death, insurmountable. Hovering there on the edge of my mind as well, something that I was unwilling to confront, was the question of who, in turn, had been able to do this to him? I felt the tug of concern, of sympathy. I was worried about him, I realised.

There were three of the king's Deathriders with him and they drew their swords when they noticed me lingering at the door. Zothar, gaining some vigour from the ministrations of Se'bak and Phaetor, gestured for them to stay their weapons. He waved his hand to dismiss me.

'My lord,' I protested, 'your injuries...'

'Are of no concern,' Zothar growled. 'Begone, child. By tomorrow they will be mere memory, to add to all the others.'

'But, my lord... Father–'

'Begone!'

I turned to go, but not before I had the chance to see one of the Deathriders affixing another weapon to the wall: a great twin-bladed axe, its brass pommel stained with years of dried blood. Another trophy of whatever battle the king had just fought and won.

It was a few days after this that I received news from Lament that my father had died. A rider crossed the desert, bearing a message from my mother. Challenged at the gates of Athrabis, inarticulate with terror, he had passed the note on before fleeing for his life back into the desert sands. I had never heard of this before, of such contact between Lament and the necropolis outside of the Games, but it must be remembered that my mother was an elder of the council and had a greater than usual influence.

The note was brought to me in my chambers by a silent member of the Mortek Guard. I regretted the missed chance of talking to the messenger, but when I saw my mother's handwriting and her wax seal, I put it out of my mind. I sat in the dusty kitchen, a fine layer of sand on the tabletop, and opened the parchment.

It was as I had expected. He had been given to the Tower and had fed the sky. All the rites had been obeyed. The dry-lung could no longer torment him.

Blessings on this day, my mother wrote, *for he goes to fill the tithe.*

I thought of the ossuary beside the palace, stacked floor to ceiling with the bones of Lament. I thought of my father, and I was surprised to discover that I couldn't bring his face back to mind. He was gone.

10

The dusk took him, as if he could not face the darkness. Selene sat with him as his life flowed away. When the crisp sunset had smeared into a seething flame, her grandfather died at last. His hand went slack in hers, but she held it still.

The three small rooms where they lived seemed larger all at once, as if she was stuck in the middle of a space it would take her days to cross. She opened the door onto the veranda at the front, breathed in the scent of the night-blooming grave-flowers as they unfurled their purple petals to the dusk. She could see over the fence to the line of the Keening Way, but the street was mostly empty now. Shuttered windows, closed doors. The air was cold, a chill wind coming in off the sea. He had been a fisherman all his life and she was glad the smell of salt spray had seen him on his way.

She sat there for a while, looking out at the city. She could hear the tolling of the hour bells, down by the Tower. The raised voices of the shopkeepers closing up for the day, complaining about business to their neighbours. The clank of buckets being filled down at the well, the Failed dragging them up from the deep water shafts. She wondered where Dardus was this evening. She saw him most days down in the agora and the sight never failed to lift her spirits. He attacked his duties now the same way he had attacked the Contest, as if he could grind them into submission. She hoped she had been partly responsible for that and that she had brought him a measure of peace and hope. Anger simmered always below the surface in him though. They were everywhere, once you learned to see them: the Failed, a despised caste dragging themselves through their miserable days. Her grandfather had always thought it an outrage.

'Give folk an example to follow and let them excel if they can,' he grumbled. 'But if not, why should they be despised for trying? In the end, what the hell else can we do, eh?'

She closed the veranda door and returned to his whitewashed room at the back of the house. It was dark in there now and there was a rank smell in the air. She opened the window, kissed his worn old face, and drew the sheet across it.

There were formalities to follow, she knew. She should tell someone, Astraea perhaps, let her inform the priests. The body would be washed and prepared, and at midday it would be taken to the Tower. She tried to imagine that moment, the old man being carried down the Keening Way. And then the ceremony, and the days that would follow, where every glimpse of the vultures rising from the Tower would make her think of his flesh being torn away.

He would have scorned all of it. 'They're my bloody bones,' he had said once. 'Let me keep them!'

He was of Sigmar, but she had no idea what the Sigmarites did with their dead. He had never told her. It was possible he didn't even know himself. He had never taken instruction from a Sigmarite priest, as far as she knew, if there even were such things.

His prayers to his god had always sounded more like curses to her and they were usually made only when he was complaining about something. But he had said Sigmar was a god of strength and bravery, standing up for the weak and fighting for what was right. Perhaps what was right was not to let his body be taken to the Tower of the Moon. He shouldn't feed the sky. His bones should not be given to that king across the desert, whether he was a god himself or otherwise.

'Sigmar guide me…' she mumbled.

She glanced to the open window, where the sky showed as a grey veil fading to black. It was forbidden in Lament to bury or to burn the dead, she knew. All must be given to the Tower, the bones cleansed by the birds and joined to the tithe. She remembered standing with Astraea a few weeks ago, as Cleon was taken by the priests, Astraea's hand clutching hers, the catch in her voice, the sense of her tears behind the carved and painted wood of the mourning mask. She tried to imagine herself standing there with one of those masks on her face, dressed in those abrasive black robes, as her grandfather was taken from her. She could not; it was impossible.

Very well, then.

It was a simple enough job to pull up the floorboards in his room. With a twist and a bit of force, the wooden nails came up with a shriek and then the whole board could be laid aside. Underneath was hard-packed earth, but there was an iron spade in the yard at the back which he had used for the kitchen garden. Selene fetched it and hammered the blade into the earth, peeling it roughly aside. She looked at his body lying there under the sheet. Then she dug the spade in deeper.

It took her all night and by the end her arms were aching. The hole she had made was no more than four feet deep and four feet across, but she hoped it would be enough. She stood there looking down into the soft grey earth, more like clay the deeper down she had dug. A couple of pale, tuberous worms wriggled in the muck, and she tried not to think of what they would do to her grandfather's body. Was that any better or any worse than what the vultures would do? Was the sky burial a cleaner thing, in a way, than leaving him to rot and dissolve in the cold, unfeeling earth? What final clasp was that for a man to feel, the wet mud clinging close?

If it didn't feel exactly right though, then it certainly didn't feel wholly wrong. His bones were his own, as he had said. Let him keep them.

With the last of her strength Selene dragged her grandfather from the bed, the sheet slipping off his corpse and tangling in his legs. She dragged it free, reeling at the stink of excrement, the sour reek of bile. She cried bitter tears. There was nothing blessed in this, nothing noble or pure. No wonder the priests kept death to themselves, jealously guarding its secrets. *The vultures*, she thought. That's what he had called them. *Damned vultures, every one!*

She rolled the body into the pit, clambered down to tuck the legs up, to lay the head on his resting arms.

'I'm sorry, Grandfather,' she said.

She could imagine his irascible reply. *Don't worry about me! Damned if I care either way now...*

He looked like a baby in a woman's belly, she thought, all curled up like that. Like someone waiting to be born again. Perhaps that's what Sigmar did, as her grandfather had claimed. Took the bravest souls and let them be born again to fight for him.

Before she filled in the hole she reached down and took the pendant from his neck. The hammer, symbol of Sigmar. She wondered if the merchant who had rescued him from the water had given it to him, or if he had perhaps made it himself. She put it around her own neck and told herself that she could feel her grandfather's strength flowing from it. His anger, his sense of decency and justice. She could feel Sigmar's strength, the god of lightning, who you praised by doing the right thing. By being strong, by standing up for those who weren't as strong as you.

'Praise be to Sigmar,' she whispered. 'Sigmar guide my hand. Sigmar take this man's soul into your care, for he was your loyal servant.'

She dug, tipped the earth, filled the hole. The day lightened. Morning was coming.

'As am I,' she said.

PART TWO

THE JACKAL KINGS

11

There was a power in the earth, and it weighed the price of all souls…

It was death to seek it, but legends claimed that for those with the deepest need, a path could be sometimes found and followed. A trail into the Underworlds, where that power could be beseeched and where everything could be risked on its whim. And yet, what father would not risk his very soul to save his son?

He rode alone from Athrabis, west, into the deepest desert. Three days and nights, without halt. Twilit skies waxed and waned as he travelled, the celestial orbs spinning in the void above. The desert scrub, the grey sand and the black stone, ever around him. Sometimes jackals and bone-crows rose from scavenged prey and fled before him, and once he saw the curled twist of a campfire in the distance; evidence of some wanderer in the wild, drawn to the wastes of Shyish for whatever inscrutable reason. For Zothar, though, these lands were not the wild. They were all a part of his kingdom. He moved through them at will.

He came to the ruins of Theres on the fourth day. Scattered blocks of wind-blasted stone, pillars listing in the dust, the suggestion of old walls and buried foundations in the heaped grey sand. He passed the broken head of a monumental statue, its virtuous, solemn face staring off into the wilderness with sightless marble eyes. He saw a jackal slink from the dunes at his approach. He paused and watched it for a while, until it disappeared into the night.

No foe had cast the city down. Fire and storm hadn't broken these buildings or ruined these battlements. It was just time; time and neglect. It was memory withdrawn and the ease of forgetting. It had been a thousand years since he had left Theres to bargain for his son's soul; a thousand years since he had returned, transformed, to lead his most loyal troops away. He had kept his side of the bargain, always; and in his cruel and unfathomable way, so had Nagash.

He guided his steed down what had once been the Royal Procession, the gateway into Theres. It was now just a faint dark line in the desert. On either side were the slumped remains of old temples and ruined tenements, the stone now bitten by the winds, the drifts of sand rising up to smother them. Ahead should have been the city courtyard and its rows of statuary, but time had withered all this to nothing. Gravewort flowered between the cracks in the stone and here and there he saw the scurry of tomb-lizards, but there was no other life, not any more. Zothar pressed his heels to his mount's flank and with a rattle of bones it cantered on. The sky darkened ahead of him. In the distance it was strobed by flashes of black lightning and from far off over the dunes came the eerie shriek of a tormented spirit seeking oblivion.

Somewhere in the middle of the city would be Neophron's tomb, he knew; the mausoleum he had raised for his son when he brought his body back from the Games at Lament. Not a trace of it remained now. Like everything else in Theres, it had been swallowed entire. He sought its rough location, knowing that it had occupied the grandest and most imposing space. He had ordered a hundred days of official mourning, while he sat slumped in his palace, stoking his rage and his grief. He remembered the madness of that time, the disbelief that his son was gone. A boy of such life and grace, so careless with his attention that he had friends from high to low amongst the citizens of the city; a young man, bold and quick, confident beyond measure...

That was what Zothar told himself, at least. He drew to a halt and dropped from the saddle, leaving his steed's reins to trail in the dust. He found a spar of broken rock, the remains of one of the old warehouses that had flanked the courtyard in the long years gone by. In truth, as he could sometimes admit to himself, Neophron could be lazy and arrogant, uninterested in the honour and glory of his city and his family. He had gone to the Games at Lament because his father had forced him, and it was only the heats that had awoken his natural competitiveness. He had wanted to win for himself, not for his city. Certainly not for his father.

'The fault was mine,' Zothar whispered into the gathering dark. 'I was the one who killed you...'

His voice scratched against the air, as harsh as the desert wind.

Often he came here to Theres, to dwell in his memories like this. Over the course of a thousand years, it had always struck him how it was these last moments of being human that had the most force and colour for him. Neophron falling in the still, silent air from the cusp of the Tower in Lament; the long days sunk in grief as his mausoleum was constructed; the hints and rumours that came his way, gleaned in the madness of that grief from the depths of the palace archives, of a possible means to bring him back... He remembered little else of his time as a mortal man, but those dread final days were ever green in his mind.

He had called for priests and soothsayers, masters of ancient lore, old crones in desert settlements who were links in the long chain of legend and myth. For hours, he would interrogate them in the throne room, dressed in his stinking robes, too wild with sorrow to wash or dress himself. He recalled one wise woman, gnarled with age, a healer for the peasants who lived in the ramshackle villages far beyond the walls of the city. She had limped across the marble floor of the throne room, unmoved by the gilded statuary, the vast censers hanging from the ceiling, the opulence and power of Zothar's rule. Zothar had beckoned her forward and turned his grey, unshaven face towards her.

'Legends tell of a power in the earth,' he said, his voice cracked and dry. He reached for wine to refresh himself, but the goblet was empty. 'A being that some say rules Shyish, this Realm of Death.'

The crone had laughed, an ill-favoured cackle.

'Aye, my lord,' she said. Her voice was a feeble croak. 'Who you seek is the Lord of Death itself, the Monarch of Souls. Old Bones, some call him… Master of Graves, *Kharos*, in the language of my folk… Who you seek is *Nagash*.'

He had shivered as he sat there, though the room was warm.

'And this Nagash will give me back my son?' he demanded. 'He can be beseeched? He can be bargained with?'

The old woman had laughed long and loud then. Slowly, shaking with age, she raised her walking stick and pointed it at him.

'*Kharos* recognises no bargains, for he is lord of all souls. They are his to do with as he wilt. You can beseech him, King Zothar, if you are brave enough to enter his domain and seek him out. But I cannot promise that his answer will be anything but your utter destruction…'

He had called for his armour and his horse before her words had even begun to fade.

'Where!' he demanded. 'Tell me – where can Nagash be found!'

'North,' the crone said, with a sly look. 'Seek out the Cave of Skulls, which breathes death into the very air. There, perhaps, you shall find what you seek.'

He remembered his journey to the Underworlds more than anything else that had happened to him in his long and violent life. Indeed, whenever his final dissolution came, he was certain it would be the only thing he would remember, fresh in his fading mind in all its dread and horror.

He rode north as the crone had bade, flogging his horse until it could run no more. When it collapsed under him, he drew his cloak about his shoulders and walked, heading far from the lands of Theres and the Obsidian Coast into the unknown. The desert faded to a bleak tundra, frosted with cold, the earth as lifeless and grey as the lowering clouds above. At night he huddled under his cloak, not daring to light a campfire. He listened to the howls of lost spirits as they stalked the land. In the morning he rose and carried on. In the distance there was only a bleak mist, the hint of low-slung hills. He headed towards them.

He found the Cave of Skulls when the last of his water was gone. The mouth was fringed with blackened teeth, each twice his height, and great hollow eyes gazed on him from above it. A thin, drear mist flowed from that mouth, stinking of the grave. He covered his face with a desert scarf and drew his sword. Without a backwards glance he entered.

Days seemed to pass as he journeyed through the dark. The ground sloped under him, and the mouth of the cave narrowed to a ridged tunnel. The stench of death increased, so foul that he had to stop and vomit before he could go on. Bats chittered in the eaves, flashing past him. He beat them back with his sword and lowered his head as he pressed on.

Spirits assailed him the deeper he went. In pitch darkness they flared with grave-light, screaming at him, clawing with their spectral fingers. Some took the guise of his parents, begging him to turn back. His wife, even, dead in childbirth when Neophron was brought into the world. She caressed him and whispered lascivious secrets into his ears that had him snarling with rage. He ignored them all. Through the blind darkness, foot after foot, as the tunnel sloped into the stinking bowels of the earth.

At last, he came to an open chamber, which was covered at one end by a web of bone. Green mist flared and twisted in the shadows around him. He held his sword up and advanced – and suddenly the web of bone shattered into a swirling, shrieking mass that surrounded him; a tide of bone-crows clattering their skeletal wings about his head. When they spoke, their voices drilled into his mind and the pain was enough to throw him to his knees.

Who dares trespass into the presence of the lord! Who values his soul so lightly he would do this thing!

Zothar pressed his hands to his ears.

'I am King Zothar, Lord of Theres! The Jewel of the Desert, the City in the Wastes,' he cried. 'I seek Nagash, King of the Dead. I have come to demand my son's soul!'

The bone-crows erupted from around his head, spinning off in a twisting, screaming mass that disappeared into the tunnel behind him. Zothar collapsed, utterly spent.

He heard something slouch from the other side of the chamber. He heard the clack of bones, the scrape of claws. He heard the beating of its wings.

When Zothar found the courage to look, he saw Nagash.

Like the skeleton of a mighty vulture, it hunched there in the cavern, its wings folded against its chest, its long, sinuous neck rearing up as it peered at him down the scimitar of its beak. Its bones were as stained and yellow as old ivory and it smelled of ancient midnights, of deserts that had been scoured clean by the wind a thousand, thousand years ago. And when he grasped his courage and looked on it, for a moment it seemed to shift in the spectral gloom and look like a man towering above him, wreathed in spirits, laughing with malicious humour through a leering mouth.

King Zothar, the vulture said. *I salute your bravery, if not your folly, for coming here. Many an age has it been since a hero has taken sword and shield to confront me in like manner...*

'I am no hero,' Zothar said, shielding his eyes. He dropped his sword. 'And I am not brave, unless it is grief that gives me courage. I do not confront you, Lord of Death, other than to ask for that which it is in your power to give.'

And what would a mortal ask of Nagash, that he would risk his eternal soul for it?

'My soul is yours, if you desire it. It is worth nothing to me. It is my son's soul that is without price to me. Neophron, as was – killed by the preening arrogance of the Jackal Kings in far Lament, on the Obsidian Coast. I would have him returned to me and anything it is in *my* power to give, you shall have.'

Lament... the vulture mused. The great beak clacked and the murderous lights in its empty eyes flared brightly. *The Obsidian Coast... And what would you be prepared to give up for this? What sacrifice will you make, for the restoration of your son?*

'Anything,' Zothar said. He spoke no lie. 'My life, my soul.'

Your city...?

Zothar paused. He looked into himself, walked for a moment in the pleasant avenues of Theres once more, stood for a while in the courtyard with its soaring statues of Theres' ancient kings and heroes. He gazed on the faces of the common folk, the people who looked to him for love and protection.

'Yes,' he said, although the word nearly choked him. 'I would rather Neophron live as a humble beggar wandering the wilds than have him spend eternity in the cold earth, his soul a lost and lonely spirit in the Underworlds. Yes,' he said. 'Take Theres and everyone in it if you must. And damn me forever for my choice!'

And you would serve me, at my command, if asked, the vulture said. *You would lead your armies in my service and conquer the Obsidian Coast in my name?*

'If need be,' Zothar said. He felt the grief swell in him, the slack, empty feeling of his sorrow. Grief for Neophron, grief for all he had now condemned. 'I will serve. I ask only one condition.'

There was a sound like the cold clash of swords and Zothar realised the vulture was laughing.

You are bold, King Zothar, I give you that, to ask conditions of Nagash. Speak, then. What is your condition?

'That Lament is left to my judgement. I will have my revenge against the Jackal Kings and will see the city pulled stone from stone. And at the last, I will drag the Tower of the Moon from its foundations and cast it into rubble.'

Then the bargain is made, the vulture hissed. *And the soul of your son will be returned to you...*

'When!' Zothar demanded. 'Bring him to me!'

You will not find him here, King Zothar... For I have my conditions too, to seal the compact between us. You will find your son now in far Lament...

'What riddle is this?' Zothar cried. He snatched up his sword. Though his spirit quailed in the presence of the Lord of Death, he took a step forward and raised his blade. 'You seek to cheat me of what we agreed!'

There is no agreement that is not made on my terms, little human, the vulture laughed. *Neophron will return to you, this I promise. But his soul will settle only for a ten-year span and will wither and die in each vessel unless it is released to find new harbour. He died in the Games of Lament, did he not? Very well – he will return to you in the Games of Lament, and as the victor you shall know him. Do not be so hasty to tear the city down, King Zothar, for if you do, you will lose that which guarantees your son's recurrence.*

'Why do you do this!' Zothar wept. 'I will do what you ask, you have my word! Why torment me like this!'

My reasons are my own and they would be far beyond your comprehension, mortal. Now, the vulture hissed, as it shuffled closer. *The bargain will be made...*

Its claws crunched over ancient bones, scattered about the floor of the cavern. Zothar tried to back away, but the fierce fire of the creature's gaze kept him pinned to the spot. He could not raise his sword. He could not close his eyes. All he could do was stand and watch in horror, as the vulture spread its wings and Nagash gathered him close.

Come to Nagash, it whispered; and Zothar saw only darkness. *Come to Nagash, and be transformed...*

When the memories had flowed and settled in him once more, Zothar rode back through the ruins of Theres and sought the desert path. He had kept his word, as Nagash had kept his. City by city, settlement by settlement, the Obsidian Coast fell to Zothar's sword. Theres was abandoned and Athrabis founded, as the seat of his power. All life was expunged, every man, woman and child cut down and rendered into new materials for his armies. What had once been a fertile corner of Shyish was now a wasteland, a bleak landscape of silence and tormented spirits. Only Lament remained with a semblance of its former life. The Jackal Kings were chased from their palace and dashed to pieces on the rocks by the sea. Over the centuries the city stewed in the ignorance of its own history. Sealed off, at the mercy of the Bonereapers, the people of Lament gradually fell into a confused worship of their overlord. At first it had amused him, but in time Zothar came to understand its use.

Let me be a god amongst them then, he had thought. *Let them quail before me, and ever feed their dead into the tithe. And let the Games continue, for eternity, and let this kingdom be a permanent wake for my son, to mourn his passing... Until he is returned to me at last.*

As he rode back to Athrabis, he clutched again at this faint hope. Nagash had kept his side of the bargain, it was true, but perhaps in time it was possible for even gods to forget what they had agreed. Perhaps one day, when the next Neophron stepped forward at the end of the Contest, Se'bak would look upon him and realise that this time his soul was a permanent thing.

I will have my son again, he thought, as he guided his steed back across the bleak sands. *And at last I can lie down and die.*

12

Five years had passed, but Selene found she thought about Lycus more the longer he had been away; as if distance had burnished him in her mind, made him more present, more real. She thought about him every day. When she was trying to get to sleep, lying on the soft down mattress in her bedroom in Astraea's house, she would hold her grandfather's pendant in her hand and pray for him.

'Sigmar, lord, watch over my friend,' she whispered. 'Keep him safe and let some of your strength flow into him. Let him not fear. Let… let me not fear for him either, but know that you will protect him, when the time comes…'

Then she would roll onto her side and tuck the pendant away beneath her shirt and try not to think of Dardus instead. The memory of Lycus made her feel angry and sorrowful all at once, her heart compressed by the love she knew she felt for him. Dardus just made her feel afraid.

No, not afraid, she admitted. *Excited…*

Her room in Astraea's house looked out onto the street at the back, a quiet alleyway shaded by an ancient woe tree. It was easy enough to unclasp the shutters and slip from the window, and then it was just a short stretch to the woe tree's branches. She lowered herself hand over hand to the ground without anyone hearing. She did this most nights now, when Astraea was asleep, and she was so practised she made barely a sound.

The alleyway was dark, and no one saw or heard her as she slipped along its length. She pulled her dark scarf up over her head, tucked her flaxen hair out of sight and padded silently along the streets of the first tier.

The gates to the second tier had been closed for the night, but it was no great trouble to scale them. When she dropped down onto the other side, she heard the hiss of a startled cat as it slunk off down the gutter and she could see the bobbing light of the watchman's lantern further down the road. She hid in the shadows for a moment until it had receded and the soft pad off his footsteps had faded away. She reached up and felt the pendant under her shirt.

Watch over me as I do your work, Lord Sigmar...

Lament was a quiet city at night. There were few bustling taverns open past dusk, no raucous laughter or drunken argument in the streets. In Shyish, it did not do to draw the attention of those things that haunted the wilds. When the dusk had faded into darkness most of the city lamps were snuffed out and people retreated into their homes. Lament, as the council were fond of reminding its citizens, was a pious and sober place. Praise King Zothar, and let us keep it that way.

She sneered at the thought. Its piety was no more than the mask of oppression. *Let us tear that mask away and see its true face...*

Dardus was waiting for her in the third tier, by the silver tree in the narrow little courtyard where she had first met him after his leg had healed. Years ago now, but she could remember it as if it were yesterday. Coming back with her grandfather's medicine, in the days when the old man still clung stubbornly to life. He was watching over her now, she knew it, the way Sigmar was watching over her too. The old house was hers no more, but her grandfather's body still lay deep in the earth beneath it. Safe from the priests and the tithe.

She had told Astraea that he had got up early one morning and headed out to the coast, claiming that he was going to do some fishing. That was the last she had ever seen of him, and she had wept as she said it. Astraea had accepted this, it seemed. After all, he was a stubborn old man, wasn't he? He wouldn't have just sat there waiting patiently for death to find him. It was just like him.

Dardus was sitting on the edge of the planter when she reached the courtyard, picking with a knife at the dirt beneath his nails. There was a canvas sack at his feet, tied with a length of frayed rope. His blonde hair was long and straggly, reaching down to his shoulders. Five years of hard physical work amongst the Failed had made him lithe and strong, but in the hardness of his face there was a hint of cruelty that sometimes scared her. She never knew what he would do, or in which direction he would turn his anger next.

'You're late,' he said. 'Didn't think you were coming. Thought the elder might have kept you home.'

'Astraea?' Selene said. She slouched nonchalantly towards him and sat down. 'She's all right, you know. Half the time I think she knows what we get up to and she's happy for us to do it. I don't think she likes this place any more than we do.'

Dardus snorted. He passed her a half-empty bottle of firewater. 'Now you're just being naïve.'

Selene took a slug from the bottle and felt it burn down her chest. Her eyes prickled with tears, but she managed not to cough as she passed the bottle back. Dardus stabbed his blade into the meat of the tree while he took another drink.

'Honestly,' Selene said. 'Since Grandfather died, I've seen her at close quarters, every day. She hates this place. Hates the council, especially that preening idiot Baeothis. She just goes through the motions.'

Dardus laughed softly. 'Well, I suppose waiting to see your son's head cut off at the next Games would put a dampener on things, that's for sure...'

Selene bristled. 'That won't happen,' she said steadily.

He looked at her askance. 'And why not?'

'Because... because Sigmar will stop it. Sigmar will save him.'

'Oh, spare us from Sigmar, not again!' he sneered. 'It's always Sigmar with you, I'm sick of hearing about him.'

'You'd rather King Zothar, would you?' she spat. She snatched the bottle from him and drank.

'At least I've *seen* Zothar. I haven't seen hide nor hair of Sigmar, wherever he is. If he's so wonderful, let him show himself now. Go on, call on him!'

Selene shook her head and said nothing. She felt the rage burning in her, harder and fiercer than the firewater. Lord, but she hated Dardus sometimes. Always sneering and mocking, but if you dared to tease him back then the anger would flare up in him like a kindled flame. Astraea had been good to her since her grandfather had died, had treated her with love and kindness, and she would defend her to the hilt. But Sigmar didn't need her protests or her defence. He was too powerful for that. Dardus' barbs were insignificant to him.

'See?' he said. 'And your grandfather didn't *really* walk off into the sea one morning, did he?'

'Come on,' Selene said sharply. She drained the bottle and let it shatter on the ground at her feet. 'Did you bring the stuff? If we're going to do this, then let's go and do it now.'

Dardus grinned and kicked the bag at his feet. She could see the gap of his missing tooth, the scar that crinkled his chin from one of the many beatings he had taken amongst the Failed. Wherever he went, provocation and violence followed.

'Right then,' he said. 'Time to make our mark.'

In the midnight dark, the Tower of the Moon was like a pillar of black ink. Nagash's Eye gave a fitful glow far above it, but for the most part the agora was veiled with shadow. No watchmen patrolled between the wooden benches or stood observing from the steps on either side. The trees moaned softly in the night breeze and there was a smell of death in the air.

'Couple of sky burials yesterday afternoon,' Dardus whispered beside her. 'Priests cleared out the bone from the platforms in the morning, I watched them while I was sweeping the roads there.'

They were crouched down by the sunken flower beds along the southern edge of the square. Night gripped them, sultry and dark. The moonlight was like a thin blanket laid across the city, tinged with green. They kept their voices low.

'How long until the next tithing?' Selene asked.

'A week or so,' he said. 'A delegation comes from Athrabis, meets the priests at the city gates.'

'How many of them?'

'I don't know exactly, but just a handful. Nothing like during the Games.'

She pictured them, the bone-men of Athrabis. She hadn't seen any of them up close since she was a child, not since Lycus had been taken away. She had an impression in her mind of their leering skulls, their empty, hollow eyes, the bones of their hands wrapped around the hilts of their blades. Every year the tithe was collected at the borders of the city, but it was priests' business and she had not seen them since. For most citizens, only the Games brought them face to face with their overlords.

'That's a full year's supply then,' Selene said. 'Why isn't it under guard?'

Dardus shrugged. She could smell him beside her, the scent of sweat and the dirty straw where he slept. The Failed had their own quarters down by the gates, although Dardus said he spent most of his nights wandering the city while it was dark. There was no one to see him then, no one to look on him with pity and scorn.

'Why would they guard it?' he said now. 'It's Lament's gift to the king, who would possibly want to steal it?' He grinned at her with his gap-toothed smile, a fierce look on his face. 'Course, we're not exactly here to steal it, are we?'

He unslung the bag from his shoulder and took out the chisel and the hammer.

The door at the base of the Tower was barred with a single lock and it was the work of moments for Dardus to shear it free. He smothered the blows with Selene's scarf and even standing next to him all she could hear was a dull thump. They stepped into the chamber. The smell was musty and dark, threaded with the faint, sweet scent of rotting flesh.

The cedar chests in which the tithe was gifted were laid at the foot of the staircase that led up to the higher levels. There were three of them, the collected bones of everyone who had died in Lament over the year just past. Two of them were locked but one was still open, its lid thrown back and the stacked bone on display. Selene saw femurs and shoulder blades, shards of skull and jaw, the flared node of a fractured ilium. Some were still stained pink with blood.

While Selene kept watch at the door Dardus took the oil from his bag. Without a pause he started pouring it all over the chests. Nervously she glanced back at him as he rummaged for his tinderbox.

'Wait...' she said. He didn't look around.

'Why?' he said. 'Getting cold feet?'

'This is… If we do this, there's no coming back. All the other things we've done, even breaking into the priests' quarters the time we stole those robes, that doesn't really mean anything. This though, we could get in serious trouble, they'd… They'd exile me, but you they'd kill. Do you understand? They'd execute you for this, Dardus. We're sixteen now, we're not children.'

He gave a bleak laugh. 'You seriously think I care?' he said. 'Let them. And Astraea would look out for you, wouldn't she? Spare you the worst of it. Who knows, maybe you'd get to join the ranks of the Failed, like me!'

She shuddered. Exile would be better, she thought. Wouldn't it?

'There are more of us than you think,' Dardus said. 'Amongst the Failed, amongst the ordinary folk. People who've seen their sons and daughters die in the Games, who've seen their loved ones ripped apart by the vultures and their bones spirited away to those monsters in the desert. They're angry, Selene. They're very, very angry, and all it will take to make them rise up…'

He scraped the flint of his tinderbox and watched the flame lick out across the oil.

'…is one little spark.'

There was a pause, a shiver of disturbed air – and then the cedar chests went up like torches.

There was a lamp burning in the hall of Astraea's house when Selene returned. She saw it when she clambered over the gate into the first tier, the stacked white stone of the other houses rising dark and silent around her. The Regent's Palace squatted empty above it all, at the very apex of the city, the ringed colonnade thick with shadows, the peaked marble roof shining very slightly in the soft, mist-shrouded light of Nagash's Eye.

When she reached the back of the house where the woe tree

spread its branches below her window, she slipped her sandals off her feet and padded quietly to the base of its trunk. For a long moment she paused, listening, but she could hear no sounds from inside the house. Perhaps Astraea had woken badly during the night again and had lit the lamp to chase away her dreams. She often did this, emerging on a wave of dread from nightmares where Lycus had returned to Lament in the skeletal guise of a Bonereaper, converted by the king into one of his own. In the mornings, her face pale and tight with exhaustion, she would confess her fears while Selene listened. There was no one else she could talk to, no one who wouldn't argue, at least in public, that what had happened to her son was the greatest blessing imaginable, even if in private they might have held their secret doubts.

Selene scaled the tree quickly and quietly and slipped into the open window, her sandals strung about her neck. She closed the shutters and was about to ease herself under the sheets when her door creaked slowly open and Astraea was standing there in her nightgown, with the lamp in her hand.

In the cast flames, her face looked wild with anxiety. Her hair, normally so sleek and lacquered, was in disarray. Selene froze in the centre of the room, her bare feet cold on the marble floor.

'I saw you,' Astraea said, in strange, faraway voice. 'Running, and Lycus too, and the Contest almost run… And there was a great flame burning in the city…'

'Astraea?' Selene said. 'Are you all right?'

Was she dreaming? Her eyes were dim and unfocused, but then as Selene took her arm and gently guided her back to her own bedchamber, they seemed to clear and she came round to herself once more. On the threshold of the chamber, Astraea turned to face her, peering down into Selene's eyes.

'He will return, won't he?' she said. 'Lycus… I dream about him sometimes, only in the dreams he is a young man, no longer a boy, and the dreams feel...'

'Yes?' Selene said.

'Well... they do not feel like dreams. They feel like glimpses of something that will come to pass, images that I've been sent to give me strength.'

Selene felt for the pendant under her shirt.

'Perhaps Sigmar is sending them to you,' she whispered. 'He gives hope to those who have none, to better guide their arm when they strike for justice.'

Astraea smiled indulgently. She never discouraged Selene in her talk of Sigmar and sometimes she even gave the impression of real interest. Selene had little she could really tell her though. Just an idea of him, an impression based on what she hoped to be true. In her mind, Sigmar was much like her grandfather; stern and unyielding, but fiercely kind too.

For the first time, Astraea seemed to realise that Selene was not dressed for bed. She glanced up as the sound of tolling bells rang distantly from the agora at the bottom level of the city, pealing across the streets and the rooftops. Very faintly could be heard the shouts and alarms of the fire watch, the bustle of water buckets being slung up from the deep wells.

'A fire...' she said absently. She looked down at Selene again and there was something cool and clear in her eyes where before there had only been concern. 'You were seeing Dardus,' she said quietly.

There was no point in lying. And yet somehow Selene knew that the truth would not be used to condemn her. Astraea already knew, she realised. More than that – she had been turning a blind eye to it, to everything she and Dardus had done. The frescoes in the temple they had defaced. The petty thefts from the priests' quarters. The bold graffiti they had scrawled on the arch of the propylon by the city gates: *Vulture Lord*.

'Yes,' she said. She wasn't ashamed. She raised her chin proudly, looked Astraea in the eyes. In the depths of Astraea's gaze, she could see the wheels and cogs beginning to turn, calculations made and unmade.

'Is he still angry?' she asked. 'At Lycus? At the Contest?'

'Yes,' Selene said. 'He's angrier than anyone I've ever met.'

Astraea nodded and turned into her chamber, the lamp still in her hand. Before she closed the door she glanced back and said:

'Good.'

13

I was sixteen when King Zothar first took me on campaign.

Since the day I had first seen the legion drawn up for war, filling the avenues of the ornamental square and marching beyond the city gates, King Zothar had taken his troops into the wastes on three more occasions. Each time I had beseeched him to take me along, to let me acquit myself in combat against his enemies, but he had always refused. With curt finality and to Khetera's leering pleasure he had dismissed me and bade me return to my chambers. I had sulked and fumed in the emptiness of Athrabis, wandering its deserted streets, kicking my heels in the empty chambers and halls. I was a young man now, I thought to myself. I was stronger than I had ever been. Though it pained me to admit it, my long years of training with Khetera had turned me into a promising swordsman. I could fight at my father's side, do honour to him and to Athrabis, and yet always he rejected me and sent me to my rooms like a child, there to await his return.

Each time the army marched back from its wars, I would watch the troops process through the gates in triumph and I would rush to the palace to see if Zothar had been injured. More often than not he had. He would sit there slumped in the bone chair beneath the map of his kingdom, patiently enduring the ministrations of Phaetor and Se'bak as they wove and knitted his injuries away. After stealing a glimpse of him, I would hurry to the parade ground and take up my sword, practising my drills, or saddle my steed and ride at spears or tilt at the lances. I was readying myself, I thought, for his next campaign. Surely next time he would call on me and at last I could show him everything I had learned. I would make him proud.

Afterwards, I would often ask him who or what he had been fighting. When we sat at those silent formal dinners, or when he called me to examine some obscure artefact from the storeroom where the relics of lost Theres were kept, I would be bold enough to question him.

'Your kingdom stretches as far as the moonlight, as long as the sun,' I said. 'The desert and the coast are yours to cross at will, and yet the army still must fight. But who, Father? Who could possibly challenge you like this?'

He would wearily bat the question away, though.

'It is not your concern, Neophron,' he would say. 'Your studies take precedence for now, your training. I would not ask an untutored child to make administrative decisions and in the same way I would not take an untrained boy to wage war.'

'I'm not untrained though!' I would protest, with all the fiery confidence of youth. 'I can fight!'

But then he would turn those blazing yellow eyes on me, and the shadow of his displeasure would descend. I would feel the cold thrill of fear and keep my own counsel; for although I had come to care for King Zothar a great deal, still I was under no illusions as to who and what he was. Though the memory grew less distinct as the years drifted by, I could still recall the indifference with which he had gestured for my mother's life. I knew as well that each year brought us closer to the next Games.

It was both a great relief then, and a great terror, when finally I was summoned from my chambers with instructions to bring my weapons and armour and such supplies as would sustain a mortal in the field for several days. Se'bak himself had come to collect me when the dawn was still a blood-streaked smear against the eastern sky.

'Take what food you need,' he croaked. 'We will not stop to rest, and the journey may be difficult for you. It would be no shame to remain behind if you do not feel yourself ready.'

I thought of Khetera's sneering laughter were I to confess such a thing. I pulled the straps tighter on my greaves.

'I'm ready,' I said.

To my great satisfaction, I was to ride with the king at the head of the army. My armour shone with the same dark lustre as his own as I took my place, and the bone crest of my helmet was the mirror of his. At my side was slung a nadirite scimitar. A shield embossed with bone was fixed to my left arm and a long cloak of rich scarlet hung from my pauldrons. As I sat there on my steed, beside the King of Athrabis, I felt unconquerable.

'Thank you, Father,' I said to him. 'I will not let you down.'

King Zothar gave the order for the gates to be opened. Behind us stretched the endless ranks of his legion, the Mortek Guard in rows and columns, the Deathriders clustered together in one huge block of cavalry. The catapults of his Mortek Crawlers were unslung and readied. The vast, four-armed giants of his Immortis Guard strode implacably into the fore.

'You have not yet seen war, my son,' he said, without looking at me. 'Let no mortal claim courage until it is tested in battle. And it *will* be tested...'

* * *

The army marched south for a day and a night, so that I almost thought we were heading for Lament. Then, as dawn rose on the second day, we turned west and headed into the rocky scrubland on the edge of the desert. Low, craggy hills rose in the distance, dark against the horizon. The land around us was a brown, bare place. The earth was parched and dry, but here and there grew clumps of sharp razor-grass, stands of a strange violet flower that shivered and trembled as if struck by a cold breeze no one else could feel.

We marched on for another two days and I heeded Se'bak's warning; it was indeed an exhaustion for me. I drowsed in the saddle where I could and ate and drank sparingly.

'Do you require rest?' Zothar asked me at one point, as my eyes drooped and I clutched the pommel of my saddle to stop myself from falling. I looked back at the vast train of the army as it stretched out behind us, the ranks of spearmen, the Death-riders in flanking screens on either side. How to ask all this to halt for even a moment, so one man could lie down and sleep?

'No,' I said. 'We continue.'

On the fourth day out from Athrabis, with those craggy hills now far on our left, I looked up from my half-dreams and saw a long line of cloud forming in the distance. Dark and billowing, with a dim rumble of thunder rising from it.

'A storm,' I said, pointing. 'Although I don't suppose it will hold us up.'

King Zothar laughed gently, one of the few times I had ever seen him demonstrate amusement.

'A storm that may indeed delay us somewhat...' he said. 'Look again, my son.'

I did as he suggested, leaning up in the saddle and shading my eyes. The land ahead of us was a featureless plain, dipping down a mile or two away into a slight depression. I saw the ripple of silver amongst the clouds, the glint of metal and brass.

'In the name of the king...' I whispered.

Zothar laughed again. He turned in his saddle to order the dispositions, but so well drilled was the Legion of Athrabis that no command needed to be given; the moment the enemy was sighted, the troops began to move into their battle formations.

It was no thundercloud, but the dust of their passing. From one end of the horizon to the other, in warring mobs and screaming hordes, came a tide of warriors that seemed without end. The rumble of thunder I had heard was the bellowed prayers they howled to the sky and the beating of their axes against their shields. It was the march of booted feet, the clamour of ten thousand hearts lusting for war.

As we got closer, our army marching on a wide front with a steady, unhurried tread, I could see the enemy more closely. They were still perhaps a mile away, spread out along the length of that wide depression. Some were clad in crimson plate, their faces hidden behind flared helmets. Others were practically naked, screeching and champing at the hilts of their weapons, their chests lacerated with self-inflicted wounds. Some rode lumbering beasts clad in brass armour, the creatures breathing a fiery fume into the air. I saw their banner held aloft in the centre of the horde; a brass icon ten feet high, dripping with blood, in the form of an abstract, sharp-edged skull.

'The disciples of the Blood God,' King Zothar said at my side. He leaned from the saddle to give directions to Khetera, who hurried off to the central block of Mortek Guard. He then twisted round to gesture towards the Deathriders on the left flank. I saw the cavalry, at least three thousand riders, break away and form up ahead of us in a thick, arrow-shaped wedge. 'Barbarians from the Buried Mountains, far to the west of here. I had wondered when their attention would at last turn east.'

'You knew they would be coming?' I asked.

'I have patrols moving across the borders of my kingdom at all times, Neophron. Nothing happens here without my knowledge. Although in your quiet corner of the land you would not think it, Shyish, like every realm, has no shortage of enemies.'

The air shook with the barbarians' cries. The stench of blood rippled like a wave from their lines. As we neared them, I could see that they had decorated their banners and icons with skulls and severed heads, with flayed skin and body parts that still dripped with gore. Whose path had they crossed already, I wondered, bringing with them such slaughter and death? And then I thought of Lament, only three days ride from here, and a sick feeling uncoiled in my belly.

What the barbarians lacked in discipline and military order, they gained in sheer ferocity. Even in the midst of Zothar's army, with the king himself at my side, I was nearly unmanned by their screams of rage and bloodlust. It was a sour thought when I realised that the only blood present that could slake their thirst was my own – they would not get a drop from Zothar's undead troops.

They came on like a thunderclap, racing across the scrub with their weapons bared – a rolling tide of humanity so steeped in blood they were more like daemons. Tall figures with shaved heads and staring eyes, their muscles swollen and engorged, their bodies lashed with chains and open wounds, chanted fell prayers to the sky. For the briefest moment I felt death draw near me. How could we possibly stand against such fury?

Beside me, Zothar was unmoved. Calmly he gave his orders. He had not even drawn his sword yet, so unconcerned did he seem. Beneath him, his steed waited patiently for instruction.

They were no more than a hundred yards from us now and the ground shook to their tread. The Mortek Guard, as smoothly as if they were on the parade ground back in Athrabis, dressed their ranks and charged their spears. There were five blocks of guard stretching away on our left, another five on our right, each regiment at least a hundred wide and thirty deep. The Deathriders had moved far out of range on either flank, still in that arrow-shape formation, and the Mortek Crawlers were by now flinging their deadly payload into the ranks of the barbarians. I saw shrieking skulls glowing with eldritch light go sailing up above us, plunging down into the horde with an eruption of bone and flesh. Some of the Crawlers threw vast blocks of black masonry, stelae etched with spells and curses that ripped apart souls as well as bodies.

Barely fifty yards separated us when Zothar at last drew his blade. As if waiting for this gesture, the Immortis Guard limbered their mighty halberds and drew up their shields, striding past us into the field of barbarians to reap a bloody harvest. Heads were cut from necks, limbs were severed, entrails were strewn on the scrubland. Twice the height of those they fought, the Immortis Guard were like a rock around which a tide has broken. They went about their bloody business with a grim dispassion.

'Forward, my legion!' Zothar cried. He raised his sword and chopped it down and I felt my steed rear under me. I spurred forward as the Mortek Guard advanced, waving my sword in the air, the warbands of our enemies only a few strides from me. Blood and thunder surged in my veins. 'Give them no quarter!'

How to describe that swirling madness, the terrifying and exhilarating chaos of battle? I felt much as I had when I had plunged into the waters of the bay during the Contest, pushed and pulled by contrary tides – only now, I swam in waves that could cut me to pieces. It was like a high, thin note was playing in the very centre of my head, a discordant whine that seemed to push the very world off-centre, muting the roar of combat, the clash of blades. It was as if I were watching it all happen and every action I made was an action made by somebody else.

Everywhere I looked there were screaming faces, contorted

with rage. Blades and axes flicked towards me; on instinct I batted them aside. Three of the barbarians, their topknots stiff with dried blood, scrabbled at my legs and tried to drag me from the saddle. I swung down with my scimitar and watched their arms go tumbling off into the dirt. My steed's hooves kicked out and I saw men's heads crack apart under them. Warriors groaned in the dirt and spat teeth from ruined jaws or hugged their spilled entrails as if mourning a lost friend. As I barrelled forwards into the great mass of the enemy, the Mortek Guard kept perfect pace – a long, unbroken line, shields up, spears snapping out to pierce flesh. I saw King Zothar in the very middle of where the fight was hottest, hewing left and right with his sword. The soul gem on his breastplate glowed like white fire and his eyes blazed so brightly that some of the barbarians were forced to look away. He left a trail of broken bodies in his wake. I cut my way through so that I could fight by his side.

Not everything was going our way, of course. These servants of the Blood God were brave and reckless fighters, utterly without fear; indeed, the injuries we inflicted seemed only to spur them on to greater and more violent sacrifice. Half-naked berserkers, bloody foam frothing at their mouths, threw themselves willingly onto the Mortek spears, dragging them aside so their comrades could charge further into our lines. I saw whole units of our troops cut down, hundreds of warriors, their bones scattered on the field and crushed underfoot. Some of the barbarians were running amok by the Mortek Crawlers, dragging the war machines' crews from their platforms, and tearing them apart with their bare hands.

But vigour and violence can only take you so far and against a truly disciplined foe no ragged warband of berserkers can hope to last. And there were none more disciplined than the troops of the Ossiarch Bonereapers.

Together, Zothar and I cut our way back to the front rank. He had suffered grievous injuries, his ribcage beaten in, shards of bone hacked from his face, but they did not slow him down. Spears and axe blades decorated the flank of his steed, but that did not seem to suffer any ill effects either. Blood was lashed across his armour, as it was lashed across mine. I looked down and was shocked to see a wide, yawning cut in the meat of my calf, blood dripping from the wound onto the ground. I had not felt the blade. I tried to stop my hands from shaking on the reins.

At King Zothar's signal, the Mortek Guard began to step back, feigning retreat. Emboldened, the Blood God's disciples rushed forwards, thinking to overwhelm us, but it was exactly as Zothar had planned. While our infantry pinned their centre on a line perhaps a thousand troops wide, our Deathriders came pouring in from either flank to surround them. I gave a roar of triumph when I saw what had happened. Five thousand horse on either side, meeting in the centre and plunging like two great bolts deep into the heart of the enemy mass. The ground shook to the beating of their hooves and the cries of rage and hatred from the barbarian horde soon turned to shouts of horror and dismay. Even those so consumed with bloodlust can be undone, it seems, when all becomes hopeless.

I was overwhelmed by the moment. I watched the Deathriders surge forwards, implacable, spears and swords rising and falling in one relentless wave. The barbarians tried to escape, howling as they ran into the Mortek Guard's unbroken line of spears. The air was misted with blood and the sky sang to their screams as they died.

'Cut them down!' I yelled, my voice hoarse. I could no longer feel my injury. I dug my heels into my steed's flank, but the king stayed my advance.

'Hold, Neophron,' he said. Every inch of his sword was spattered in blood. His armour was notched, and his mount's legs were stained red to the knees, but he was utterly calm. 'The King leads from the front when the matter is most pressing, but it would be unseemly to participate in such slaughter.'

He held his sword aloft and the Mortek Guard advanced.

The Blood God's sons sold their lives dearly that day. Futility often gives strength to the arm, but in the end, there could be no doubt of the outcome. Before the light began to fail and before the frail, grey skies of Shyish darkened into night, the last of them was silent, and the cold earth drank its fill.

I was able to rest for a while after the battle. The Bonereapers moved amongst the dead for the remainder of the night, stacking their enemies' weapons and armour in the centre of the battlefield, while the great juggernauts of the Gothizzar Harvesters shucked the meat from the corpses. The rent flesh was cast aside, and the pink recovered bone was stored in the grooved baskets on their backs. It was a sight to turn the stomach; I did not look on it longer than I had to. Some of those the Harvesters farmed were still living, incapacitated by their wounds, and the sound of their torment as they were torn apart was unbearable.

I lay down on the dun grass beside my steed for a while, nursing my wound, drifting in and out of a fractured sleep while the army gathered its casualties around me and prepared for the march back to Athrabis.

Phaetor inspected my injury, but the knitting together of flesh instead of bone was beyond his skills. He stood there beside me, looking almost confused as he stared down at the bloody blade strike in my leg. The bone fronds on the back of his skull twitched and quivered. His sickly green gaze faded as he tapped his bony fingers to his jaw, puzzling over it. Fortunately, Se'bak had some skill in the art of healing; there was little he had not gleaned from his centuries of study, the library at Athrabis being an almost inexhaustible resource. He produced needle and thread from his robes, his bones creaking as he crouched down beside me.

'You come prepared for everything, Se'bak,' I said. 'I dread to think who you might have practised on first...'

I tried not to cry out as the needle pierced my skin. Although all the Bonereapers could face you with only one expression, all the sympathies and ambiguities of flesh pared away to simple bone, I always knew when I had amused Se'bak. The lights of his eyes pulsed, the jaw opened a sliver, the facsimile of a smile. But when he spoke, I found the mirth dying in me.

'There have been Neophrons past counting,' he said, slipping the thick twine back and forth, sealing the wound. 'You are not the first to earn an injury in combat.'

I thought on this while he bandaged me up.

'Did any of them die in battle?' I asked. 'Before their time, I mean. Before the end of the Contest?'

Se'bak dissembled, but I pressed him on it.

'It has been known to happen,' he admitted. 'Not for a hundred years, that I can recall. Why else do you think King Zothar has you trained so vigorously in the arts of war before letting you participate in it?'

'And their souls?' I said. 'What happened to them if there was no... no vessel for them to move into?'

Se'bak lowered his gaze. 'Alas,' he said in a hissing whisper, 'they were fated to wander the wilds of Shyish until their appointed moment. Lost and tormented, moaning their agonies across the sands... Once, I recall, King Zothar bade me try and capture one of these lost souls before it could be reincarnated, hoping that my arts would be able to–'

'Enough, Se'bak,' the king said. He came and stood over me, looking down at me as Se'bak finished dressing the wound. 'If my son is sufficiently rested, I would talk with him.'

Se'bak, with effort, levered himself to his feet and bowed.

'Of course, my liege,' he said. He turned to me. 'Come and see me in three days for the dressings to be changed,' he said. 'Mortal flesh is weak, after all.'

When Se'bak had left, Zothar remained standing. The screams of the dying barbarians still trailed pitifully through the night air as the last of them were torn apart, flesh from bone. Around us, the army went about its preparations with brisk efficiency, but they gave us a wide enough berth for the privacy of our conversation. My head was spinning with fatigue and with the loss of blood, but I made an effort to concentrate.

'You are not otherwise injured?' Zothar said. At last, he turned to face me, looking down at me lying there in the scrub. I sensed him wrestling with his mood, weighing his words before he spoke them. He stood with his hands resting on his sword hilt, the point planted in the ground. He still bore his injuries, but he would not let the Boneshapers repair him until the army's casualties had been seen to and the legion was safely back at Athrabis.

'No, Father,' I said. 'I hope… I hope I didn't shame you in the fight?'

Zothar shook his head. 'You acquitted yourself admirably,' he said. He glanced at me. 'A little impetuous, perhaps, but from what I recall blood does run hot in combat. But you have made a fine warrior, Neophron. As you were before. And as you will be again…'

I swallowed, closing my eyes against the pain, the exhaustion that fogged my mind.

'You have won a great victory,' I said.

'Against this rabble? No, this was a mere skirmish, against madmen and fanatics. In the days when I first took up the bargain of Nagash… then I fought true battles.'

With a sharp snap, he sheathed his blade.

'You see, though,' he said, 'what is necessary to maintain my rule? It must ever be defended, by sword and spear. Vigilance is the price of power.'

'Yes, Father.' I thought back to the moment we had approached the plain when the scale of the enemy horde had become apparent; what Zothar had dismissed as a rabble. 'Father,' I said. 'If we hadn't stopped them here, then...'

'Yes?' he said. His eyes flared in his skull. 'You begin to understand, do you not?'

'They would have reached Lament,' I said quietly.

A soft, creaking laugh escaped him. 'And what do you think they would have done there, hmm? These blood-crazed killers, these barbarians?'

My mind recoiled from the picture. 'They would have slaughtered everyone...'

'They would have slaughtered the lucky ones,' he corrected me. 'The rest would have been subjected to the most appalling tortures until death came as a sweet release. Do you see now how favoured your city is? Lament, a soft place of white marble and pleasant gardens, with its council, its fishermen, its sacred tower... Dreaming away in its blessed ignorance, guarded by the blades of my soldiers, with no idea how many enemies beset it?'

I roused myself, the fatigue fading away for a moment. 'They must be told!' I said. 'What if... what if the unthinkable happens and you meet an enemy you cannot beat, my lord? They must raise troops for their own defence, they–'

'There is no enemy I cannot beat!' Zothar snarled, flying at me. 'None!'

I covered my face in terror. Crouched over me in the moonlight, his bones shattered, his eyes aflame, he looked as if he had stepped from the dark bounds of a nightmare.

'Forgive me, lord!' I cried.

'Lament drifts along in ignorance because I will it so!' His voice was harsh and grating. 'If they knew the scale of the dangers in the realm at large, the city would collapse. I would have refugees begging for admittance to Athrabis or fleeing along the coast in the vain hope of finding safer lands beyond the horizon. Lament is as I want it, no more and no less!'

'Yes, Father,' I said. I stopped my voice from shaking.

'Now,' he said, straightening. 'Rest. In the morning we will depart. Se'bak will see to your recovery and when you are fully healed you will perform a certain task for me. A test, if you will, of all you have learned in statecraft and kingship.'

'It will be my honour to serve.'

He laughed again, and it was a cruel, mocking sound.

'We will see. There have been certain issues recently, with the collection of the tithe in Lament. You will go there as my representative,' he said, as he began to withdraw. 'You will enforce my will, and you will determine if this is a situation that requires… a more punitive approach.'

'What issues?' I said.

Zothar paused before he strode away into the darkness.

'Rumours have reached me,' he said, 'of a name from the mists of the past. Someone who perhaps does not favour the relationship between Lament and Athrabis. Someone calling themselves "The Jackal King".'

14

It was a moonless night, Nagash's Eye cloaked in a veil of cloud, when Dardus led the others to the coast.

Four of them came with him, meeting by the great arch of the propylon before the city gates. Dardus crouched in the shadow of the walls while he waited for them to arrive, a tattered cloak about his shoulders and a knife tucked into his belt. He had tied his hair back and sucked nervously at the gap of his missing tooth. The city slumbered around him, with here and there a night light burning on an open porch, or a tallow candle flaming in the upper window of a tenement. The night guard had been strengthened in the months since he had set fire to the tithe, but he had been following the patterns of their patrols for weeks now. He was safe for another few minutes.

He shifted his weight as the blood slackened in his weak leg. He hoped it wouldn't hold him up; they had a long journey ahead of them before the night was through. He fingered the blade of his knife. For a moment he wished Selene was with him, but then the risks of being caught were high. He didn't want her to be caught. His own life he would throw away on a whim, but he would do what he could to protect her. That sense of caged wildness, her steely spirit...

He turned his mind away from her. There was a clink in the shadows behind him. When he turned, he saw Amyntos and Docia slipping along the edge of the wall towards him. They were dressed in dark tunics and Docia had an empty canvas sack slung over her shoulder. Like Dardus, they were both barefoot. The Failed had little to their name and sandals were a luxury denied to them.

'You're late!' Dardus hissed. 'Where the hell are the others?'

'Calm yourself, lad,' Amyntos grumbled. He was twice Dardus' age, but near half his size. Some joked he had duardin blood in him, but Dardus dismissed such nonsense; everyone knew duardin were a myth. Docia scratched at her patchy, close-cropped hair and shifted the position of her bag.

'They'll be here,' she whispered. 'Nightwatchmen were patrolling by the Tower earlier – they've set a guard to it now. They'll need to wait for them to pass by before they can cross the agora.'

Dardus nodded and bit at his fingernail. Burning the tithe had provoked more of a reaction than he'd expected, if he'd expected anything at all. If he was being honest with himself, he'd only done it to impress Selene; it was the worst thing he could think of, far worse than breaking into the priests' quarters and stealing their robes. But then the deed was done and he had fled with Selene as the bells began to toll, the priests scrambling to put the fire out before the whole Tower was gutted.

There had been uproar in the city after that; it had been astonishing. Rumour had it that when the priests met the Bonereapers outside the city gates for the tithing a week later, one of them had been cut down as punishment for their failure. No one knew what was going to happen next. That imbecile on the council, Baeothis, had recommended executing some of the Failed to make up the shortfall in bone. The council was split, but Astraea had eventually talked them round. He had Selene to thank for that, he was quite sure...

Still, the damage was done. The city was tense, feverish. Nothing like this had ever happened before. Who was to say the council wouldn't change their minds about the Failed when the Bonereapers returned? If they did, then Dardus would be damned if he'd let them take his life without a fight.

Vulture Lord, he'd scrawled on the walls of the agora once. It had amused him to see the priests frantically scrubbing it away the next morning, flitting about in their hooded robes like bonecrows. But then the following night the graffiti had returned, only this time it read *Jackal King*... He had no idea who had done it. It certainly hadn't been him.

There was anger abroad in this city, he knew. It only took a few muttered conversations to find like-minded members of the Failed, those bitter at their second-class status, reduced to poverty and menial labour only because they'd had the guts to take part in the Games. Who was to say there weren't people outside of the Failed who were equally angry? Those horrified at the deaths of their loved ones in the Contest, or grief-stricken when a child was demoted into this despised caste. Selene was one of them, for a start. Who here, apart from the feeble and the pious, actually wanted to see the bones of their wives and husbands, their mothers, fathers, and children, stacked like firewood and handed over to those creatures in the desert?

It's not fair, he had wept in self-pity, after he had fallen from the Tower.

No, it certainly wasn't, he thought now. *So, make it fair.*

After another minute or two, Hesper and Markus came hurrying from the alleyway on the other side of the propylon. Once again,

Dardus noted how rat-like Hesper was, with his greasy dark hair, his pinched little face. Markus strode towards them not with confidence but with an alarming sense of indifference. He had been one of the Failed for decades; he must have been fifty years old if he was a day and it was clear that life or death had little meaning for him now. There was a slack, vacant expression to his lean and craggily handsome face. His eyes were as dull as if he'd just woken up from a deep sleep.

Dardus looked at them all in turn. The bored, the angry, the desperate, the indifferent. Was this a resistance movement they were building? He couldn't even say himself. It was all happening so fast.

They hardly seem like resistance heroes, he thought. *But they're what we've got...*

They climbed the gate posts and dropped down on the other side, sprinting quickly along the line of the outer wall towards the east. The white marble was dull and grey in the midnight dark, and the ground underfoot was black. Something wailed sorrowfully in the distance, a rising scream that faded away on the chill breeze. Hesper looked alarmed, but the others gritted their teeth and hurried on as they headed to the coast. Around them, as Lament passed into the darkness, the bare and empty lands of Shyish were as pitiless as the velvet sky.

The fishing boat was tied up where Amyntos said it would be, dragged up onto the black sand of a little cove beyond the bluff. One of his duties was to bring the catch in when the fishermen returned, and he knew this part of the coastline well. Dardus flicked the rope from the encrusted mooring post and pushed them off. The boat was no more than fifteen feet from bow to stern, but there was enough space for them all to huddle together amongst the nets and fishing spears.

The waves slapped greasily against the hull and an icy wind came coursing across the water. Dardus shivered in his cloak as the others hitched the sail. He remembered the swim towards the end of the Contest. Pelleus, the look in his eyes as the flense-fish rose behind him. The red slick of blood on the surface of the water...

There was breeze enough to take them south for a mile or two and when it slackened they each manned an oar. The sea stretched off to portside, a corrugated field of grey that was lit here and there by sparks of pallid luminescence. The coast on their right was a dark line slipping past in the gloom.

'How do we know they'll still be there?' Docia said. Her voice was loud in the moonless night.

'They'll be there,' Dardus muttered. 'They know we're coming.' He turned to Markus. 'You've got the grave-sand?'

'Aye,' Markus said. He tapped the pocket of his tunic and Dardus could hear the clink of phials. He wouldn't have trusted anyone else with it – certainly not Hesper. They'd robbed five different healers to get the grave-sand together; he'd be damned if he'd watch Hesper scurry off with it.

It took them another two hours, but at last they came to the point where the coast curved in towards a spread of open beach – a wide crescent of sand that glittered like crystal in the moonless light. Dardus pushed the rudder to the side as the others dragged and fumbled with the oars. The waves cut and broke around the prow and then the sand was shushing under the keel. They leaped out into the knee-deep water and dragged the boat ashore.

Lights burned up ahead – two or three, the caged flame of lamps, the flutter of a torch. Dardus could hear voices, the bark of laughter, the clink of glass. He swallowed hard, his mouth dry.

'Give me the grave-sand,' he said to Markus.

He slipped the bag of phials into his pocket. Hesper's teeth were chattering, although whether that was from the cold water they had waded through or simple nerves, Dardus didn't know. He looked at the others.

'Don't say anything to them, let me do the talking,' he said. Then, with no need for any more delay, he girded himself and stalked up the beach as the others followed.

The merchants' caravan was a few yards beyond the tideline; a circle of gaudy tents, with a campfire blazing in the centre of them. Three men in soft, rich robes sat around this fire, sharing a bottle of ruby wine. Two massive aurochs, which were used to pull the caravan's wagons, were hitched off towards the side, placidly chewing the cud. There were other men with swords standing just beyond the fire's cast light, motionless in the shadows. They wore boiled leather jerkins and metal skullcaps. Ghurish mercenaries, Dardus had been told the last time he was here. Grim fighters, loyal only to coin.

'Hail, Impastus!' Dardus cried as he drew near. He stood tall, his hands at his side and his palms open before them. He forced a grin onto his face, exaggerated the limp in his weak leg. 'I said I would return, and here I am!'

One of the merchants stood lazily and arched an eyebrow. He was short and thickset, a long scar feathering down to his jaw that made him look more to Dardus' eye like a streetfighter than a dealer in spices and gems. His robe was midnight blue, fringed at collar and cuff with soft grey fur. The guards drew their weapons and stepped into the light of the campfire, but the merchant waved them away.

'Ah, young Dardus,' he said. 'A man of your word, I see. As, of course, I am of mine.'

'I had no doubts, Impastus,' Dardus said.

'You have brought some friends, I see?' Impastus glanced over at the others, who clustered nervously behind. 'You are not anticipating trouble, I hope?'

'Merely extra hands to carry the merchandise,' Dardus laughed. He clinked the phials in his pocket. 'I have the payment, as promised.'

Impastus chuckled lightly. 'Straight to business, I see. You won't observe the formalities with us?'

He sat down on his camp stool again and poured himself another glass of wine. It was clear he was in no hurry. No doubt it amused him to keep someone as insignificant as Dardus waiting. The other two merchants, dressed in robes of similar quality, raised their glasses in salute. Dardus felt a drop of sweat bead and trickle from his forehead. He kept the grin fixed in place.

'Alas, no,' he said, as if this was the greatest sorrow to him. 'Time is pressing, and I would be back home before dawn.'

'Indeed,' Impastus sighed. 'Such is the world these days, with no time for the finer things. All is strife, and conflict, and money to be made...'

He waved to the guards and two of them disappeared behind the wagons. After a moment they returned bearing a wooden chest which they laid on the ground beside the campfire. Dardus crept closer as Impastus opened the lid. Inside were stacked two dozen swords, a score of knives and daggers, even a pair of nadirite cudgels. The blades were old, worn things, certainly not castle-forged, but they would do. They would do very well indeed...

Dardus took the bag of grave-sand phials from his pocket and handed it over, not taking his eyes from the weapons. As Impastus took it though, the merchant snapped his hand forward and grabbed Dardus' wrist. He felt the strength in those fingers, the power of someone who had only reached his position after years of sordid back-alley beatings, who had clawed his way up from the very bottom. His eyes were hard as he stared at Dardus' face.

'Business is business,' he said, 'but there is only one condition to the trade.'

'Name it,' Dardus said through gritted teeth. He tried to pull his hand away, but the merchant held it tight. He could sense Hesper fidgeting behind him, Markus pondering in that cluttered mind whether he should try and intervene or not. *Stay where you are, you fools*, he wanted to shout.

'King Zothar gives us permit to pass through his lands,' Impastus said quietly. 'We pay the tithe, as we must, but otherwise we have easy passage. It would be… *awkward*, to say the least, if he were to learn of our arrangement.'

'He won't.'

'I need your word – such as it is,' the merchant said with a smile. His fingers tightened on Dardus' wrist.

'You have my word,' Dardus spat.

A moment passed, drawn out, tense. Then, with an easy grin, Impastus released him. Dardus staggered back and rubbed his wrist, but he forced the smile onto his face all the same. He beckoned the others near, taking the canvas bag from Docia. There were two more bags inside it. Quickly, they began to fill them with the weapons.

'Is King Zothar your god too?' Docia asked the merchants as she knelt to the chest. There was a burst of laughter from them; even the guards couldn't help themselves.

'My sweet child,' Impastus said, wiping his eyes. 'There is an old saying – "It is a wise man who fears the gods." Let us just say that I am a wise man and leave it at that.'

'I fear him…' Docia mumbled.

Dardus could see the balance in her eyes shift. She was tipping from Markus' indifference to Hesper's panicked anxiety. She was on the very edge, he knew; all this, the idea of resistance or rebellion, or whatever it was they were doing, was the only thing that kept her going now. She had looked ahead towards the long, dim acres of her life as one of the Failed, and it had horrified her. She would do anything to escape it.

'You are right to fear him,' Impastus said. He swallowed his wine. For the first time Dardus saw a flicker of uncertainty in the merchant's face. 'You worship him as a god, but I think perhaps he is even more terrible than that.'

Dardus turned sharply to the others. 'We've got what we came for,' he said. 'Dawn's only a few hours away, we need to move.'

'Good luck, my friends,' the merchant called as they carried their bags back down to the beach. He raised his wine glass, toasting their bravery – or their foolishness.

They waded through the cold water and pushed the boat out into the sea, striking the oars when the keel slipped back off the sandbank. The lights of the merchants' campfire receded, a lonely amber glow wavering in the middle of the grey and restless night.

'Best put our backs into it,' Hesper whined. He pointed across the ocean, now on their right as they headed back along the coast. The horizon had pinked with light; dawn was on the way. 'We've still got to get all these weapons back into the city.'

Dardus smiled to himself, hacking at the oar. He thought of the caves above the bluff, which Selene had told him about. Last resting place of the Jackal Kings…

'They're not going into the city, it's too risky,' he said. 'If they're found, we're dead. No, I know exactly where we can keep them. Keep them safe, until the time is right…'

15

The council hall was a spacious, uncluttered chamber, but Baeothis paced it like a bone-gryph trapped in a narrow cage. There was a long marble table in the centre of the room, twenty feet from end to end, and he stalked around it, unable to settle.

'Priests have been attacked in the streets!' he cried. He thrust his arm out indignantly, as if demonstrating the evidence of this outrage. 'Slogans and insults scrawled on the very walls of this building!'

To give him credit, Astraea thought, his shock wasn't performative; he was genuinely horrified by all this. When he wrung his hands in distress, he wasn't doing it for the benefit of the other elders, or to help press his case. Lament had long been a calm and quiet city. The council's function was on the one hand purely administrative and on the other hand purely symbolic. Everything that had arisen in the last few months, since the tithe had been burned, was beyond unexpected. No one knew how to deal with it, least of all Baeothis. For all his exhortations that something be done, he was stumbling about in the dark as much as the rest of them.

He strode now behind Astraea's chair, his jaw thrust out, his black hair dishevelled. He gripped the back of her chair. When he spoke, his voice was low and troubled.

'I have just received reports that during the night someone dared to scale the Tower of the Moon and steal – actually *steal* – bones that had only recently been cleansed by the vultures for the next tithing. Which, can I remind you, is now only eight months away!'

Astraea could feel his hands shaking through the back of her chair.

'Well then,' Melissta said, an expression on her face of stunned disbelief. She tucked a lock of hair behind her ear, shrugged, gestured vaguely at the room. 'I simply don't know, I mean… well, it's a disgrace, isn't it?' She looked at Kaitellin, who sat side-on to the table and was resting his chin on the pommel of his walking stick. He was deep in thought and said nothing. Astraea met Haephastin's eye, but he shook his head almost imperceptibly. He reached for his wine and drank deeply, tipping the goblet back to hide his face.

'Thanasis,' Astraea said, addressing the priest who sat at the other end of the table. 'What does the Holy Order suggest?'

The priest's hood was drawn over his head, but beneath the shadows she could see the planes of his emaciated face: the beak-like nose, the lips drawn back to reveal teeth that sat loosely in his darkened gums. He turned to face her with all the languid detachment of someone on the verge of starvation. Like all the priests in Lament, he was ever striving towards the perfect condition of King Zothar and his Bonereapers.

'Our position,' he said in a whisper, 'is simple. These are blasphemous crimes without precedent in our history. Not since the days of the Jackal Kings has the order of Lament been so disturbed.'

'And your proposed solution?' she said.

Thanasis seemed to drift for a moment, lost in his thoughts.

He took up the flask that sat before him on the marble table, a concoction of syrups and liquors that was the priesthood's only sustenance. He sipped carefully. As a girl, Astraea remembered the other children disgusting each other by claiming that the priests drank the run-off from the rotting bodies on the platforms in the Tower. The thought came unbidden to her now. She remembered her own religious instruction when she was young, sitting bored in classes with Baeothis and Melissta, retching at the smell of the priest's breath when he stood over her to recite the Ossuary Prayer. Baeothis with his hand always up, desperate for approval. He had been so keen to please, even then...

She looked away from the priest and towards the open colonnades at the side of the chamber, which looked out onto the clean, commodious streets of the first tier. The light was bright this morning, filtered through a layer of cloud as thin as muslin. The white marble of the city seemed to smoulder with an inner flame. Everything was still and quiet out there, the streets dipping gently on the incline towards the gates of the second tier. So many public and private buildings in Lament were built on these open plans, she had lately realised, free-standing, with access to the open air, although Lament was only truly warm during the season of the Games. Was it so that the breeze could gently and unobtrusively waft away the smell of the dead? It had never occurred to her before. From the roof of the Tower, death flowed across Lament like a smothering blanket.

Thanasis capped his flask and cleared his throat. Astraea looked back to him, dreading what his next words would be. Baeothis had regained his seat and leant forward eagerly.

'Our proposal should not, of course, be seen as an ultimatum,' the priest said carefully. 'The perpetrators of these crimes must be rooted out and punished as a matter of course – and I would suggest a public flensing, at the very least. But if this is not resolved *immediately...* then we would have no choice but to make a petition to Athrabis for aid.'

There was silence around the table. Haephastin looked sick, his eyes wide. Kaitellin did not move. Baeothis, after what he must have thought was a suitably reverent pause, thumped the table with his fist.

'Exactly!' he cried. 'Let the Soulmasons of Athrabis root out this corruption, this disorder! That'll put the fear of Zothar into these miscreants, I can guarantee it!'

Astraea felt as if she'd swallowed a mouthful of ice water. She could feel it stabbing down into her stomach.

'You would invite the Bonereapers into the city,' she said. 'Outside of the Games, to do... what, exactly?'

'To find answers,' said Thanasis with a cold smile. 'To interrogate, to arbitrate, to... *punish*.'

'And we all know where to start,' Baeothis growled. He looked at them each in turn. 'The Failed have had it too easy in this city for too long. We all know perfectly well that they're behind this.'

'Too easy?' Astraea scorned. 'Are you even listening to the words you're saying?'

Baeothis threw his chair back and got to his feet, stabbing a finger at her.

'There was practically a riot down at the wells on Procession!' he shouted. 'My own son had his arm broken by thugs who said the wells were for the Failed only. Are you seriously telling me they're not now fomenting open rebellion?'

Astraea narrowed her eyes. 'At least you still have your son to care for.'

'And yours sits at Zothar's right hand,' Baeothis said. 'Do not dare pretend that is anything other than the greatest honour imaginable.'

Astraea felt the words sink into her like knives. She did not trust herself to make a response and so reached for her own goblet and drank deep. The wine was like dust in her mouth, like sand.

'You never went in for the Games when you were a lad, did you, Baeothis?' Haephastin said lightly. He gave a dry smile. 'Big strong fellow like you, I thought you would have been a natural choice.'

Baeothis gave a dismissive wave as he took his seat again.

'I was no great athlete in my youth,' he said airily. 'I make no more excuses than that, it would have been...'

'Too much of a risk?' Haephastin offered. There was a guileless look on his face that Astraea knew well. 'After all, one of the Failed wouldn't have had the opportunity of entering city politics, would they? And certainly not with their father's assistance...'

Kaitellin laughed quietly and Baeothis had the decency to look abashed.

'None of us took that risk,' Kaitellin said. Was that sadness in his voice, Astraea thought? Regret? 'It stands to reason, otherwise none of us would be sitting here now. Either we would be dead, or we would be Failed.' He looked around the room, smiling with his gentle, old man's smile. 'Or who knows, perhaps one of us would have been Neophron, for a decade at least? No, no,' he said, 'I have always felt the way the Failed were treated was an injustice of sorts. Death or a life sentence, for being brave enough to try in the first place.' He sighed. 'But it is what it is. The Games have an ancient foundation. You may as well try to lift the city up and rebuild it further down the coast as try to change such an old tradition. It is our culture, for what it's worth. It is our way of life. Zothar wills it.'

He fell into silence again, contemplative, leaning on his stick.

'Think of it from their perspective,' Astraea said, 'hard as that might be. We have two peoples in this city, living side by side. We have citizens, with all the benefits and protections and opportunities citizenship brings. And we have an underclass beneath us, treated like scum. Is it any wonder they're angry, after centuries of this?'

'They are scum!' Baeothis said.

'Why, for Zothar's sake?'

'Because they failed!' he shouted, thumping the table again. 'It is precisely for Zothar's sake, blessed be him. The Failed brought shame on their families in the eyes of our god and they brought shame on their city!'

'And when the Games come round again,' Astraea said coldly, 'will you allow your son to compete? Or will you keep him safe from that risk and everything that comes with it?' Her voice caught in her throat. 'For let me tell you that victory in the Contest feels as much like defeat as failure.'

'Be careful, elder,' Thanasis whispered at the other end of the table. He sipped at his flask again. 'You skirt very close to blasphemy. The Games *is* Lament. The Contest *is* Lament, as King Zothar wills it. There is no other way.'

'There was once,' she said.

She thought of Dardus, Selene's friend. And then, unbidden, she thought of Selene; her cool, unshakable certainty in Sigmar. The god of lightning. The god of justice.

There was the scuff of a sandalled foot as one of the council attendants hurried into the room. His face was dark with sweat, his eyes troubled.

'What is it, Aegeus?' Kaitellin said.

'There's a delegation approaching, sir,' the attendant said, catching his breath. 'From Athrabis, from King Zothar!' He looked at Astraea. 'And they're led by your son.'

16

Dardus was picking at the calluses on his hands when the call went up, leaning with his broom against the city wall just off the Procession, down by the apothecaries' quarter. He heard the cry rising from the gates and he could almost feel the wave of shock and fear that rippled away from it through the streets. A woman passed him as she came running down the Procession, a child clutched to her chest. He saw one of the healers in a shop at the corner of the street close his shutters and draw the inner bolt on his door. There was fever in the air, a sense of poise and uncertainty. The hot, silent moment before the storm breaks.

Two old Failed were pulling a waste cart just ahead, trundling it down the street. They looked at each other and dropped the shafts, scurrying past him as they hobbled for the alleyways that wound and climbed up to the gates by the second tier.

'What is it?' Dardus cried at them. 'What's going on?'

One of them turned before he ducked into the alleyway. 'Bone-reapers!' he hissed. 'They're here. Hundreds of them!'

Fear took him then. His tongue cleaved to the roof of his mouth. He swallowed, felt for the knife he had hidden under his tunic. Was this it? Were they coming for him at last? For all of them?

He took up his broom, clutching it to his chest like a shield. Maybe the priests had asked for help and Zothar was finally sending a force to crush them all? He thought of the weapons he had stashed in the caves above the bluff. The north wall rose up on his right-hand side, thirty feet of dusty marble with barely a foothold to be seen. He couldn't scale it, but he didn't fancy his chances trying to pass through the main gate either; it was forbidden for the Failed to leave the city unless they had specific permission, or duties to attend to.

He stopped and listened. He could hear the sound of marching feet in the distance, the crunch of dust and sand, the blunt metallic clink of weapons. He felt as if he was encased in a column of cold water. It was like the flense-fish rising from the depths of the bay all those years ago, paralysing him with fear. All of a sudden, he remembered Lycus' voice rolling gently across the water, calm and steady, talking him out of his panic. The memory struck the flint of the anger inside him and lit a spark that had him moving at last.

No point in dying in ignorance, he thought. *I may as well see what they're going to do first. Let them cut me down in the agora if they must, where everyone can see…*

He threw the broom to the ground. He doubted he would need it now.

Hesper came rushing up to him when he reached the end of the Procession, his rodent face drawn with fear.

'Have you heard?' he said. 'There's a hundred troops at the gate. It's Neophron himself leading them!'

Dardus grabbed his arm. 'Lycus? Are you sure?'

'Sure as I can be, I saw it with my own eyes! A human leading them, sitting on one of those bone creatures. Couldn't be no one else now, could it?'

'No,' Dardus said. 'I don't suppose it could...'

Together they slunk through the streets towards the northern flank of the agora. They passed groups of people coming in the other direction, hurrying past with their heads down. How different it all was from the Games, Dardus thought, when everyone in Lament had been desperate for a glimpse of the king. But that had been an expected event, something anticipated and planned for. This was quite different. The city was on edge and the troops of its overlord could hardly be expected to calm the situation down.

'What do you think?' Dardus asked. The street opened out into the broad prospect at the front of the city, the acre of marble flagstones and shaded walkways. 'Are they coming to kill us all, or just give us a fright?'

'Can't rightly say,' Hesper admitted. 'Beating up priests and causing a ruckus is one thing, but I think they're here because of the bone. We've hit them where it hurts, Dardus, and they won't stand for it. What did you do with the last lot we stole?'

'Stashed it with the rest, in the bottom of the wells at the other end of Procession. I was waiting till we had enough for a bonfire in front of the council hall.'

They clambered the raised white steps that formed a proscenium in front of the temple. From there they could see the Tower of the Moon over on their left; the open plaza beside it where the market stalls had been set up; the low, single-storey houses of Antigonas Road on the other side, running in parallel. Normally at this time of day folk would be strolling through the stalls picking up provisions for their evening meals or passing the time with cups of Hysh-flower tea from the tea sellers who wandered the crowds with metal urns on their backs, a rack of clay cups balanced on one arm. Now though, there were people milling by the stalls, gathered in uncertain groups on the edge of the square or wandering fitfully to the grid of streets and alleyways on the other side.

Marching with alien precision down the Grand Avenue on the far right of the square was a column of Bonereaper troops – at least a hundred of them, as Hesper had said. Their spears were shouldered, and their shields were on their backs, but the sense of threat and menace that radiated from them was palpable. Suddenly, the stash of old swords and notched daggers in the caves above the bluff seemed pitiful things. How on earth would you fight something like this?

He saw Lycus then, riding at the front of the column as it passed from the Grand Avenue into the square, sitting proudly on an immense armoured warhorse that was some strange blend of different bones. Nearly six years and two hundred feet stood between them, but he would have recognised that face anywhere. The face of the boy who had cheated him of his prize. The face of the man who rode here now like a conquering hero. The face of his enemy.

You can't… You can't fight them if everyone's so afraid of them, he thought.

'You have to show them,' he muttered to himself. 'Show people what they're really like. You have to make everyone hate them instead.'

'Eh?' Hesper said at his side. 'What do you mean?'

'I've got an idea,' Dardus said. He drew away down the steps, heading back into the quiet streets by the northern wall. 'Give me an hour, and then go to him.'

'Who?' Hesper whined.

'Lycus – Neophron. Go to him, tell him you've got information. Tell him to search the houses on Antigonas Road, on the other side of the Tower.'

'What for?' Hesper called, as Dardus hurried off into the back streets. He had an hour to get to the wells at Procession, then to sneak around to the southern edge of the marketplace. Plenty of time.

'Tell him that's where he'll find the missing bones!'

Two days to cross the desert from Athrabis to Lament; time enough, I would have thought, to prepare myself for seeing everything and everyone that I had left behind. But as Lament came into view, coalescing from the desert sands in a spread of gleaming marble, the mist-spray lingering from the turbulent coast to smother it in a sea-green gauze, I knew that it was not. It had been nearly six years since I had won the Contest and yet everything that had happened to me since that day made it feel like a lifetime ago. I would almost have said that it had all happened to someone else. Perhaps there was a grain of truth in this? After all, was I not Neophron now? I was no longer Lycus, son of Cleon and Astraea. That boy had passed away when the last Neophron was beheaded; his soul had moved aside for the soul that had entered him. Was that not the case? For if not, what was the point and purpose of all of this, from beginning to end?

King Zothar had decided to send me at the head of a company of troops, a hundred spearmen of the Mortek Guard. He anticipated no difficulties in my visit and neither did I, but, as he had already made clear, a king rules as much by the exercise of symbol as of naked power. It would not do for Neophron, the Regent of Lament, to enter what would one day be his city alone.

I would have happily taken direction in this, bowing to my father's command without a further thought. But for reasons that I couldn't fathom he sent me with Khetera as my second. First Hekatos of the Mortek Guard, my military trainer and tormentor for all the years I had been in Athrabis, Khetera took the king's order without comment. Both of us had been summoned by Zothar to the map room in the palace. As his wishes were relayed, Khetera had saluted smartly. But then, as we left the palace together, he to his barracks and me to my chambers, the Hekatos had muttered in his dry, sibilant hiss: 'I will keep my eye on you, boy. The sight of your mother and your home will unman you, I have no doubt. Any sign that you break the king's trust will be met with my blade.'

I had said nothing, turning to go, but my hand had itched for my sword. I did not know what Zothar meant by pairing us like this, but I promised myself a time would come when such insults from Khetera would no longer go unanswered.

I had asked Se'bak why Khetera hated me so much, visiting the Soulmason deep in the Mortisan laboratories in the northern quarter of the necropolis. Like all of the main buildings in Athrabis, it was a bleak and soaring confection, a riot of spire and buttress in green-black bone, with arched windows high above the streets like screaming mouths and gargoyles and death's-heads grinning down from gutter and rail. Here, deep in his research, was where Se'bak sifted and blended the souls of those we conquered in battle, taking the base elements, and combining them in forms that would help our own troops perform most effectively in the field. It is a fact often realised too late amongst those who fight the Ossiarch Bonereapers that even the costliest victory does not diminish our forces. Quite the contrary – not only can our troops be reassembled, and our casualties made up, but the army grows with the bone of those we destroy. To fight the Bonereapers and lose is only to hand them greater and greater strength.

'Khetera is a proud and wilful character,' Se'bak said, as he pottered with phylactery and phial. He sifted through the clutter of his workbench, his ancient, brittle skull lit with eldritch green light from his aetherlamps and laboratory flames. 'He was, in days long past, one of King Zothar's most brilliant generals. Loyal to a fault, ambitious, glad of war. If you think of him as such in life, then imagine what he became in death.'

I enjoyed watching Se'bak at his work. I had become fond of the old Soulmason, in my way. He had always treated me with an easy kindness, although sometimes I couldn't help but think that I was just another specimen he was content to have at hand so he could observe and study it. How many Neophrons had passed through Athrabis in all these centuries? Was Se'bak equally kind and gracious to them all? It didn't matter, I supposed. He was kind enough to me and that was all I cared about.

'He chafes at the king's commands, then?' I said.

Se'bak lightly slapped my hand away from the parchments I had been toying with.

'I would say otherwise,' he said. 'Khetera will follow a command to the letter, in all things. In almost all things, I should say. He believes Nagash has made us unconquerable, and as the Obsidian Coast is ours to command, why not the whole continent? Why not the whole Realm of Shyish, even? I suspect he believes that King Zothar's grief over the death of his son is an endless distraction from our true purpose. If he were to forget Neophron and let the boy's spirit fade away to its final rest, then King Zothar could turn his attention beyond the desert and the coast and find new kingdoms to conquer.'

'He is easy enough with his threats,' I said. 'And many is the time I've felt he was on the verge of killing me in training. Do you believe my life is at risk?'

'No, no, not at all,' Se'bak said. He mused for a moment, clacking his teeth. A little scurf of bone dust drifted from his jaw. 'He would not perhaps go so far as to cut you down himself, but I would not be surprised if he were keen to manoeuvre you into a position where death came by another's hand.'

He seemed troubled. I remembered what he had said before, after the battle with the Blood God's disciples.

'And if Neophron's soul is lost outside of the Contest, with no chosen vessel to enter?'

'Oh, a dark time that would be, indeed,' he said. 'Once before, I can recall it. Spells and rituals without count to locate it and the entire army scouring the Obsidian Coast from end to end... Athrabis itself fell into near disrepair. Many felt that the king had lost his mind. His own soul gem became weak, to the point I feared it would dissipate entirely. No, I cannot think that Khetera would risk such a thing again, but...'

'But you cannot be certain?'

Se'bak gave me a shifty look. I smiled at the old Soulmason, feeling guilty at pushing him into a corner.

'No matter,' I said. I hopped off the stool where I had been sitting and tested the weight of my injured leg. The wound had almost fully healed. 'I don't fear him.'

'Ah, but you should,' Se'bak said steadily. 'In life he was a brutal, violent man. In death, he is without mercy.'

Despite my concerns, Khetera did not provoke me on the march. He was silent for the most part, concerning himself only with the disposition of the troops, but ever I felt his eyes on me as I rode at the head of the column. It was fortunate perhaps that I found myself unwilling to pause on the journey and rest. I feared Khetera's scorn at my mortal weakness, but I feared his knife in the dark more.

We crossed into the borders of Lament late in the day. The light was still clear and forceful, but the cold, sallow dusk of Shyish was near. A few farmers or fishermen, returning to the city at the end of their working day, saw the column approaching and hurried for the gates. I sent a handful of troops running ahead to announce my presence and called the column to a halt.

'Why wait?' Khetera demanded. 'Let the mortals scurry like rats in a panic as they try to please their masters.'

'You forget, Hekatos,' I said. 'This is to be my city one day. I would not have the people hold me in fearful awe.'

Khetera, standing at the side of my steed, gave a cruel laugh.

'It will be Neophron's city one day,' he said. 'When his soul takes permanent refuge, as the king believes. I shouldn't think your head will be the one to wear the regent's crown though. Rather, I look forward to seeing that head tumble across the flagstones when the king removes it from you...'

I smiled, as if his words had amused me. In truth, I could think of no retort. Khetera was right; there were only four years now to the next Games.

We entered the city with hurried pomp and circumstance, a discordant blast of ill-trained trumpeters, the drummer clattering their instruments by the propylon. I waved them silent, leading my steed down the Grand Avenue, the Mortek Guard marching steadily behind me. The streets were quiet as we approached the agora. I saw few faces looking from the windows above as we passed down the road. This was an unexpected moment; apart from during the Games, the king's troops had not entered the city for time out of mind. Certainly, no one could recall when Neophron himself had entered Lament with the expectation of ever leaving it again.

I saw my mother standing with the other elders where the Grand Avenue opened out into the wide central square of the agora. Khetera's words were loud in my mind, and I refused to let the sight of her unman me. I tried to look her over as I did the other elders, as if they were no more than petty dignitaries beneath my notice, but when I saw the lines of sorrow in her face, how drawn and tired she looked, the tears already brimming in her eyes, I could not help myself.

'Mother,' I said. I dismounted, my voice thick with emotion. 'I have returned.'

What must I have looked like to her? I was but a boy when she had last seen me. I was a young man now; hardened by combat, clad in the bone-fringed armour of the Ossiarch Bonereapers, a sword at my hip and a hundred troops behind me. I was taller than her and when I embraced her, she seemed frail and bird-like in my arms. She buried her face in my neck and wept openly. It was only the thought of Khetera watching that kept me from weeping too.

To hell with you, Khetera, I wanted to say. *This is my mother, my city. This also is my family.*

After a moment she composed herself and held me at arm's length, smiling so that the lines of worry were wiped clear from her face.

'Lycus,' she said. It was the first time I had heard my true name spoken for almost six years. 'Welcome home.'

'Alas, the visit cannot be longer,' I said.

One of the elders shouldered his way past the others, bowing reverently. He was a big man, older but well-built, with dark pomaded hair and the easy smile of someone keen to ingratiate themselves. His name was Baeothis, I remembered. One of my mother's colleagues on the council.

'My lord!' he cried. 'On behalf of the council I welcome you most fulsomely! The Regent's Palace shall of course be made ready for you.'

He snapped his fingers at one of the other elders, a woman my mother's age with fine auburn hair. Melissta, I thought. It was all coming back to me. She scurried off towards the thoroughfare that led up to the higher tiers of the city.

'Anything I can do personally,' Baeothis said, 'you have, of course, only to ask.' He warily eyed the soldiers standing at attention behind me. 'Your, uh… your men, do they require anything that we can provide for them…?'

'Do not trouble yourself,' I said. I felt the power of my command returning to me, the grandeur of my position. I turned to Khetera, who stood there rigid and unmoving. 'Hekatos,' I said, 'the troops are to remain in the agora for the moment, and I would have an honour guard to accompany me to the Regent's Palace.'

I took my mother's hand and ignored the other elders.

'For now, though,' I said, 'I would speak with my mother a while.'

'Yes, my lord,' Khetera said, emotionless. 'It shall be done as you command.'

I left the square with my mother, heading towards our home high in the first tier. I could feel Khetera's glowing eyes boring into my back every step of the way.

17

How small it seemed when I entered my old home. My chambers in Athrabis were bigger than the whole house. In fact, compared to the city in the desert, Lament seemed no more than a spit of land beside a continent. I removed my helmet and, with a strange mixture of sentiment and apprehension, looked into my old bedroom while my mother brewed us some tea. The furniture was the same, the way the sallow afternoon light filtered through the shutters, but I recognised nothing else.

'Selene lives here now,' my mother said. She came and stood beside me at the door. I saw that she had washed the tears from her face and had composed herself once more. 'Her grandfather died a few years back and she had nowhere else to go. She's been such a help to me.'

'Is she here now?' I said. I tried to make the question seem off-hand, unconcerned, but I couldn't disguise my nerves. My heart leapt at the thought of her face.

'No, but perhaps she can see you later,' my mother said. 'I know she wants to talk to you. There's so much to talk about, Lycus. So much that's been happening here.'

She handed me my tea and together we sat in the parlour at the front of the house. The shutters were closed, but I could hear the sound of people passing nervously along the thoroughfare towards the lower city. I had left two of the Mortek Guard at the door and they must have been an intimidating sight.

I found that I didn't know what to say. I was ten years old when I had last spoken to my mother. The talk of a child with a parent is easy and unselfconscious compared to the conversation of a young man.

I could smell the Hysh flowers blooming in the garden, the sharp, bitter fragrance of the gravewort growing between the cracks in the paving stones on the road. My mother was staring at me in a way that made me feel ridiculous all of a sudden; like a boy again, playing at dressing up. The armour I wore, the sword on my hip, only so many props in some childish game. I had killed people, I wanted to tell her. I had fought monsters the likes of which you couldn't imagine, cannibals and killers all, and I had prevailed.

'I've heard about the tithe,' I said, bluntly. 'I'm sure I don't need to tell you that whoever is responsible has been playing a dangerous game. My father will–'

'Your father?' she said. She was taken aback; I realised what I had said.

'I meant King Zothar, he–'

'Your father died in that room behind you,' she said. Her voice was like stone. 'The dry-lung was so thick in him at the end, I'm sure it was a relief. I wrote to you, but I had no reply.'

'I'm sorry, Mother,' I said. 'I meant to write back, truly I did, but… you don't know what Athrabis is like, the easy formalities are more difficult there.'

'Is that what you call it? "Easy formalities"?'

'That's not what I meant!'

'Then what did you mean?'

I gave a bark of exasperation and stood up to open the shutters. The cool air flowed into the room. I felt hot, as if she'd cornered me and I couldn't see a way out.

'I'm here to enforce the king's will, Mother,' I said. 'That's the reason I've been sent to Lament. As I'm sure you know, the king's will is absolute. This disruption to the tithe has to stop.'

'Or what?' she scorned. I was shocked to hear her tone. 'We can't die any faster, and the vultures cleanse our dead at their own pace.'

'Are you so naïve?' I said quietly.

I turned to her, saw the mirthless smile on her face. She sipped her tea, thinking, calculating. It made me feel immensely uneasy.

'I am not so naïve as you think, Lycus. I know what the king would do if he felt the tithe was at threat. But I must say to you that the threat is real, and I don't believe it will get any better. People in Lament have accepted their lot for centuries, but there comes a point when change is in the air, and nothing can be done to stop it. I believe we are at such a point now. It kindles in the streets and in people's hearts alike, and I do not know if the fire can be put out.'

'This is madness!' I said. I lowered my voice in case the guards at the door could hear. Whether they lacked the will to inform on me or not, I didn't care to risk. 'You don't know the position this puts me in!'

'It's not about you!' she cried, casting her cup to the ground. 'Though it pains me to say it, and though the sight of you in that armour is like a dagger in my heart! Every day is a torment to me, knowing that it is one day closer to your death. But there are others in Lament who have felt the yoke of the Games for far too long. They are no longer willing to live in harness.'

'The Failed?' I said. I thought of Dardus. I wondered if he were still alive. I could not bring his face to mind other than as a frightened mask, out there on the waves of the bay. 'They are rebelling? Against every ancient custom and rite of the city? It doesn't make any sense, what in the name of Zothar can have possessed them?'

'The name of Zothar...' she muttered. 'Perhaps that is what has gripped them. The fear of that name. The dread of what it promises. Or perhaps they just want lives in which they can cover themselves with a shred of dignity.'

I was at a loss. I wanted to tell her, to make her believe, that King Zothar had greatness in him, that his sacrifices were unnumbered to keep Lament safe from those who would destroy it – the mindless barbarians, the orruk hordes, the dread servants of dark masters... *He has great love in him*, I wanted to say. *He does all of this out of love and grief for his son, that's all. He is not what you think he is.*

'You have always been too sure of yourself, Lycus,' she said sadly. 'Too arrogant, always wanting to be the hero of your own story. You have no idea of the risk you really took, running in the Contest, but I have no doubt that if you had become one of the Failed instead of the victor, you would have turned every corner of your mind towards escaping that fate.'

'That's not true,' I said. I was angry now. None of it had gone the way I thought it would. Whatever I had expected would happen between us, whether we would have reminisced happily or just sat in perfect and contemplative silence together, I didn't expect this recrimination and blame. I felt sick and weary.

'You made the wrong choice,' she said, 'and now you are in an impossible position. Are you so blind as not to realise that this is what King Zothar wanted? To force you to make a choice, a terrible choice!'

'That isn't true!' I said. 'And if it was, then it was only because he knew I would make the right one!'

There was a sharp rap at the door, the sound of a spear shaft being knocked against the wood. I hurried to the door and opened it, to see Khetera standing there with his bony fist around the scruff of a young man's neck. The lad was scrawny and dressed in little more than rags, a pinched, emaciated face with black beady eyes that made him look like a rat. He was clearly one of the Failed.

'What's this?' I demanded. 'Who is this man?'

Khetera shook the poor creature. 'This mortal claims he has information about the attacks on the tithe. Says he will only pass it on to you, in person.'

'Let go of him,' I commanded. I looked him in the eyes and bade him speak. 'What is your name?' I asked. 'What information do you have?'

'Hesper, if it please your lordship,' he cringed. Sweat trickled from his brow and the presence of the Bonereaper troops obviously terrified him. 'Word that's come to me, my lord, that I overheard I mean. None of my doing, I swear, but I heard it said that there's a house down on Antigonas Road where the stolen bones from the Tower are being held. Criminal elements, lord, rebels, and rioters! I'm a pious man, my lord, and would do my duty by the king...'

Khetera gave a hollow laugh. 'Always these mortals turn on one another when they fear their life is at risk. What is your command?' he said to me. '...My lord?'

I looked back at my mother, standing there in the shaded hall, leaning against one of the marble pillars. Our eyes met. After a moment I looked away.

'Lycus...' she said.

'Order the troops to begin searching the houses,' I told Khetera. I picked up my helmet from the ground and prepared to leave.

* * *

A crowd had gathered by the time I arrived in the agora. The afternoon was shading now into dusk and the sky had taken on a flat and depthless sheen. The light in the square was brittle, flavourless, and made everything feel as if it had no real substance to it.

The troops had been through every house on Antigonas Road, bursting through the doors and ransacking the rooms, tossing furniture and blankets out of the windows. Families stood in anxious groups by their front doors, waiting for the destruction to end. Anyone who protested felt the hilt of a blade or the rim of a shield in their stomachs. Before long the folk who lived there had meekly surrendered their right to privacy and respect.

I was shocked at how comprehensively the Mortek soldiers had followed my orders. Antigonas Road ran in parallel to the southern edge of the marketplace, on the other side of a wide, tree-lined thoroughfare that connected to the Grand Avenue. It was from those trees that Selene had watched me scale the Tower, I realised, in the final moments of the Contest. The Tower, bleak and forbidding, like a shard of Athrabis planted in the centre of Lament, stood not a hundred feet away across the flagstones. I felt judged by it, somehow, as if mute stone could pass comment on my actions. I wanted to call the troops back, but I had given the order and must see it through.

'Regretting your decision?' Khetera whispered at my side. 'I knew you were soft, mortal. Fear not, though – command is so often just a case of standing silently by while others do your dirty work for you...'

'There's no need for violence,' I said, trying to sound stern. Khetera always made me feel the gulf of time that separated us; the centuries of bloodshed that he was steeped in and the paltry sixteen years I had stood on this earth.

'There is every need for violence... my lord. What else do you think power is, but the use of force?'

I tried to stand there proud and unmoved, one hand resting on the hilt of my sword, as I had seen Zothar stand so many times before. I watched the crowd on the other side of the square, some craning their necks to get a better look at the ransacked street, others staring on in sullen rage and disgust. Failed and citizens alike, united in their resentment of what was being done here. I began to worry that someone would be foolish enough to throw a stone or draw a knife. What did they think would happen then? They had no idea how quickly they would be cut down, how mercilessly.

'How has it come to this?' I muttered to myself. 'How has this been allowed to happen?'

'Weakness,' Khetera croaked. 'Always, the weakness of mortals, not to take the hard decisions when they must be taken.'

There was a cry from one of the houses at the far end of the street. It was a flat-roofed structure of plain whitewashed stone, only one storey, with a little kitchen garden neatly arranged in front of it. There was a water bucket set up by the front door and one of the Mortek Guard had pulled out a canvas sack that had been hidden in it. He opened the bag and tumbled out a stack of dripping bones into the street.

There was an awful groan from the crowd when they saw what had happened. I felt it echo in my gut. A horrible cold feeling descended on me. I watched two Mortek Guard drag the owners of the house out into the agora and throw them to the ground: a young man and a young woman, husband and wife, who clutched at each other in terror, each hoping the other would be the anchor against the wave that was about to engulf them. I walked over with a sense of crushing inevitability. Khetera did not leave my side.

This was the test, I knew. This was what King Zothar had sent me here to do.

The young man saw me approach and clambered to his knees.

He had a soft and gentle face, I thought, kind grey eyes that beseeched me for mercy. The young woman, as if stunned, hid her face behind the long trail of her blonde hair. She had no illusions, I thought. I saw the elders of the council approaching from the thoroughfare that led up to the second tier. I saw my mother, her black hair coiled in a single plait that lay across her shoulder like a snake. I could not meet her eyes.

'Please, my lord!' the young man was begging. 'I don't understand, this is nothing to do with us!'

His voice was hoarse with fear. Beside him, the Mortek Guard who had found the canvas sack had gathered up the bone and brought it over. I saw lengths of femur, shards of skull, the fan of a broken ribcage.

'We're pious citizens, I swear!' he cried. 'I've never seen that before in my life, I would never desecrate the Tower! We worship King Zothar, please have mercy!'

I did not know what to do. I felt every eye in the crowd on me, dark with hatred. I felt my mother's grim and determined stare. I felt the satiric attention of Khetera at my side. Perhaps most of all, although he was many miles distant, I felt the weight of King Zothar's gaze crushing my heart, as heavy as all the stones in the Tower of the Moon. I was standing where he had stood six years ago, I realised, when he had cut off Neophron's head without a moment's thought.

The sky was darkening now. The streams of cloud, thin and insubstantial things, rippled and fled. The velvet night of Shyish came fading into view.

'I beg you, my lord,' the man whispered. 'Spare us. I know your name, my lord, you are Lycus, son of Astraea. Do not do this, please! You are from Lament, you are one of us!'

The moment clarified. The crowd receded. My mother disappeared.

'My name is Neophron,' I said, through gritted teeth. 'I am of

Athrabis, the necropolis, the dread keep of King Zothar. And you have profaned him by this theft of what is his by right.'

The woman cried out once. I nodded to Khetera, who drew his blade, and then I stepped away. I did not want him to see the tears in my eyes.

18

Two twin torches bracketed the doors into the Regent's Palace. Each was a six-foot length of black wrought iron and the brands at the top guttered with a fierce and unruly flame. The light they cast onto the walls of the palace made it seem carved from fire, all the soft white marble stained with orange and red, fuming there against the blackness of night. It was the palace of he who would one day come and take Lament as his rightful inheritance; the palace of Neophron, when the wheel of soul-incarnation stopped at last, and the son of King Zothar found himself anchored in a permanent life once more.

Selene looked up at the mighty pillars that supported the roof, a hundred of them ringing the colonnade from end to end, each of them more than four feet thick. She saw the slab-like lintels high above her, the carvings on the architrave of scenes from Lament's ancient past, blurred now by the passage of time into no more than a faint discolouration in the stone. It was the palace, she knew, of the Jackal Kings of old. It had lain empty until this night for a thousand years.

Two of the Bonereaper soldiers barred the way, spears at their shoulders. Although every instinct in her body told her to turn and walk away, she approached them with as much confidence as she could muster. She wondered if these were the same who had dragged those people from their house earlier that evening, casting them to the ground so their heads could be cut from their shoulders. The scene still lingered there behind her eyes, the appalling horror of it, the dread that found no release. The sword was raised and came down without pause, with not a hint of mercy or regret, or even base satisfaction. And then two people were dead, their blood thick against the flagstones, and Lycus was walking away...

The Bonereapers crossed their spears as she came near. *Sigmar guide me*, she thought. *Guide my words, and turn his heart towards the good, for all our sakes.*

'I would see your lord,' she said. 'Neophron, as he is called. He will see me. Tell him Selene is here and would talk with him.'

One of the soldiers, eyes pinpricks of green light in its hollow skull, opened the door and marched off into the interior of the palace. While she waited, Selene turned and looked down on Lament spread out before her: the three tiers of the city stacked one atop the other like the layers of a cake, the palace at the very apex of it all, the Grand Avenue twisting and turning as it looped from gate to gate, from the mansions and manses of the first tier all the way down to the huddled dwellings of stone and wood in the third. She could see the agora down there, spread out near the city gates like a wide white sheet, the black blade of the Tower reaching almost as high as the level of the first tier. Lamps and torches burned in windows, but the streets were empty. No one was abroad this night apart from the silent ranks of the Bonereapers, patrolling the streets, making their presence known.

She had never been this high above the city before. Beyond the walls, looking north, she could see the wastelands of Shyish, the thorny scrub and the endless grey plains of the desert. Green lights flickered out there, flashing against the horizon. Were those the walls of Athrabis, she wondered, dozens of miles beyond the simple stone of Lament? She could almost feel its brooding malice, King Zothar's dark attention turned towards them while he waited for his 'son' to bring him news. Was all this talk of rebellion mere dissatisfaction, he would want to know, or something more serious?

Selene thought of all the people huddled in their homes tonight, all of them dwelling on the sight of that young couple beheaded in the square. No one believed they had stolen the bones. They had been planted there, she was sure; false evidence to justify an execution, to show those who lived here that they were utterly at the mercy of Athrabis and always would be.

She touched the pendant under her tunic, felt the strength of her rage temper into a cool, clear flame.

Soon, King Zothar... she thought. *Soon you will see what people pushed to the limit are capable of... The jackal is at bay, but that is when it is most dangerous.*

'Selene,' a voice said.

She turned, looked through the open door to where a dark-haired young man stood in the hall of the palace. He was war-like, grim of face, a lean hardness to his limbs as he raised a hand to beckon her in. He was drinking from a goblet of wine, and he was wearing a plain tunic, the kind that would go under armour, still with his greaves on his legs.

Selene paused. The moment seemed to elongate. She felt stretched, somehow, distorted between two times that she couldn't place. She saw a boy climbing the cliffs above the bluff, and she saw a young warrior without pity, whose hand ached for a blade. And then the moment snapped back and both points became one. She knew who this was now, although never in her life would she have imagined she could have looked on him with such confusion. She did not recognise him; he had changed so much.

'Lycus,' she said.

She felt the blood rush to her head. Her face was hot, and she didn't know what to do with her hands. She had known him her whole life, but it was like she was being thrown on the mercy of some barbaric warlord, some tyrant from the wastes who had sacked the city and demanded tribute. Lycus gulped at his wine and threw the goblet to the floor, rushing forwards suddenly, embracing her. Selene gasped, felt his body shaking, could smell the wine on his breath, the sweat of long travel. Carefully she held her arms around him, holding him, waiting for him to compose himself.

'Selene,' he mumbled, 'you cannot imagine how I have longed for this moment. How long has it been, by all that's holy...?'

He sobbed once. He seemed totally unconcerned by the two Bonereaper troops who still stood guard by the doors. Was he drunk, she wondered? She thought of a boy kept prisoner in a city of the dead, six long years spent without human contact, six years of nightmare and horror. The emotion was too much for him. Coming back here had broken him.

Another charge to lay at your door, Zothar, she thought. *You have taken someone innocent, utterly without guile, and you have crushed him...*

Selene ushered him into the palace and closed the doors, quite as if it were she who was welcoming a guest and not the other way around. Slowly, Lycus gathered himself together. He turned his back on her while he wiped his eyes and stooped to pick up the goblet from the ground. He refilled it from a jug that sat on a small table of polished glass beside the door.

'Come,' he said, turning around and giving her a lopsided smile. His face was dark and mottled, glistening with sweat. 'There are more private rooms towards the rear of this awful place, we can sit and talk, you can tell me everything.'

He gestured at the hall around them, his voice echoing back from the vaulted roof that disappeared into the shadows above. Torches fumed along the walls on either side, so distant that their light barely reached the centre. The hall was a cavernous space, the floor made of black marble threaded with green veins, and there was a faint grit of sand underfoot. There was no furniture, no decoration save for two grand frescoes on either wall, which had crumbled and fallen to pieces over the ages. All Selene could see of them was the fading colours on the plaster, the suggestion of battle or strife.

'This is a mere ante-chamber,' Lycus said. He laughed, gestured with the goblet and sloshed wine over the brim. 'All this for me, can you believe it?'

'Lycus,' she said, 'please...'

'That lickspittle Baeothis had it cleaned up, practically ran up here himself to make sure I wasn't inconvenienced by a speck of dust. Of course,' he mused, 'I say it's all for me, but it's not really, is it? It's for whoever comes after me and whoever comes after that, and so on. Neophron after Neophron, stretching off into the future, forever and ever and ever, until one day... It's a scary thought, isn't it?'

'People here are very scared,' she said quietly. 'They're frightened and they're angry, and those two poor souls murdered in the market square have not calmed things down.'

Lycus flinched. She saw the pain flicker across his face, like lightning as it trembles in the distant cloud.

'That couldn't be helped,' he said. He turned his back on her, drank from the goblet again. 'They had profaned the Tower, stolen what is rightfully King Zothar's. That's why I'm here,' he said, as he turned again to meet her eye. Something of the warrior came back to him then and it was Selene's turn to look away. She thought of Sigmar, girded her heart with his strength. 'I am to stamp Zothar's authority on this city, make it clear in no uncertain terms that such profanity will not be tolerated.'

He almost sounded like he believed it. But then he grimaced, as if the words choked him.

A voice came from the shadows in the far corner, near where a high window admitted a slow channel of cool air.

'Is that right?' it said. 'And if a young man seeks to reclaim the bones of his own father, that counts as blasphemy against your king? For that's what he was, the man you killed – a son grieving his father. So I understand, anyway.'

Dardus stepped from the shadows. His long, unkempt hair was tied back and there was a sourly amused look on his face. The torchlight gave depth and colour to his sallow skin. Selene walked over and took his hand and he bent to kiss her brow. She saw Lycus look from one to the other, confused, until the realisation dawned. He masked it with another swallow of his wine. When he spoke, it was with a terrible false humour.

'Dardus!' he cried. 'My old friend…' He took in Dardus' tattered clothes, his air of cynicism and squandered hope. 'There was no need to sneak in like this, I would have welcomed you with open arms!'

Dardus gave a satiric bow. 'Alas, my lord, such as myself are not permitted beyond the third tier.'

'I would have given permission,' Lycus said. 'You know I would.'

'No, my lord,' Dardus said. He did not take his eyes from Lycus' face. 'I do not ask permission to move through my own city.'

Lycus laughed once, frowning as he did so. He raised the goblet, saw that it was empty.

'My friends,' he said. He stepped to the jug by the door, saw that it was empty too. 'I would call for more wine, but I sent the servants away, something... always something unnerving about the dead serving you food and drink, if you're not used to it...'

'And how is Athrabis?' Dardus said breezily. He strolled around the hall, gazed up at the faded frescoes, the peeling gilt of the cornices. 'Lament must be such a climb down for you after so many years.'

'Not at all...' Lycus began. 'It's–'

'And in such elevated company,' Dardus continued. 'I apologise that you have to lower yourself to conversing with such scum as me.'

Selene stepped forward before Dardus provoked him too far. She could feel the tension crackling between them, the long years of Dardus' resentment. He might be reckless and brave, but she knew that Lycus had changed beyond compare. There was steel in him now, a sense of violence. If it came to it, Lycus would prove the deadlier.

'Lycus, forgive us, but we are not just here as old friends,' she said. 'We need your help. Lament needs your help.'

He smiled and looked down at the floor, holding his empty goblet in both hands.

'This is more than petty theft and vandalism, isn't it?' he said. 'I could sense it, in the agora. The crowd, the way they looked at us.'

'"Us"?' Dardus said. 'You truly are one of them now, aren't you?'

Lycus spread his hands. 'I am Neophron,' he said sadly. 'You know that. I am the son of King Zothar, one-day Regent of Lament and Lord of Athrabis.'

Dardus grinned. 'For a few years more, anyway.'

'That's as may be, but until then – I am King Zothar's word in the city.'

Selene went to him and took his hand. She could sense Dardus bristling behind her. As much as she loved Dardus now, when she felt Lycus' hand in her own something shivered and tore inside her. His green eyes, so dark, were like shards of emerald.

'King Zothar is not what you think he is,' she said. 'The Games are not what we have always believed, a way of honouring and worshipping him. He is not a god and what Lament is forced to endure has become monstrous and cruel. We are nothing more than a wake for his dead son, and we cannot escape it unless we seize our freedom for ourselves – for he will never give it to us. Never.'

Lycus gave an incredulous laugh. He staggered backwards as if struck and for a moment Selene thought he might fall.

'How can you say that!' he protested. 'You have no idea what you're talking about, none.'

'You think this is fair!' Dardus cried. He plucked at his filthy tunic. 'I live like an animal because of your king! The Games are no more than an excuse to keep Zothar's heel on all our necks, to create serfs so debased by this miserable culture they think their oppression is just and holy. Well, it is not!'

'And what would you have me do about it?' Lycus snarled. 'Do you think killing those people in the square was easy for me? I did not wield the blade, but I felt the blow, let me tell you. Zothar commands and I obey, there is no other choice.'

'There is every choice,' Selene said quietly. She drew the hammer pendant from under her tunic and held it up for Lycus to see. 'There is the easy choice, to collude in this tyranny. Or there is the hard choice, to do what is right. To fight back. To refuse to play any part in it.'

Lycus looked at the pendant.

'Your grandfather's,' he said, understanding at last. 'Sigmar wills it, then, does he?'

'Sigmar…' Dardus scorned. 'All gods are tyrants to me, I care not for their insecurities, their petty lust for worship. I have seen Zothar, though. I know that if he is not flesh and blood, he is still a thing that can be touched. And anything that can be touched can be hurt.'

Lycus lowered his voice. Selene saw real fear creep into his eyes.

'What are you saying?'

'Lycus,' she said, beseeching him. She clutched his hand. 'You are my oldest friend. You are part of this city, part of me. We need your help.'

'We need you to kill him,' Dardus said. 'Kill Zothar. Free Lament.'

'The Jackal Kings…' Lycus whispered. 'The name from the mists of history.' He looked at them both. 'You are the Jackal…'

Selene shook her head. 'A name, nothing more. I don't know who has plucked it from myth and scrawled it over the city walls, but the sentiment is the same. Lament would be free again, as it was once, under the Jackal Kings. And only you can help it become so.'

'Or what!' he shouted. 'What do you think you can do against the might of Zothar?'

Lycus flung the goblet across the room. He covered his face with his hands and staggered into the shadows.

'If we don't get what we want,' Dardus stated, 'then the tithe is cut off completely. We will destroy the Tower, burn every corpse in Lament before it has a chance to be cleansed.'

'You are children,' Lycus cried. 'You have no conception of what Zothar is, what he does for this city! By the Eye of Nagash, do you have any idea of the scale of Athrabis? Do you even know what happens to the tithe?'

His voice echoed and crashed around the empty hall. Selene, her heart thudding in her chest, looked to the closed doors in case the sentries chose this moment to intervene.

'There is an ossuary at Athrabis,' Lycus said, 'that is filled from floor to ceiling with the bones of the tithe from this city. From floor to ceiling, bones stacked upon bones, for hundreds and hundreds of years. Zothar does not need the tithe, he never has. It is nothing to him.'

He stabbed a finger towards the walls; north, west, and south.

'Lament is an oasis of calm amidst a maelstrom,' he said. 'One month ago, not two days ride from here, I fought in a battle against a foe so appalling that you would have rent your clothes in piety and gratitude towards King Zothar if you had so much as glanced upon them. Lament is safe because of King Zothar. You cannot imagine his true greatness, because you see only the smallest fragment of it and in your confusion, you mistake it for tyranny. If it is, then it's the tyranny of a parent over a wayward child, the child too ignorant to understand the depths of the parent's sacrifice.'

He looked at her with tears in his eyes. Selene felt her heart wrench. She clutched the pendant, held it to her lips, her eyes squeezed shut.

'Then there is no hope of freedom,' she whispered. She glanced up at Lycus; the tears were now running down his face. Her gaze was as hard as flint. 'But there is still hope of justice.'

'Selene, please,' he said, his voice hoarse. 'I will pretend we never spoke of this. I will say nothing of it to the king, but you must relent. Zothar would rather see the city destroyed than defiant to his will, I know it. Please, let the tithes continue unmolested.'

'Damn you, Lycus,' Dardus said. 'You always were a coward and a cheat. If fate had put me in your shoes, I would have stretched every sinew to save this city.'

'That is exactly what I am doing,' Lycus said. 'You're just too blind to see it. Now go, please. The guards will not challenge you, Dardus. Give my name to any in the city who does.'

'Most gracious of you,' Dardus sneered. 'My lord.'

'Selene...' he said.

Their eyes met. Selene kissed the pendant before tucking it away again beneath her tunic. Lycus nodded and when he spoke his voice was flat.

'I hope we don't have to meet again,' he said. 'Not until the Games.'

He turned away and crossed the wide, empty acre of the hall. Selene watched him go, until the shadows had swallowed him.

'Goodbye, my love,' she whispered. 'Sigmar save you, I pray.'

The guards said nothing as they left but Selene shivered as she passed them all the same. She could not bear to look on them. Dardus held her close, his arm around her shoulders, and she allowed him to lead her away. She could feel the violence of his heartbeat, the tension in him, the rage.

'It's not over,' she said. 'I trust him, even now. He will do the right thing.'

Dardus snorted. 'Lycus? He's shown us what he really is. He pretends a warrior's bearing, but he's terrified all the same.'

'Aren't you?' she said.

'Maybe,' Dardus smiled. 'But my fear gives me strength.'

They came to the sloping flagstones of the Grand Avenue, the high mansions flanking the road with their spacious gardens, the classic austerity of their plain and elegant frontages. A few yards down the road, the gate to the second tier was guarded by two watchmen. Dardus moved to slip away into the shadows; Lycus' word or not, he would find his own way back. Selene took his hand and they kissed for a long moment. In that kiss she could feel all the sadness and anger of this evening pass between them.

'What should we do?' he asked. 'Hope seems vanished, but Lament is still enslaved.'

She shook her head. 'No, not vanished, just withdrawn. Just waiting for the right moment.'

'Which is?'

'The Games,' Selene said. 'Four years to prepare. Four years to stockpile weapons, to train, to seize control of the council, and then to put pressure on Athrabis. Zothar will come in person for the Contest. When he does, then our chance will arrive.'

'We'll kill him ourselves,' Dardus grinned.

'Sigmar wills it,' Selene said. She kissed him goodbye and watched him slink off into the darkness. She composed herself and carried on, heading to the gate. The night was fragrant around her and the wastes of Shyish beyond the city walls seemed suddenly very far away.

We'll kill him ourselves, she thought. *And we'll save Lycus before it's too late.*

PART THREE

THE CONTEST

19

The light from the guard's lamp wavered and spat, the wick fizzing in the clasp of the dirty oil. A twist of smoke rose and ribboned back towards her. Astraea held the scarf lightly across her face and concentrated on not slipping as she passed across the slick cobblestones. A drop of water fell from the ceiling not a hand's breadth above her head and spattered onto her shoulder. The smell down here was appalling; despite the scarf she could taste it at the back of her throat. Excrement and urine, rotten food, the stale tang of misery and guilt.

They came to the end of the passageway, to a thick oaken door reinforced with iron bands. The guard took a key from his belt and twisted it in the lock, and then they were through into another passageway equally mean and squalid as the first. There were iron doors on the right-hand side of the corridor, with small metal grilles at head height. Astraea glanced into each one as they passed. Sometimes she caught a glimpse of a body in mute repose, or of someone pacing the close confines of their cell. Most of them were empty though. Lament was not a city with a broad criminal element, and she had gone to some lengths to ensure that anyone caught protesting the tithe was given a sentence of simple house arrest rather than incarceration or exile. The city gaol, deep in the bowels of the council chambers, was a place where only the worst and most dangerous offenders were thrown – people who, Astraea had argued, posed the most serious risk to the peace and prosperity of Lament. People like the man she had come to see.

They came to the last door at the end of the passage. The guard hung his lamp by a hook on the wall and withdrew. Astraea thanked him and peered through the grille into the dank cell beyond.

'Good morning, Baeothis,' she said. 'You asked to speak to me?'

The elder flung himself at the grille, his eyes wild. There was a week's growth of beard on his chin and his pomaded hair was lank and dishevelled.

'Astraea!' he croaked. With no one to talk to, it was like his voice had shrivelled in his throat. 'By all that is holy, you have gone too far! You must let me out, I demand it!'

'You're in no position to make demands,' she said. 'And you're too dangerous to let out… at least for the moment.'

'For Zothar's sake!' he said. He pushed the tips of his fingers through the bars of the grille. They were pale, she thought, like the tuberous worms she used to dig up in her garden, when she still had time to consider such things. 'Dangerous? What madness is this, I am an elder of the council, a loyal servant of Lament!'

'From your position on the council you have exhorted nothing but violence and repression,' she said. Her voice was calm, as if they were merely discussing routine administrative matters. 'You would have the Failed punished as one, without discrimination, for the actions of a few firebrands. I cannot allow that.'

'You witch!' he cried. 'You are in league with them, I have always known it! You and that damned priestess…'

Baeothis drew back and composed himself. When he spoke again it was with all the mellifluous persuasion of his earlier days.

'Astraea, please, look it this rationally. It is mere weeks until the Games. King Zothar and his troops will be here for the Contest, and if he notices even the slightest irregularity, what do you think his reaction will be? Hmm?' He chuckled richly. 'After all, you can hardly throw him in gaol as well, can you? It's not too late. Release me, readmit me to the council, and I will see that the other elders issue you with a full pardon. I swear it.'

'You misunderstand,' Astraea said. The lamplight bowed against the contours of the passageway and the water that dripped down the walls glistened like ice. 'The council does all this at my command. I have set myself as First Elder, and Lament will suffer under your malice no more.'

'But what about the Games!' he wept. 'The Contest!'

'Alas, you will have to miss it,' she said. 'A great shame, for it will be the last Games of Lament... and the final Contest.'

'You will bring ruin on us all!' Baeothis cried. 'You would set yourself up as a queen above us!'

'No,' she said sharply. 'No, not that. I am no queen. But Lament had kings once, did it not? When my son returns, perhaps it will have a king once more.'

She turned to go, taking the lamp with her. Behind her, the passage-way descended into gloom.

'A king,' she said again. 'A jackal, to watch over us.'

The rest of the day was taken up with council business, the dull routines of administration. With Baeothis gone, however, Astraea had found it far easier to stamp her authority on the other elders. It was an irony that King Zothar's adoption of her son was what had slowly pushed her on the road towards rebellion, secret though it might be for the moment, but at the same time it had given her a far greater degree of influence than she would have enjoyed previously. There was no official term for it, but to many of the elders, as well as to the common folk, she was seen as the mother of Neophron the same way King Zothar was seen as his father. The others deferred to her, and they had accepted her claims that Baeothis was seeking to seize control of the city and set himself up as regent. After all, the evidence she had had Dardus plant in Baeothis' chambers was certainly compelling – manifestos scribbled on reams of parchment, weapons for an uprising against the council, stacks of bone stolen from the tithe. His stridency against the Failed went against him. For everyone who considered it in the light of this evidence, it did rather seem like he had been protesting a little too much…

There was only one weak link left in the council, she knew. She looked around the table, taking each of them in turn. She dismissed Haephastin, more sunk in gluttony and indolence than ever. Melissta had been unnerved by Baeothis' fall; seeking to avoid guilt by association, she had now become one of Astraea's most vociferous supporters. Kaetellin, as gnomic and inscrutable as ever, seemed content to let events play out as they must. He had always been a great favourite of the Failed on the council and Astraea's mild reforms to their conditions had met with his approval.

No, she thought, gazing around at her colleagues, the afternoon light falling in a wan sheet through the pillars of the colonnade. *The weak link is the priest – Thanasis.*

He met her eyes. Under the shadow of his hood, he smiled at her, sitting there at the other end of the table as still as a corpse, the flask of nourishing liquor in front of him. He could not be frightened or bought off. He could not be arrested on false charges, not without provoking the rest of the priesthood and those more pious citizens who still trusted them. As they sat and talked of the dullest municipal issues – street lighting, drainage, structural issues on the west wall – Astraea idly turned over the possibilities of murder and assassination in her mind.

Dardus would do it, she knew. He would be delighted to be given such a task. And yet his pleasure in the job would make him reckless and clumsy. Rather than seeming to die quietly as a result of illness or accident, Thanasis would end up dead in some bloody spectacular, with multiple witnesses putting Dardus at the scene. There could be no suspicions raised about what they were doing, not yet. Four years of planning had gone into this moment; four years of building up supplies and weapons, of infiltrating the city guard, of secretly mobilising the Failed and those citizens sympathetic to their cause. They only had to hold their nerve a little while longer.

'And now we come to the Games,' Thanasis said. The subject seemed to energise him slightly. He sat forward, sipped from his flask, pressed his bony fingers to the sharp bridge of his nose. 'They are approaching rapidly, and I fear our preparations are running behind. The volunteers must be organised, the lots taken to make up the shortfall…'

'Haephastin,' Astraea said, 'if you would be so kind as to start organising the lots. The shortfall is generally much greater than we always expect.'

'Indeed,' Thanasis said piously. 'Such a shame, a sad reflection on our times, when the young cannot summon the same zeal to contribute as their forefathers.'

'I can't think why,' Astraea said coolly.

Haephastin, dragging himself through a drunken haze, slumped forward in his chair and nodded eagerly.

'It will be done!' he slurred. He reached for his goblet and knocked it over, spilling a dribble of wine onto the table. 'Damn thing,' he muttered. 'Aegeus! Aegeus, damn you, come and clean up this mess!'

'And what about your own preparations, Astraea?' Thanasis said. There was a supple concern to his voice, entirely feigned. 'This will be a most significant Games for you, will it not? To see your son, young Lycus, make the ultimate sacrifice and be absorbed into the holy body of King Zothar... You must be so proud.'

He smiled and she saw the grey teeth in his blackened gums, glinting from the cast shadow of his hood.

'It will, and I am,' she said. She inclined her head, as if acknowledging the priest's concern. 'It will be a great day, and I assure you that my preparations are nearly complete.'

When the day's business was done, Astraea left the council chambers and headed deep into the warren of streets up against the southern wall. She pulled her cloak about her as the light dimmed, the cold Shyishian breeze rippling in from off the desert and the sea. The city wall was high on her right-hand side, the sloped marble mottled with dirt, the base of the walls smothered in drifts of sand. She entered a dirty, ill-kept alleyway with only a single broken aetherlamp at the far end. The buildings crowded her on either side and only the narrowest sliver of the evening sky was visible above.

She had turned around so that the walls of the second tier were rising up off to her left, the marble pinked by the last rays of the declining sun. Just visible beyond them were the high roofs of the more salubrious quarter of the city. If she tipped her head back she could even see the walls of the first tier at the very top. For those in the first tier, at the very apex of the city, the agora and the Tower were the only parts of the third tier they would regularly visit. The grand public buildings, the temples and council offices, the granaries and warehouses, were all clustered around Lament's central square. The rest of it, the streets where the Failed and the city's poorest people actually lived, may as well have been in another part of Shyish altogether.

Soon, she thought as she approached a wooden door in a squat and unobtrusive stone building off the alleyway. *It will all be changed, changed utterly...*

She knocked and waited a moment, then turned the brass ring of the handle and entered, closing the door behind her. Inside was a narrow hallway of unworked stone, a flight of stairs leading down into the darkness. Astraea took a taper from a cup on a little wooden table and lit it from the solitary candle that burned in a sconce by the door. She followed the stairs down and at the bottom came out into a narrow chamber with a low roof of fired brick. There was a plain woollen rug on the floor. Two torches burned from brackets on the walls on either side. At the other end of the chamber there was a waist-high wooden altar, on which rested a decorative hammer worked in gilt and silver and a leather-bound book open in the middle.

Selene was standing there, consulting the book. She was wearing long, dark robes, the hood thrown back, the hammer pendant around her neck. She turned and smiled as Astraea entered. For a moment Astraea thought she looked like a girl again, like the young, carefree lass who had played with Lycus when they were children. Now, there was a fierceness and a directness in her that Astraea sometimes found difficult to confront. Her pale hair was cut close, and her face was lined and austere, although she was only twenty years old. She was no longer a young girl, Astraea thought. She was a mother now. She was a priestess of Sigmar. She was Sigmar's Word in Lament.

'How was the meeting?' she asked, as Astraea bowed at the altar. Selene looked back at the open book, running her fingers over the words. It was a copy of *Intimations of the Comet*, picked up from the same traders from whom they had been buying weapons. To Selene it was the most precious thing she owned, more precious even than her son.

'The usual,' Astraea said. 'Nothing significant, although Thanasis reminds us that we need to press ahead with the arrangements for the Games.'

'He has a point.'

'Indeed,' Astraea sighed. 'We at least have to make it look like it's proceeding as normal. How is young Arius? That boy was a whirlwind when I left him this morning, I hope he's calmed down since then.'

Selene smiled. 'Kalista is with him just now,' she said. 'He loves that old maid, more than he loves his mother, I'm quite sure.'

'Nonsense,' Astraea said, although she thought there might be a grain of truth in it.

Dardus and Selene's son was a wonderful child, a delight to Astraea and a boy that reminded her in strange ways of her own son. More than once she had found herself wishing that Lycus had been the father. They had been so close when they were children, but she was surprised at her own sentiment to imagine that Selene and Lycus might have one day grown up and fallen in love.

She had never been able to fathom the relationship between Selene and Dardus. It seemed something based not on love, but on mutual hatred – not of each other, but of the world they found themselves in. It bound them together, gave them purpose, and it had produced this child, Arius. But could a child born and raised out of nothing but hatred ever thrive? It troubled her. It troubled her as well to see how fervent Selene's faith was, although it was a faith that Astraea herself now shared. Sigmar was a stern god, she thought, but he was at least a just god too.

She wondered what Lycus was doing now. There in far Athrabis, did he lie and think of his family and friends back in Lament? That moment four years ago had been a torment to her. To hear him speak of Zothar like that, to see him turn away with such merciless indifference when his creatures had killed that young man and woman in the agora. But he was not lost to them yet, she knew. She believed in him still.

She turned her mind away from such sorrows.

'Is Dardus leading the patrol this evening?' she asked as Selene closed the book.

'You know Dardus,' Selene said. 'He always wants to lead them.'

'I'm torn between worrying that these patrols in the desert just draw attention to ourselves and that they're essential if we don't want Zothar's troops to catch us unawares. Who knows what spies he might have in Lament? The priests, certainly. Thanasis would pass information on in a heartbeat.'

'The priests will have to be dealt with when the Games come,' Selene said. She began lighting the candles on the altar. 'We need people in position to kill them when we make our move.'

Astraea felt chilled at the casual way she said this, but she agreed all the same. And she would shed no tears for Thanasis.

'There is so much still to do,' she said.

'There is,' Selene answered, and then she turned from the altar with the hammer in her hand.

She was no longer Selene, an orphan girl Astraea had taken in because of her friendship with her son. She was the priestess now, stern and unyielding, without mercy for those who blasphemed against her god. When she spoke, it was in a voice like thunder.

'Kneel!' she said. 'Kneel before Sigmar!'

Astraea, trembling, knelt. Selene placed the hammer carefully against her brow. The kiss of cold metal, the weight of gold and silver, and Sigmar's weight behind it. The weight of a god.

'Do you feel him in you?' the priestess intoned. 'Do you feel his strength flowing through you!'

'I do!'

She held the hammer above her head and her voice cried out to the heavens – to blessed Azyr, the Golden Realm, where Sigmar sat in judgement on a throne of wrought gold and coruscant fire.

'Sigmar, lord, bless your faithful servants! We are but sparks of the lightning on a benighted shore, but ever we burn to your holy purpose. Give us a measure of your power, lord, that we may smite your enemies unto death!'

Astraea sank into the sermon; it was a like a balm washing over her soul. She felt the purity of Sigmar's grace descend on her. She felt his anger, his love. There behind her closed eyes came the briefest flash of an image of destruction; of Lament in flames and her fighting in the rubble, outnumbered, on the very cusp of death. Content.

20

We came to lost Theres after a hard ride across the desert. We had left Athrabis at first light the day before. The city disappeared in the dust-haze behind us and the grey dawn fell like a sheet of water onto the cold and empty wastelands. They stretched on before us, a rucked field of dunes and sand drifts and buried ruins.

Vultures cut across the bleak sky as we rode, black specks that turned and slowly wandered south. I wondered if they were the same birds that flocked the pinnacle of the Tower in Lament? As we rode on in silence, I thought back to the agonies of my last visit to the city, four years ago. The young couple Khetera had beheaded in the square. The look on my mother's face when I referred to Zothar as my father. The pain of seeing Selene kiss Dardus, so severe I thought it would break my heart.

They had asked me to kill the king and I had refused. I had breathed not a word of it to anyone, but it was a secret that festered in my soul. I remembered departing with my troops from Lament, still stunned at what had happened as we headed back to Athrabis.

As we marched out through the agora, the people had hidden themselves away or thrown dark and sullen looks at us from their windows. The whole town was as grey and silent as the Shyishian dawn. Khetera had been grimly amused as he marched at my side and we had exchanged not a single word on all the miles back to the necropolis. I had brooded on my failures, and, though it pained me to admit it, on my successes as well. I had done what King Zothar had ordered. I had done my father's bidding. When I reported to him in the map room, saluting him as strict and formal as any common soldier, he had dismissed Khetera and stood for a long while gazing up at the vast bas-relief of his empire.

'Were you required to… enforce your authority?' he had asked me, still with his back to the room.

'Yes,' I said.

'Who?'

'A man and a woman,' I told him, 'who had looted bone from the Tower.'

'You made an example of them?' he asked.

'…Yes,' I said.

'Then you have done what I commanded. You have enforced my will.'

He had turned to me then and reached out a skeletal hand to rest it against my shoulder. I remember thinking, in some faint spark of insight, that it was almost as if he were turning his back on his empire, hanging there on the wall of his chamber. He was reaching for his son across all the clouded centuries, gesturing towards that which he had once lost, and repudiating everything he had gained in its stead. And was it possible that in those smouldering yellow eyes, the fuming lights of his long unlife, there was something like a buried spark of love – a faint flame still kindled in the depths of his soul? I had to look away. I felt overwhelmed by what I had done, by what had been demanded of me from both my father and my friends. And then his hand fell from my shoulder and he had turned again to the map upon the wall, and without another word from him I knew I had been dismissed. For days afterwards I felt the weight of his hand, as if he were pressing down on me still.

Lament had been quiescent in the years since, but I knew the king had his doubts that the spark of rebellion had been fully extinguished. He had eyes and ears in Lament that I could only guess at, and he brooded on it still. I dreaded the thought of being dispatched there again, to wield the sword of his authority. Who else would have to die? Who else would I have to kill before Lament could slumber again in its complacent dreams of peace and order?

Two pillars rose out of the haze ahead of us, as the day began to wane. We passed through them, and as we rode on I realised we were moving along the remains of an ancient avenue. I could see the foundations of buried buildings long since tumbled into ruin, the lonely spar of a broken wall, the empty plinth for a statue that had been carried off by the elements across the untold centuries. The sky ahead of us was gorged with light, but as the day fell away the horizon blurred and faded into the slack, drear evening of Shyish.

These then were the ruins of lost Theres, the king's city from when he had been a mortal man. From this avenue he had set out to seek the power in the earth that could restore to him his son. Instead, he had found Nagash, and he had made a bargain that had held him in its clasp ever since.

I felt a torpor sink onto me, more profound than that brought on by the long ride. In the ruins of Theres I saw a true glimpse of the ages and their relentless weight. Zothar was as old as this dead city, but he lived still, in his way. Theres had been utterly smothered by time, though; I felt as if every year of the millennia had settled on my shoulders.

We walked for a while through the ruins, leaving our steeds

by the side of the buried avenue. Zothar pointed out aspects of the city as we passed, features that time had rendered invisible to me, but that must have cast some faint shadow in his mind as he spoke. Here was where the city had held its feasts on holy days, worshipping some chthonic deity that had long been forgotten in the passing years. Over there was the theatre where troupes of players had performed during local festivals, cathartic dramas that re-enacted moments from the dim history of Theres in the Age of Myth.

As we walked, I felt what may have been flashes of memory ripple through my mind. Did I imagine the crowds of people walking these streets in days gone by, or did I recall them? Was it my imagination that called up the sight of these buildings in the days when they were whole, or was it my memory? I could not say. The memories of Neophron, if that's what they were, had always been vague and insubstantial things to me. I could never convince myself they were anything other than the flights of a frightened mind, wrenching details into a familiar pattern to stop itself from being overwhelmed by what was so strange and unusual.

'And here,' Zothar said, his voice little more than a whisper above the desert wind, 'is where I buried you after the Games in Lament. I raised your mausoleum, your monument, so that none should ever forget the son that was born to me, and who died in service of his city.'

He swept his hand out to indicate a bare acre of scrubland and dust, the hint here and there of stones breaking through the sand. It was as strange and pitiful a sight as I had ever seen.

Zothar turned away, as if too moved by what he looked upon to continue.

'Many are the times I have returned here,' he said. He stood looking towards the horizon, where the dusk now bled away into night. The last fingers of the sun reached out to press themselves against the nadirite of his armour, calling up a dull, smoky glow from the depths of the metal. 'To commune with what I have lost, and... and with what I have gained.'

'Gained, my lord?' I said. I stood beside him, my head lowered in respect of his memories.

'Strength,' he said. 'Power, immortality. I must acknowledge that the bargain of Nagash impressed benefits on me, as well as a curse. I could not have conquered all that I have without them.'

'There are none who can defy you, lord,' I said.

'None. Nagash, in all his infinite cruelty, kept his word. And yet, as the centuries pass and as I welcome each version of my son's soul into my care once more, I have long wished that the Monarch of the Dead will show me mercy at last. As thanks for my service to him, my loyalty. As you know, I have long hoped,' he said, 'that one day Neophron would return to me permanently. His soul has ever been a seed on the breeze, tossed through the winds of time, but perhaps one day it would finally come to rest on stable ground. It would take root once more and grow.'

He turned towards me and took my shoulder. I looked up into the dark hollows of his eyes, the smouldering yellow flame.

'I believe,' he said, 'that day is upon us now.'

I could barely trust myself to speak. 'My lord?' I said. 'What do you mean?'

He looked away.

'More than any other soul in the last thousand years, I believe you are the closest to Neophron that I have seen. I think... I think you may be Neophron, fully returned to me.'

For a moment I seemed to step away from myself, to see it all from another angle entire; this cringing skeleton, this freak of mantled bone. It was a grotesque sight and the madness of it almost deranged me – but then my perspective altered once more. Like a sleeper waking heavily in the night and turning on the pillow, I soon slipped back into the strange dream of being Zothar's son. He was the king once more before me. He was my father.

He released my shoulder and walked slowly back to the empty patch of ground where the mausoleum had once stood.

'You have fought for me now in four battles,' he said, 'each time distinguishing yourself further.'

I nodded, recalling the skirmishes we had fought last summer against an orruk warband that had tried to cross the Howling Crevasse; the bloody and prolonged engagement the year before that with the duardin of the Emberforge Lodge, in the north-western corner of the kingdom. It was no idle boast to say that I had graduated from a scared boy who barely knew what he was doing, to a bold warrior confident in the face of the enemy. The kingdom of Athrabis was protected by my actions. Lament was made safe by my skill at arms.

'You have proved yourself a dedicated student of mathematics, history, literature,' Zothar continued. 'At the same time, you are bold and willing, your mind quick, your body fast and supple. In the midst of stress and troubles, there is an ease in your mind that speaks of great character. You remind me in every way of my son, for good and ill. And more than this,' he said, looking at me again. 'It cannot be explained by any other means, but… but I *feel* that you are him. I feel that you are anchored in that body more permanently than you ever have been before.'

He touched the soul gem on his breastplate. His jaw, that hook of bone, hung open but he did not speak. I saw him groping for the words, for emotions he had not been able to express for centuries.

'If there was still a heart in my breast that was capable of it,' he whispered, 'I would feel… I would feel that I…'

He shook his head and turned again to the bleak horizon.

I did not know what to say. I too was moved – by his pain, by his inability to confess his feelings; perhaps even by his inability to experience them in the first place.

'If I truly am Neophron,' I said, 'then what does this mean? For Lament, for the Games?'

My heart raced. I thought of Selene, my mother. I even thought of Dardus, although in the days since I had last left the city, I would have been glad to see him dead. The Regent's Palace appeared before my eyes. I would return to my home; I would rule it in Zothar's stead. I would be Neophron reborn, Regent of Lament.

'It could be free...' I said. Quickly I added: 'It is of no more consequence to us now if I truly am who I was always meant to be. There is no need for the Games, for the Contest.'

Zothar waved the point away, off-hand.

'No,' he said. 'If you are truly Neophron, then I have no more need of Lament at all. Let it be destroyed like all the others. Let it join Acharnae and the Painted Jewel and every other city and kingdom I have cast to ruin in my time. A last offering to Nagash, as thanks for his eternal blessing. The day of the Games draws near, mere weeks away, the time when your soul would normally sunder itself and seek new refuge. When we return to Athrabis, Se'bak will examine you and confirm it for us.'

'But – but the regency, Neophron's palace! I could rule there for you, Father, I could be your Law in Lament!'

'I already am the Law in Lament,' he said. His voice was as cold as the breeze. 'As I have said before, a king rules through the exercise of symbols as much as power. The regency is a symbol, something to make the people of that place feel connected to a greater whole. Nothing more.'

He laughed quietly.

'They gather their weapons and make their plans,' he said, 'those who feel themselves oppressed. But I know well what they intend. If you truly are Neophron returned, my son, then this will be the last Games ever held there. I will march on the city and destroy it, for it is of no more use to me.'

He walked back towards the avenue, where we had left our steeds. Mutely I followed.

'After all,' he said, 'why would you want to be Regent of Lament, when you could be Prince of Athrabis?'

We were a day from lost Theres when they attacked us. The evening was drawing near, and I had turned in the saddle to ask if we could pause and rest a while. Normally I would have forced myself on. After campaigning with the Bonereapers I had become used to matching their relentless pace, but King Zothar's words had set my mind into a panic that I could barely contain. I couldn't think, could not imagine how I could persuade him to spare Lament and all of its people. I felt exhausted and wanted only to lie down and turn this awful problem over in my mind. Then, as the light began to change, I saw a puff of dust curling up from an outcrop of stone ahead of us, a jagged thatch of obsidian that burst from the sands like some monstrous plant.

Something about the way the dust moved set my nerves on edge. The warrior's instinct, which had been beaten into me over the years, roused up in my blood.

'My lord?' I said – and then an arrow came flying from the rocks.

I wrenched my reins to the side. The arrow clattered from my pauldron, and I felt the fletching whip my face. I saw five riders spur themselves from the rocks, one already drawing on his bow for another shot, the others tearing their swords from their scabbards.

'The king is attacked!' I cried, as if the sentries of Athrabis, still forty miles away, could hear me. My blood was up, though, and the brazenness of the attempt infuriated me. I spurred myself forward, risking a glance to see the king drawing his scimitar, his jaw wide in some silent scream.

The riders came on, ragged-looking men in patched tunics. They cried and yelled, waved their swords above their heads as if acting the part of warriors. I thought them perhaps some ill-trained gang of outlaws, bandits of the waste who had wandered far and found themselves well out of their league. But then, as I charged them, my steed hammering the grey earth under its hooves, the fading sky purled with amethyst clouds above, I saw Dardus at their head. His face was twisted with rage and hatred, the wild hair streaming back from his shoulders, his sword pointed directly at me.

These were men of Lament, I realised.

Four more riders came haring around from the other side of the rocks, trying to outflank us. It was a sound manoeuvre and for the briefest moment I felt a touch of apprehension. But then King Zothar had surged forwards and was amongst them, hacking left and right with his scimitar, his steed barrelling the horses out of the way. I saw blood flash against the purple sky, the screams of dying men.

I met Dardus' blade against my own, easily turning it.

'Traitor scum!' he cried.

He thundered past and tried to wheel around me, but by then I was into his fellows.

I blocked one swing from a man with wild grey hair, stabbed forward and thrust the point of my sword through his jaw. He cried out and dropped his weapon, both hands up to cover his wound, his half-severed tongue lolling through his fingers. The next rider reared up as I swung hard from left to right, the blade catching his horse across the face. It screamed and bolted, the rider tumbling backwards and falling badly to the ground. I trampled him under my steed's hooves, pivoted, spurred forwards and used my momentum to pluck another rider from his saddle.

I turned wildly, looking for Dardus, but all I could see was the trail of dust as he fled, heading back towards Lament. King Zothar had dispatched all of his assailants with ease and no more than two or three other riders had escaped to join their leader.

The blood cooled in my veins. I looked on the wreckage of the fight, the dead men of Lament strewn across the dust. I had fought and killed many a foe over the last few years, but I could not think of these men as enemies. I was gripped with an immense sadness as I looked down at them. Even the thought of Dardus at their head did not make me feel any less overwhelmed.

I turned to the king, but he was gripped in such a rage that I quailed before it.

'Have I not been lenient, my son?' he screamed. 'Have I not been just and faithful to our compacts? And this is my repayment! This audacity will not go unpunished, I swear it!'

He hacked his steed forwards and tore off across the sands towards Athrabis. It was all I could do to keep up. The fate of Lament, I knew, depended entirely on what happened next.

21

The hour-bell had just struck midnight when Dardus burst into Astraea's house. Selene had put Arius down for the third time that night, the boy being restless and unsettled, when there was a scuffing tread outside the front door, a crash as it was flung open. Selene slipped out of her son's room at the other end of the corridor, just as Astraea emerged from the parlour. She had not been able to sleep either, it seemed. The night was a tense and fragile thing, hanging over the city like a web.

She saw Dardus collapse into the hall, grasping at one of the pillars for balance. His face was mottled with fatigue, his hair drenched with sweat. She ran to him, lifting his head up.

'Astraea!' she hissed, trying not to wake the child. 'Help me get him into the parlour. And fetch some water!'

Arius began crying, but Kalista, the maid, went to him. Together, Selene and Astraea dragged Dardus into the room at the front of the house, laying him down on the couch. When Astraea returned with a cup of water, he drank greedily. He seemed to recover some of his strength and sat up, rubbing the exhaustion from his eyes.

'What happened?' Astraea said.

'Lycus…' Dardus groaned. 'And Zothar himself!'

'They crossed your path?' Selene demanded. 'They knew about the patrol?'

Dardus shook his head. 'An accident more than anything. We had looped round near the walls of Athrabis and were heading back when they came from the desert to the west.' He eyed her carefully. 'I saw the opportunity, and I took it.'

Selene felt her heart lurch. 'Is he…?'

'He lives,' Dardus said, as if nothing could deject him more. 'They cut us apart, as if we were nothing, damn them… Lycus hacked down Markus as if he were a dog on the roadway! Amyntos, Docia and I managed to escape, and the rest are feeding the vultures now. Docia hasn't returned, we lost her on the ride…'

'Sigmar save us,' Astraea whispered. 'Then they know… Zothar knows now that we oppose him, and he will move openly against us…'

'Why?' Selene cried at her husband. She shook him by the shoulder. 'Why did you do it, would you leave our child fatherless?'

Dardus shrugged her hand off. 'The chance was there in front of me,' he muttered. 'I could have ended this in one swing of my sword.'

'Against Zothar himself? You are more of a fool than I thought!'

Dardus swung his legs from the couch and got unsteadily to his feet.

'The deed is done regardless,' he said, grimacing. 'We have to move. The priests must die tonight, the weapons be put in the right hands. Zothar will ride for Lament by first light if he's not riding here already. We must prepare!'

Astraea stood from the edge of the couch. 'He's right,' she said.

'Any advantage of surprise we might have had during the Games is gone now. We must prepare the city. Thanasis and the priesthood must be arrested at once.'

'Arrested?' Dardus sneered. He reached for the sword on his hip. 'Let the gutters run with their blood instead. Let everyone know that we're serious.'

Selene drew back, her mind racing. Her blood was like fire in her veins. It was all happening too fast, too recklessly…

She stood at the window, her hands up to her face – and then, as she stared out over the darkened city, she seemed to see a great light unfolding across the sky, a golden light against the drear and sallow clouds, lancing from the heavens. The rumble of thunder rang deep in her bones and the pendant was hot against her skin. Unbidden came to mind the words from the first volume of the *Intimations*: 'For Sigmar speaks thus with a strong hand above my head, and though the road be dark, ever shall his light guide my steps, even unto the darkest chambers of mine enemy.'

She saw a dark city lit with an eldritch green glow, vast out of all imagining; and in the centre of it, gleaming like a star, an inextinguishable point of light…

'No,' she said. She turned back to face them. She felt as if her voice was coming from somewhere over her shoulder, from a point deeper and further away than she could possibly imagine. Astraea looked on her with reverence. Even Dardus could not meet her eye. 'We must not give up on Lycus yet. He remains our best hope.'

'Lycus has betrayed us!' Dardus said. 'He cleaves to Zothar, he always has done. Lament is dead to him.' He gripped his sword. 'This is all we can trust now.'

Astraea wrung her hands, her face wet with tears.

'If we could only speak to him,' she said, 'if we could turn him to our cause…'

Dardus was scornful. 'You would issue him an invite, would you? I'm sure Zothar would be content to wait while he dawdled over a cup of Hysh-flower tea!'

'He cannot come to us now,' Selene said. Her heart felt full beyond measure. 'But I can go to him.'

'Into Athrabis?' Dardus said, incredulous. 'On your own? But… it would be suicide!' He threw his arm out. 'You would leave our son motherless?'

'No,' Selene said. 'I will not be alone. Sigmar will walk with me, every step of the way.'

I was so exhausted by our pace that I sought my chambers as soon as we returned to the city. In moments, all was in an uproar; I heard the harsh cries of commands being issued, the clash of weapons and armour out on the streets. Zothar had ridden immediately for the palace, where I imagined him pacing the map room, his scimitar in hand, transported by rage. For although he often gave the impression of long and thoughtful contemplation, of distraction into the lanes and byways of his long memory, I knew that Zothar was capable of the most profound and impetuous anger as well. I had seen it often enough; as hardened as I had become over nearly ten years in his company, he still had the power to terrify me. I was glad to be away from him for the moment, to seek refuge in the one place where I could be entirely on my own.

I cleaned and put aside my weapons (I was a good soldier by this point) and lay on the bed to think about the skirmish in the desert. The blood of those I had killed would not wash from my hands. I saw Dardus again, snarling with hatred, his sword extended towards me. I saw the grey-haired man, the look of abject sorrow on his face as my blade went through his jaw. Had he woken up that morning thinking that this was how his day would end? Had any of them? Had I?

I must have dozed for a while, the rigours of the journey overwhelming me. I dreamt of Zothar's screaming skeletal face, the sands of the desert. I dreamt of a cavern deep beneath the world, where a vulture made of bones hunched and plotted, brooding in its elemental malice. I saw Nagash's Eye, the moon, stuffed with the souls of all those who had died in the Games, all screaming at me to save them…

I woke with a start. It was dark and the air was still. The city beyond my chambers was silent. The army had not yet left, I knew, but the ranks had been dressed and the Deathriders had saddled their steeds. Zothar was waiting for the dawn. He would leave at first light, timing his arrival at the gates of Lament for dusk, when the sight of his army would prove even more terrifying.

Symbols, I thought. *It is not just the army itself that defeats an enemy, but what the enemy perceives that army to be…*

Without thinking, acting purely on instinct, I snatched up my sword and leapt from the bed. There was someone in the room with me. I was not the only living thing here.

'Show yourself!' I commanded. 'Death is near you if you do not!'

'Death is always near us,' a woman's voice said. 'For are we not of Shyish, and are we not both people of Lament?'

She stepped from the shadows in the corner of the room, her head veiled by a scarf, her eyes as wild and compassionate as I had ever seen them. There was no one it would have surprised me more to see.

'Selene!'

I dropped the sword. The room fell away for a moment, and all Athrabis with it. I wanted to take her in my arms, to embrace her, but then the cold reality of where we were was stark in my eyes again. I took her shoulders, held her at arm's length, as if I could force her to turn and go back the way she had come. It had been four years since I had last seen her. I had not expected her to be before me again until the moment King Zothar struck off my head at the end of the Contest.

'Why are you here?' I said. 'How? In the name of all that's holy, the city prepares for war! Have you any idea how easily you could have been caught?'

She reached up and drew her hand lightly across my face.

'What better time to pass unseen, when all eyes are looking in the other direction?' she said.

She staggered into my arms, and I could see how exhausted she was. The journey from Lament was a hard march, but on horse it could be reached in a few hours, if the rider did not spare the whip. She sat down on the edge of the bed while I fetched water, some of the plain soldier's fare that the Bonereapers allocated to me.

'How did you find me in this labyrinth?' I asked, as she ate and drank. 'It would be like wandering Lament looking for a pin you knew was hidden there.'

'Sigmar guided me on the path,' she said. 'There was...' She faltered, as if reaching for words that were just out of her grasp. 'I cannot explain it, but it was like there was a light glowing in the midst of all this darkness, and I only had to follow it. You were that light, Lycus,' she said. 'And Athrabis is a greater darkness than I would have ever believed.'

She shuddered, clearly recalling the journey through those miserable streets – hiding in doorways, slipping through the shadows, every nerve exposed to the awful danger of discovery.

'But why?' I demanded. I sat down beside her, held her hand. 'You know about Dardus, the fight in the desert? He tried to kill me,' I said.

'He tried to kill Zothar,' she countered. I saw a flash of fire in her eyes. I remembered the way she had held him as they left the Regent's Palace all those years ago.

'And does he truly think Lament can win a war against Zothar? For he has played his hand now, and war is come whether he wants it or not.'

'He believes it,' she said. 'As does your mother.' She looked at my face, her eyes searching mine. I felt her hand squeeze my fingers. 'As do I.'

I felt crushed, oppressed by the weight of such futility.

'So, the Jackal Kings have risen again, have they…?'

'Just the ordinary women and men of Lament,' she said defiantly. 'Those who cannot stand the yoke of the Bonereapers a moment longer. Those who choose death and freedom, rather than slavery.'

'By all that's holy,' I protested, 'if you've passed through these streets, then you must have had at least a glimpse of what Zothar can muster to his banners? Do not do this, Selene. Do not range yourself against him, for he will utterly destroy you.'

'And you think there is still time for anything else?' she said. Her voice was calm, as if all this was at the end of the discussion and the decision had already been made. 'We fight because we must, and we have right on our side. That is worth more than his whole legion, I know it.'

'Do you think being right will comfort you when Lament is in ruins and the rubble is stained with your blood?' I said. 'How many troops does being right bring to the war? How much cavalry, how many war machines?'

'Sigmar does not bless those who choose the easy way,' she said. 'And the right way is always the hardest.'

'Sigmar…' I sighed. I realised how much I must sound like Dardus. 'You place your hope in a god who has no power here. None.'

'The greatest power Sigmar holds is in people's hearts,' she said softly. 'And his dominion is everywhere.'

I took her hand again, raised it to my lips. 'Why are you here, Selene? What can you hope to achieve?'

She kissed me then. I had never felt such softness, such ease. I felt all the sorrow and misery of Athrabis wash away from me, and then she was drawing back and standing to go.

'We are on the brink,' she said sadly. 'All have given up on you, Lycus, but you know I never shall. I trust you. I love you. I always have done. I always will.'

'What can I possibly do?' I said. I was drenched in misery. 'War is come down, and Zothar will not be swayed, I promise you.'

'If he is truly your father,' she said, 'then let him listen to his son. Sway him with a son's words. And if he is not, then do as you must. For all of us.'

She disappeared back into the shadows, slipping from my chambers and out into the drear streets of the city. I prayed then for her safe return, but if pressed I could not say who I prayed to. Perhaps it was to her god, to Sigmar, who had given her the courage to come in the first place.

Let him watch over her, I thought. For no one else will.

I thought about her words as I lay there in the dark, as the hours ticked over towards the rising dawn. I was Zothar's son, by all the rites of my people. Zothar believed that I could be Neophron returned, the final incarnation of his lost child. If so, he would not need Lament and its fate would be sealed. But if not, then there was a chance the city could be spared. He needed it, more than he could ever admit. Grief and sorrow had tied him to Lament, through all the ages of his long unlife. He could not so easily cut that bond.

Selene could be spared, my mother, everyone who lived there. There was only one person who could guarantee it either way…

I left my chambers as the light began to stain the eastern sky. My sword was heavy in my hand.

22

The streets thrummed to the march of troops as I made my way to the Mortisan laboratories. I passed columns of infantry moving up from their barracks in the north-western quarter, heading to the mustering grounds in the central square. There were war machines lined up, row upon row, on the vast promenade of the avenues; Mortek Crawlers having their counterweights slung and their frames reinforced. I marvelled again, despite myself, at the scale of Zothar's forces, their obedience, and the efficiency with which they prepared themselves for war. What could Lament possibly put up against all this? Dardus and a rag-tag band of rebels with rusting swords? It would be a massacre. A bare company of Mortek Guard could clean the streets of any resistance, let alone the entire legion.

Fear put speed into my pace. I hurried on through the spectral streets, the green lights of the aetherlamps pooling on the black cobblestones. I could almost feel Zothar's anger radiating from the palace in the distance, tempered now to a cool, hard flame, but no less deadly for all that.

The Mortisan laboratories were, in contrast, a place of industrious peace and rigorous contemplation. Behind the forbidding exterior of the building, hunkered like some great, spiny beast against the northern quarter of the city, its spires stabbing the sky like spear blades, I found as I always did a sense of dusty quiet. I pushed through the great double doors and entered a world of shadows and silence, broken only by the far-off wailing of some tormented soul as the masons pared away whatever elements they needed from it. My footsteps echoed as I crossed the empty hall.

I found Se'bak in his study, where he was, as ever, surrounded by scrolls and volumes of ancient lore. On his workbench were the cluttered materials of his experiments, phials and crucibles, glass alembics, a mortar and pestle. His staff was leaning up against a listing bookshelf and he looked preoccupied as I entered, plucking through the papers on his desk. I saw that his short sword was lying in front of him, still sheathed in its scabbard. I tried to step back from myself and see him as he really was; as something dark and unnatural, and not with the broad and generous affection I normally felt for him. He was a malign thing, I tried to think. A monster, ancient beyond imagining. Not even a body resurrected, but a soul housed in some flaking amalgam of bones. I tried to hate him, but I could not do it. He had always been kind to me when he had no reason to be so. He had been my tutor and he had been my friend. I felt a great weight settle on my heart.

'Ah,' he croaked. 'There you are, my boy. I had sent word to you, and here you are, faster than I would have imagined.'

'You sent word, Se'bak?' I said as I approached. 'I did not receive it.'

'You didn't? Well,' he said, 'no matter, you are here now. King Zothar has charged me with a vital task, and I must say he was brisk with the ordering of it. He came back from your visit to old Theres in some heat. You did not argue, did you?'

He turned his ancient skull to face me. I gazed into those flickering red lights, the pinprick flames of his eyes. I could see where the suture lines between the bones had darkened with centuries of dust and dirt, where the bone itself had yellowed with age and begun to flake. What fell magics, I wondered, kept such a thing together? Again, I tried to conjure a feeling of disgust, but it died inside me. All I felt was a great sympathy.

'We did not,' I said, 'although there was trouble on the way. We were attacked, by men from Lament.'

'From Lament?' He shook his head. 'Then that explains the preparations, and his impatience.' He tapped the sword on his desk. 'I am armed and as ever I am ready to accompany the army. But let us hope cooler heads prevail…'

I came and stood by his desk.

'Se'bak,' I said. 'The king wishes to know whether I am truly Neophron. Lament stands on the brink, dependent on the truth of it either way.'

'Lament's fate has ever hung from such a gossamer thread,' he said sadly. 'The soul is the strongest thing in all creation, it is true, but in many ways it is a thing less substantial than the very air. Even in the laboratories of the Mortisan Order, with all my experience, I have often wondered at the phantoms we deal with. Can you hold it, hmm? Can you see it?'

'No,' I said. 'But I can feel it.'

'Indeed, indeed…' he said, musing. 'Not the blood in their veins, but the fire of their spirit, the sense of themselves as an apprehending thing, both enmeshed and apart from the world around them…' He looked at me kindly. I wondered if he had been walking for a while in the old memories of the life he must have once lived. 'It is the gift of the living,' he said, 'to feel the life quicken inside you, my boy.'

'And is this life inside me my own?' I said. 'Or is it Neophron's?'

'King Zothar certainly believes so,' he said, peering up at me. There was something hard and dark in his gaze then, as if the answer was already known to him. 'And he has commanded me to determine it. We approach the ten-year mark, after all, when Neophron's soul prepares to migrate to its next vessel. It is at this moment that, like the corpse-fly emerging from its chrysalis, we see it in its entirety.'

'How will you tell?' I asked, dreading the answer.

'The soul gem in my staff,' he said, reaching one of his hands for it. 'Pass it to me, my boy. It will scry the very depths of you, as it did when you were first chosen. This time it will see the soul in its every aspect. Do not be afraid,' he said. 'This will not hurt as much as you would expect…'

He knew. He had always known, since the very moment King Zothar's blade had struck the head from Neophron's shoulders, nearly ten years ago. Either I was truly Neophron returned or I was no more than another temporary vessel; whatever signs Se'bak could read, they had been written there as clear as day on the lineaments of my soul when I was a child, as he approached me in the agora of Lament. Perhaps expedience had made him keep this truth to himself, at least initially. I liked to think that it was the bond that had grown between us that made him keep it to himself in all the years that followed.

I found suddenly that I did not want to know myself. I hadn't prepared myself this far, but I had thought that if I were to do anything it would be after Se'bak had confirmed whether Neophron truly lived in me or not. If not, then let me die. Let the Games go ahead and let Lament soothe itself with the accustomed ritual. But now, standing before him, I only wanted to be free of it all. I did not want to know that I had become only a host for another soul, something that would live through me forever. By the same token, I did not want to know that for the last ten years my life had been no more than a resting place in that soul's eternal journey. I thought of Selene.

Se'bak held out one of his hands for his staff, gesturing for me to pass it.

I reached for where it was leaning against the bookcase, and when I looked down into his eyes I saw the soft red lights take flame. The understanding passed between us. His jaw hinged open as if he wanted to speak, but there were no more words to say.

'Se'bak,' I said. There were tears in my eyes. 'I'm sorry.'

I let the staff drop from my hand. As the Soulmason reached for it, I drew my sword and struck.

I cannot stress enough the trepidation I felt as I made my way to Zothar's palace. Troops still marched along the streets and formed up in their mustering yards and it took me longer to navigate my way there than I would have liked. I used the time to clean the blood from my face where Se'bak had struck me in his death throes, to pat down the bone-dust from my tunic. I carried my helm under my arm and ran as fast as I could. When I reached the grand stone steps that led up to the palace doors I was as tired as if I had just ridden all night from Theres.

I paused on the top step before I went in. I looked south, where the high walls of Athrabis at the far end of the avenue were as silent and forbidding as a cliff face. I hoped Selene had managed to escape, that through whichever wicket gate or sally port she had managed to sneak through, the journey home was safe.

'Sigmar bless you,' I said under my breath. I glanced to the sky, but Sigmar was not there, or at the very least he hid himself from such as me.

I could hear the crack and roar of Zothar's voice from the other end of the hall, the polished acre of black marble that seemed as long a distance as I had ever walked. The sound of my footsteps floated up to the shadows of the vaulted ceiling far above. I clutched my helm, felt for the hilt of my sheathed blade, and tried to present a soldierly appearance as I marched into the map room. I hoped Zothar, in his passion, would overlook the cut on my forehead, or assume it had been dealt during the skirmish with Dardus and his renegades; after all, I hadn't seen him since that moment.

He was stalking from one end of the map room to the other when I entered, screaming and gesticulating at his underlings. Khetera stood there at the side of the room, as stiff and straight as an arrow, Phaetor the Boneshaper with the tendrils wavering like deep-sea fronds on the back of his skull. There were Hekatoi from the other regiments standing at attention too, all of them bearing the brunt of Zothar's ire. He raged against the traitors of Lament, the renegades and their feeble rebellion, the last scions of the Jackal Kings who he should have crushed a thousand years ago as payment for his son's death.

'Nagash can take their bones,' he screamed, 'for I would not sully my legion with them! I will build a pyre of Lament and let their vultures feast and watch the bone-crows pick amongst the leavings when all are dead!'

He was so transported by his rage that he drew his scimitar and in one hard sweep brought it down onto the table in the centre of the room. The smoky crystal was cleaved clean in two, the noise like a thunderclap. I glanced to the wall of trophies, taken from all the foes who had felt that ire over the years. I wondered what Lament could possibly contribute to that collection. My mother's diadem, perhaps. Selene's robes.

Zothar turned and saw me enter. For a moment his rage faltered.

'My son,' he said. 'I have summoned Se'bak for the examination, but he sends no answer. Have you seen him?'

'No, Father,' I said. 'I have come direct from the Mortisan laboratories and there was no sign of him.'

Zothar cursed. 'Lost in his research, no doubt, the old fool! Dawn rises, and time draws short! I would have my answer on the state of your soul...'

'Father,' I said. I glanced nervously at Khetera and the other Hekatoi, pushing my way through them to stand at his side by the ruins of the crystal table. I lowered my voice, as if speaking in confidence. 'Father, give me this chance, as you gave it to me before. Let me go to Lament, with strength in force. Let me cut the thorns from this rebellion and spare you the fruit – for the love of your son, do not risk all in Lament's destruction yet.'

The proud skull turned to face me. The yellow lights of his eyes dimmed as he looked down on me. I caught a glimpse of myself in the polished nadirite of his breastplate, the reflection distorted, skewed, so that I looked like some gangling, half-formed thing beseeching a being of austere power and grace. I held his gaze in that moment, sure that he could see the murder of Se'bak written across my face and that it was only some lingering affection for me that prevented him from cutting me down. I did not flinch.

'I may be Neophron fully returned,' I said. 'Or his soul may have made only a temporary refuge in me, as it has done so many times before. Time presses on us and we cannot wait to test this before the rebels grow bolder. Father, let me stamp your will on Lament, that it may be spared for your purposes until we know for sure either way. Let us not be hasty here.'

The moment balanced on the edge of a blade. I think it was then, more than at any other time, that I truly felt myself a creature of flesh and blood amongst these dry and lifeless bones, for in that room, I was the only one who needed to hold his breath against the outcome of Zothar's decision.

'Go,' he said at last. 'Take Khetera and five regiments of Mortek Guard. Phaetor, go with them. Invest Lament. Give them this choice – that the ringleaders shall be surrendered and killed and as recompense every adult over the age of twenty-one will give up the bones of their left hand to the tithe. If they refuse, then the Legion of Athrabis will return in force and not a stone of Lament will be left standing.'

He dismissed us and turned away. As the weight of his gaze was removed from me, I felt as if I had been released from a cage. My legs were trembling, my hands shook, but I managed to disguise it. I placed my helmet on my head and saluted, as if no more than a faithful soldier eager to obey his lord's commands.

I summoned Khetera and together we left the palace to organise the troops. At the door, the wide stone steps spread out before us, Khetera looked at me. The teeth in his skeletal jaw seemed almost like they were smiling.

'Always,' he said. 'Always this weakness when it comes to his son. It will be his undoing at last.'

23

She tried to snatch a moment's rest when she returned to Astraea's house, but as hard as the ride across the desert had been, Selene could not sleep. Lying on her bed, the sallow daylight dying in the western sky, she felt tormented by her memories. She thought of Lycus as a boy, climbing the bluffs to the cave of the Jackal Kings. She saw again that shattering moment when Neophron's head was severed and Lycus was claimed as King Zothar's son. Those scenes drifted before her eyes like the afterimages of a vacant dream.

She kept thinking back to him, sprawled there on his cot in the gloom of those awful chambers, deep in that terrible city. She had tied her horse by an outcrop of rock half a mile distant and there had been such commotion and disorder in the streets that it had been easy enough to slip through the open gates into Athrabis. She had seen columns of Bonereaper soldiers rushing down radial passageways, troops of cavalry on those monstrous skeletal steeds clattering their hooves down the avenues, but no one had noticed her as she crept from doorway to alley, sneaking further into the city than she would have believed possible. At every moment she expected to be stopped, for drawn swords to pierce her in a dozen places. She had been gripped by such terror as she slunk through the streets, as if she were walking through the very bowels of the Underworlds, that she had almost turned and ran. It was Lycus that had kept her going, more so even than her faith in Sigmar. She could sense the light that flowed from him, the goodness of his heart. It had been like a beacon calling her onwards through the darkness. He was their last, their only, hope.

She remembered the feel of his lips against hers, the breath that caught in his throat. She meant what she had said. She loved him and she had done so for as long as she could remember. There was goodness in Dardus too, she knew, but it wasn't the same. His cynicism, his rejection of everything Lament stood for, had enthralled her since she was a girl, but as she lay there on the bed she writhed against her guilt. Dardus had buried himself in his anger and what had once made him seem dangerous and exciting now seemed pitiful. He had never been given the chance to be anything other than sardonic and cruel. Even the love she felt for him, weak and insubstantial as it was, hadn't been enough to free him from his rage.

She sighed and tried to gather her emotions together, but sleep was a phantom to her. Selene swung herself from the bed, too exhausted to do anything other than sit and wait.

How had it come to this? Rebellion, the threat of war, the certainty of destruction.

Lycus, she thought. *Please, in Sigmar's name, spare us from this if you can. Turn Zothar's wrath from Lament, or strike him down and save us all...*

The bells began to toll down by the city gate. She heard the rush of feet out on the avenue, a lone and despairing cry. She felt drained by horror all of a sudden, and her hands shook as she quickly dressed.

Dardus spun around as she entered the parlour. He was standing there with Astraea, who looked like she was going to be sick. Dardus himself was almost delighted; there was a fey look in his eyes, a wild sense of joy in the way he bounded over to her.

'They've arrived!' he said.

He clenched his fist, bared his gap-toothed grin. The bells continued their clamour in the lower city; all was in uproar.

'Who?' Selene said. 'What's happening?'

'The Bonereapers,' he said. 'They've sent an army. Our scouts have seen them They're two miles off yet, but it's war, there can be no doubt. Lycus is leading them once more. It's safe to assume that he does Zothar's bidding... I'm sorry to say that your mission was in vain, Selene.'

He did not seem sorry in the slightest. He smiled at her, as if she would be as delighted by this news as he was.

Selene sat heavily on the couch. She stared at the bare grate of the fireplace, at a patch of the rug where the thread was wearing thin. She couldn't think. Her mind flew in different directions, alighting on nothing but a deadened sense of dread. Lycus had failed them. She had failed them.

She reached for her pendant. She called up the image of her grandfather, his gruff assurance. He would have met this moment the way he met all the others in his long life, with scorn and with a strong right hand.

'What do we do?' she said.

Astraea, who had seemed to cringe into the shadows at the news, now stepped forward. The fear had fled from her. Now, at their darkest moment, she assumed the role of the council elder once more. Selene found herself thinking of the graffiti that had sprung up around the city over the last few weeks: *Jackal King*. Perhaps they should have looked to a Jackal Queen to lead them instead?

'I give the order now,' Astraea said. Her voice was grave. 'And let no one misunderstand it. The priests must die tonight, before the city is surrounded. Dardus, see to it – alert everyone we've placed in the city guard, raise every sympathiser and distribute the weapons.'

Dardus, who had moved the weapons in from the caves above the bluff as soon as Selene had set off on her mission, gave a savage cry.

'The vultures will feast on their flesh,' he laughed. 'Have no fear!'

'And make sure Baeothis…' Astraea closed her eyes and pinched the bridge of her nose. 'We can't risk him being a rallying point for the priesthood,' she said quietly. 'For… for the others on the council.'

'I'll see to it personally,' Dardus said.

'Sigmar save us,' Astraea whispered. 'That we are forced to this extremity…'

Selene rose from the couch. Though her hands still shook she raised them in benediction.

'If it truly is war,' she said, 'then let Sigmar not save us, but give strength to our arms that we may smite those who are against us. From this moment on, let us draw on his power.'

Torches flared on the walls of Lament as we approached. I halted the army half a mile away in the scrubland. I could see men running back and forth from the gates as they were closed. Screams cut across the night air, the clash of swords. I saw the glow of a fire far over in the eastern quarter, throwing up a flickering light against the bellies of the clouds. Dusk had just passed across the land and night was almost on us. The air was wan and cold, and as we stood there waiting, the darkness seemed to gather over us like a grave-shroud. The rugged hills behind the city looked for a moment like the planes of a vast, howling skull, eager to swallow it down. I shuddered and girded myself for what must come next.

I gave the orders for the dispositions, one wing of the army fanning out towards the line of the coast a couple of miles distant, the other drawing up in column to feign an assault on the main gate. I had five thousand troops behind me, but I had no intention of using any of them if I could help it.

Khetera came and stood beside me. I looked down at him from the saddle of my steed, trying to assume an authority that at this moment I did not feel.

'This gives every impression of a city that is fighting itself,' he said. His harsh, whispering voice was as dry as the breeze, but I could hear the amusement behind it. 'Perhaps our work is already done for us, and the rebels have turned on each other? Typical of mortals,' he laughed. 'The moment of crisis comes upon them, and they break in their fear.'

I looked to the walls, saw the torches flitting along the battlements. It was a torment to me not to know what was happening, whether or not Selene and my mother were safe. Was Khetera right? Had the council turned against them? Did rebel fight loyalist in those quiet marble streets? Did the gutters run with the blood of Lament's people? I could see the flat roof of the Tower of the Moon looming over the agora, the black stone stained red by the light of the fires.

I was conscious of the Hekatos watching me, drumming the bones of his fingers against the hilt of his sword. The army, arrayed in its ranks and regiments on the scrubland behind me, felt like a great weight pressing down on my shoulders.

'You have ever been loath to heed my instruction, boy,' Khetera said, 'but my decision would be for an assault on the main gate immediately. Any defence they could muster would be brushed aside with ease.' He gazed contemptuously at the walls of the city, structures that had feared no enemy for time out of mind; they would pose no difficulty to him, I was quite sure.

'Let us at least hear what they have to say for themselves,' I said, spurring my steed forwards. I turned and called for Phaetor, the Boneshaper, and for two Mortek Guard to carry the king's banners. 'I will go with an embassy to speak to them. If the situation is as dire as it seems, then perhaps the gates will be opened to us, and no blood will be shed.'

'A pity,' Khetera sneered. 'But not a surprise, mortal. To see your fellows cut open will always be too much for you to bear.'

'Your insolence does not provoke me as much as it once did, Khetera,' I said, pivoting my steed so it butted up against him. He stood his ground, to give him credit. 'Am I not Neophron? Am I not King Zothar's son, Prince of Athrabis? Perhaps in time, when my father relinquishes his own soul, the decisions about the army will pass to me. There are far-flung outposts on the very fringes of Zothar's kingdom in need of a garrison, I'm quite sure, and a commander to lead them.'

'Time,' Khetera hissed. 'I have all the time there is, child. From now until the day Shyish itself fades into the oblivion that awaits all things, and its grey sands and drear skies are but bitter memories on the very edge of the void. You, mortal, will last only as long as these scrubland weeds we walk across. Do not speak to me of time.'

He pushed the head of my steed roughly aside and stalked off towards the walls of the city. I slipped from my warhorse and followed, like a chastened boy hurrying after an aggrieved parent, my teeth gritted with rage. Phaetor, gangling forward with his bony stride, came up from the body of the troops with the two Mortek Guard, the banners held between them.

'Come, then,' Phaetor said. His skull seemed always twisted into a leering smile, as if every task was the greatest pleasure to him. 'Let us take our embassy to the mortals. It is always amusing to hear them beg for their lives.'

'I will hear no one beg,' I said. 'The terms I offer will be fair.'

'Your father's terms, young Neophron? Or your own...?'

I gave no reply, just stalked on with anger in my heart.

In moments we were before the gates of Lament. The torches paused in their flight along the battlements, and I could see scared faces staring down at us from twenty feet above, half in darkness, half in light. The flames so coloured them that it made it seem as if each wore a mask of blood. I did not recognise any of them, but some intuition told me that they were of the Failed. This gave me hope that Selene and my mother might be safe. Dardus, surely, would not have allowed any harm to come to them.

'The gates are closed to your kind, traitor!' a cry came down. 'Turn your troops around and disappear back into the desert. Lament is a free city now.'

'I would speak with you,' I called up to them. 'You see the forces I bring with me, but I would have us talk before they are unleashed. If the talk goes well, there will be no need of violence. Call the council to the gates.'

I felt Khetera bristle at this, but he was silent. I watched the eager conferring between the men and women on the walls.

'The council has fallen,' a voice called back. It sounded young, torn with malice and bloodlust. My heart faltered. 'They were traitors to the people and although they sit in their chambers still, I doubt they'll be leaving them any time soon!'

Coarse laughter followed this. I swallowed nervously. The banners crackled on their spears behind me, snapping in the chill sea breeze.

'What of Astraea?' I said. 'My mother. She was always on your side, the side of the downtrodden, the Failed. If she lives, then I would speak with her.'

'She lives,' the voice called back to my great relief. 'She leads us now, but she will not speak to the likes of you, traitor.'

'This is Neophron, Prince of Athrabis!' Khetera screamed suddenly. 'Scion of King Zothar! You bring insult on the king and will pay with your lives!'

I did not doubt for a moment that Khetera's passion was more for the insult and not for the prince. Nevertheless, I saw the effects his words had; the rebels recoiled from the wall and in the torchlight I could see the dread passing like an illness amongst them. Bravado could only take you so far. All of a sudden, their walls must have seemed very thin indeed.

'What of Dardus?' I called quickly. 'I know he has influence amongst you. Send him out to parley, before injury follows insult. I offer the full protection of our banners. He will come to no harm.'

Khetera turned to me as the rebels spoke in husky whispers to each other.

'You fool!' he whispered. 'You play your cards like a beggar sitting over a meagre hand, when you could brush this scum away and win all at a stroke!'

'Silence,' I told him. 'Just… just wait.'

Khetera drew away in disgust. I watched the guards on the wall, praying for them to make the right decision. Even now, I did not know what I would do if Dardus actually came out to talk. I could plan no more than a moment ahead at a time, but I knew that of all people in Lament, Dardus would be the least open to reason.

A sick hope started to brew in me, the awful lines of a strategy that might just work. I could convince Khetera that Dardus was the real power in Lament, the ringleader behind the rebellion. As foul a deed as it would be, utterly betraying the pretences with which I had called him out, I could cut Dardus down and spare everyone else who lived here. I would be cursed by such an action, I felt, but better to bear the curse so that others might live.

The guards on the wall finished talking. I held my breath. The young voice called out again:

'He will speak.'

A long moment followed, in which I began to fear that Dardus had lost his nerve. Then, after what felt like an age, the gates of Lament slowly opened, and a figure stepped onto the scrubland outside the city. He had a sword at his hip, a canvas sack thrown casually over one shoulder, and he was so stained with blood it was as if he had come fresh from the slaughter. I recognised Dardus at once, but I was shocked at the change that had come over him since we had last met. Then, four years ago, he had been a mocking and sardonic figure, but there was something almost bestial about him now. He cared not for life or death, I saw. Fire and destruction were all he lusted after. I steeled myself to strike, silently asking whatever gods might be listening to spare my soul for this betrayal.

'Lycus,' he crowed. 'In armour resplendent, and with all the might of Athrabis at your back. I imagine you're very confident of yourself, but you're not inside the city yet, are you?'

'If you think this is all the might of Athrabis,' I said, 'then I'm sorry to disabuse you. This is a mere patrol compared to what King Zothar could send against you. I'm here to make sure this goes no further.'

I loosened my sword in my scabbard. Dardus stopped ten feet away, grinning, the lights of the flames flickering in his eyes. His tunic was drenched in blood. His hands were rusty with it. I was about to challenge him when another figure stepped from the gates, the great doors swinging shut behind her.

'Selene,' I whispered, my voice hoarse.

She came with an undimmed countenance, striding confidently to stand by Dardus' side. She wore crimson robes and in her hand she held a golden hammer that was encrusted with blood.

The girl I had spoken to not a day before seemed to have fled. In her place was this severe and unbending young woman. My gaze faltered.

'It will not go any further,' Selene said. 'For it has already gone as far as it must. Lament is free and will not suffer under the heel of Zothar any longer.'

'Blasphemy!' Phaetor cried. I held up my hand to silence him.

'Selene, please – you must see reason. Whatever defences you think you have, Zothar will sweep them aside in an instant. And he will, you know this. He will show no mercy.'

'Then why should we lay down our weapons and expect it in return?' she said. 'Why trade a moment of freedom for a lifetime spent living at the whim of that monster. If we all die fighting for what is just, then we die at Sigmar's command, not Zothar's.'

'Sigmar!' Khetera cried. He gave a choking laugh. 'Now much that was obscure becomes clear to me! Do not think that Sigmar is any less of an empire-builder than King Zothar, or Nagash for that matter. Sigmar would take Lament only as the first step on a conquest of his own, child. He is no just god.'

'Sigmar sees all,' Selene said. She met Khetera's gaze and did not flinch. 'He judges the qualities of the heart, and the courage of his followers. And neither will be found wanting in Lament.'

I felt almost paralysed with dread now. Everything was spiralling out of my control and reason felt like a faint thing to offer to those who were prepared to die. I turned to Dardus.

'There are innocent people in Lament who only want to live in peace,' I said. 'Would you condemn them to death too? It is not too late to turn back. The council can reconvene, the priesthood can mediate between you...'

Khetera, his voice grating like the sand across the desert stones, said, 'You waste your time, boy. You know Zothar's terms – the deaths of these rebels, and every adult in the city to give their left hand to the tithe. Now enforce them or let us tear this city to the ground!'

Dardus laughed. 'Those are the terms you offer? Strange to say, but I don't find them particularly enticing. Here, traitor,' he said. 'This is what we offer in return.'

He tipped out the contents of the sack onto the dirt. Two severed heads rolled in the dust, agonised expressions frozen onto their faces.

'Baeothis, elder of the council,' Dardus said. 'And Thanasis, chief of Zothar's priests.' He gave the heads a desultory kick. 'The council will not reconvene. The priests will not mediate. Your mother is the council now, Lycus. She leads us. Who knows, perhaps after a thousand years, Lament will find itself with a Jackal Queen…?'

Khetera's sword came singing from its scabbard and he struck at Dardus without a word.

My own blade chimed with the blow as I blocked it. I felt the force of it shuddering up my arms. As Khetera backed off I circled around to stand between him and Selene. Dardus had drawn his own sword and it was only the fierce glow in Khetera's eyes that stopped me from turning to see what he was going to do with it. I had no doubt Dardus would have been perfectly happy to plunge it into my back.

'This is the choice you make, mortal?' Khetera whispered. 'Treason, and your father's trust thrown back in his face?'

'No one needs to die here,' I said. 'Lament has kept faith with King Zothar for a thousand years, we can solve this if we only put down our weapons and talk!'

I heard Selene, the flat certainty of her voice. All hope died in me.

'Lament will never go back,' she said. 'Never. It is too late.'

'She has made your decision for you, boy,' Khetera whispered. 'Now, prove yourself a man at last – and fight!'

There was no art to it, no easy deployment of the tactics Khetera had drilled into me over ten years of beatings. There was only desperation and the terror that, if I failed, Selene would be killed on the spot. I swung my blade at the Hekatos, but all I cut was the threads that bound me to Athrabis and King Zothar.

Khetera darted to the side, his sword in perfect guard. The two Mortek soldiers dropped their banners and drew their swords. Phaetor crept back, no weapon in his hands but the magics with which he could unravel bone. I launched myself in towards Khetera while Dardus and Selene faced the others, swinging my blade high and trying to break his guard with the sheer force of the blow. He turned it easily aside, struck me with a backhand across the face and sent me sprawling into the dust.

'I would be lying if I said I hadn't longed for this moment,' he said. 'Alas, that it will not last as long as I hoped.'

So began the most desperate fight I had ever had. I knew full well what Khetera was capable of, and it was all I could do to keep his sword at bay. An arrow came streaking in from off the wall and pierced the skull of one of the Mortek Guard, giving Selene enough time to smash the jaw from its face and bring her hammer crashing down onto its forehead. For my part, I cut and parried, looking for a break in Khetera's defence. There was none.

'You embarrass me, child,' he laughed. 'I thought I had trained you better than this.'

He swung low and I blocked it, sweeping his sword up the length of my blade to open a cut across my jaw. I flinched, fell back, had barely enough time to block the lunge he aimed straight at my heart.

'It will be my pleasure to drag your carcass back to Athrabis and lay it before Zothar's feet.'

I threw myself into a flurry of blows, dread and fury giving me a strength I didn't realise I had, but Khetera turned everything aside. He pivoted as I swung, faded from the length of my lunge, stepped, and parried and counter-attacked, until I had two more cuts on my right arm and my left leg. Blood roared in my ears and fatigue crept into my bones. My sword was heavy in my hand. Khetera himself was undimmed, as if he had done no more than perform a few drills on the parade ground. His mocking laughter rang around that little patch of land before the walls of Lament. I thought of everyone watching me, waiting for me to die. For perhaps the first time I understood the terror of our enemies when they faced the Ossiarch Bonereapers. For how could you kill something that does not live? How even wound something that feels no pain?

'I would ask for your surrender,' Khetera said, 'but I'm afraid I must make an example of you, here before your friends. I have to show them that the defiance of King Zothar is a bill paid in coin they cannot afford.'

He was fast, too quick for me to match. He swung and I tried to block, but to a great clatter of the nadirite blades, my sword went sailing from my grip. I watched it plunge point first into the dirt.

'On your knees, Lycus of Lament,' he hissed. He held the point of his sword under my chin. All it would take was the gentlest pressure to slit my throat and spill my blood into the sand. 'Let your people bear witness to the wages of treason before they experience it themselves.'

The hammer smashed into his shoulder and sent him spinning round, with a spray of shattered bone. Selene stood there above him, bloodied, unbowed, while Dardus held Phaetor at bay. The two Mortek Guard were no more than a pile of severed bones and Zothar's banner had been trampled into the dirt.

I dived for my sword and brought it up in a great, sweeping arc to take Khetera's arm off at the other shoulder. He snarled in rage, scrabbling at me with his remaining hand, his jaw clacking, his burning eyes like shards of fire. Selene smashed down with a second blow, crushing his spine.

'May Zothar… grind your bones… to dust!' he cried.

Slumped in the dirt, he still reached for me with his shattered arm. I held up my sword, thinking of all the years I had spent dreaming of this moment – Khetera at my mercy and the killing blow at hand. Nights I had spent as a child, seething in my chambers, rehearsing the words I would say to him so he would understand the depths of my hatred. But there was no time now for such boyish fancies. War was at hand, and it is a pitiless master.

I swung and cleaved his skull in two.

Phaetor had woven his magics even as we fought, and already the Mortek Guard were slowly knitting back together; bone clinging to bone. Dardus, his face streaked with sweat, held up his blade.

'Stop, Phaetor!' I cried. Something in my voice gave him pause; he crouched there, like an animal at bay, the lights frantic in the eye sockets of his skull, the bone tendrils quivering on the back of his head. 'Go, now – take word back to my father,' I said. 'Tell him what has happened, tell him I…' The words would not come. 'Tell him that I ask for mercy, for Lament. And if he would give me forgiveness, it would be more than I deserve.'

Phaetor slowly nodded and backed away. In moments he was scuttling off towards the ranks of the army, where it stood at attention in the scrubland.

I looked at Zothar's banner, a dusty rag on the ground at my feet. I thought of my father's rage, of the crystal table cut in two. I thought of the Legion of Athrabis marching from the gates of the necropolis. Most of all I thought of Se'bak and my blade cutting through his skull, the way the lights had dimmed in his eyes as he clutched my tunic.

'Lycus,' Selene said. She laid her hand on my shoulder. 'Come, we must get back inside.'

I nodded. I turned from the trampled banner and followed them back into Lament. When the doors swung closed behind us, it sounded like a bell tolling nothing but our doom.

24

When they came to tell him of his son's betrayal, Zothar made no response. He stood by the broken halves of the crystal table in the map room of his palace and dismissed them: Phaetor, the Hekatoi of the regiments he had dispatched to Lament. The Boneshaper had bowed and scraped, with that leering look etched onto his skull. When the doors were closed Zothar had turned to the embossed map that covered the entire wall on the far side of the room.

Zothar's kingdom, he thought. *Held in the name of Nagash, who is All...*

He stood with his hands behind his back, staring up at the map and letting his thoughts flit where they may. He looked at the ridges and hills of the Quietus Reef, where the peoples of that rocky landscape had worshipped an ancient, twisted oak tree, planted there in the Age of Myth by Alarielle herself, so they claimed. Zothar had stormed their forts, burned their villages and put them all to the sword. He had immolated the tree, seen its roots torn up, the ground salted behind him. The Quietus Reef had been silenced, for Nagash.

He looked at the valleys where the Kingdom of the Painted Jewel had once ruled from the mountains far in the east to the first dunes of the desert. In the centre of their greatest city was a shard of brightly coloured crystal, taller than a man, lit with a strange refulgence that flowed between ice-blue and sea-green, from the vibrant red of sunset to the mouldering amethyst of the dusk. They had believed this wondrous jewel was a gift of the heavens, a shard of the worlds beyond the Void, thrown down to bless them with its celestial beauty. Zothar had torn down the ramparts of that city, killed its population and shattered the Painted Jewel into a thousand pieces. Even now those shards lay scattered beneath the tides of the desert sands and the foundations of that city were no more than jumbled rock smothered by the endless wastes of time.

Acharnae was no more. He still sometimes, deep in his memories, heard the screams of its people as they begged for mercy. He gave them none. Proto-civilisations of nomads and wanderers had been chased down and murdered in the dirt by his troops. Villages had been torched, their people flensed so the bones could be used in his armies. Great maritime empires from across the sea launched fleets against him, but when they met the spars of the Obsidian Coast they were overwhelmed and destroyed. For a thousand years Zothar had marched and killed, conquered and administered, extinguishing all life wherever he found it in the service of Nagash.

Even lost Theres…

He remembered staggering from the Underworlds, screaming, fingerbones raised to scour the planes of his skull. Malicious souls had flitted round him, the first necromancers he would use as his Boneshapers and Soulmasons. The laughter of Nagash had echoed cruelly in his mind. Other men perhaps would have been driven mad, but Zothar was not like other men. Even in death, his soul cleaved to its purpose. He would have his son returned to him and if he had to kill everything in Shyish to do it, then that was merely the terms of the agreement. And he was a man of his word.

All else was faded detail to him now. He chose not to dwell on it. Returning to Theres, standing by the tomb of Neophron. Cutting down all who came near him, and the souls of those necromancers taking new form. Bloodshed and violence and each man and woman he killed renewed by the Boneshapers, their souls blended and squeezed back into strange configurations. When enough were dead, the rest bowed to him again – but it was not sufficient. Flesh was too weak for what Nagash had ordered. All must become as he was, so the conquests could continue…

He drew a line now with his finger from the coast to the city by the shore. Lament, where Neophron had died. Once a powerful city-state, a place of great learning and culture, the seat of the Jackal Kings. He had allowed it to live, all these years. He had permitted its continuation, chained to it by Neophron's recurring soul.

When Phaetor had told him what had happened outside its gates, he felt the pain of Neophron's death renewed. He seemed to see again his body falling from the Tower of the Moon at the end of the Contest, on the cusp of victory, his fingers slipping from the stone. That moment, poised, suspended, as if every second was a lifetime. The crowd had held its breath and Neophron had not made a sound. Just the call of a vulture from somewhere over the city, a single bird crying, as if relishing the prospect of the feast.

Sometimes Zothar felt he was trapped in that moment still, waiting for his son to hit the ground. His boy, the child he had raised alone, his life. What was a child to a father but a part of his soul, running free? A shard of what had once made him good. And now it was shattered on the flagstones of Lament. It would always lie broken there. He would never come back.

Was Lycus truly Neophron renewed? Se'bak was still missing and could not tell them. Zothar feared the worst about the Soulmason. Either the boy knew about the true state of his soul, or he did not want to know; either way, he had acted accordingly and now Se'bak could tell them nothing. Then Lycus had fled to Lament, to the lands where he had been born, amongst the people who had first raised him. Khetera had been destroyed, the rebels had seized the city. A priestess had been there, Phaetor had claimed. He had brought back a confused testimony, but the name of Sigmar had been heard on her lips.

How had it all slipped so easily from his control?

Zothar turned from the map and left the room, striding through the palace with no real destination in mind. He felt all Athrabis as a weight pressing on his mind and every moment he tried to tear his thoughts back to the present he seemed to see his son falling backwards from the Tower instead, dropping through the afternoon air, the crowd silent and the vulture crying.

He looked up at the ribbed ceiling, hundreds of feet above him. He saw the dust and sand gathered in drifts at the base of the obsidian pillars. He saw endless corridors and passageways and rooms around him, and when he burst at last from the doors of the palace into the streets of the city, he saw avenues and roads that led nowhere, for no one. All of it sickened him, suddenly. He thought of Neophron's mausoleum in lost Theres, smothered by time and the sands. But that was not his mausoleum, he thought. That was merely a gesture towards it.

He stared at the spires of the city, the necrotic black marble, the twisted bone. Gargoyles sneering from the heights, archways carved to the likeness of skulls, vast boulevards that could hold columns of troops five hundred abreast. The green fume of the spectral light, the mournful breeze twisting through its empty streets – no, he thought, *here* was Neophron's mausoleum.

Athrabis, no more than the centrepiece of a thousand-year wake for a dead boy who would never come back.

Zothar felt as if every ounce of Athrabis had collapsed onto him at once. He screamed, a nightmare shriek that would have curdled the blood of anyone living who could have heard it. If he had had eyes, he would have wept for all he had lost and all he would never regain.

Nagash would never return him. He was a fool to think so. The cruelty of the King of Death knew no bounds.

Better to let him die, he thought. *Better to relinquish his soul, and let it wander where it will. Perhaps that way it will one day find the peace I have been unable to give it.*

He looked to the sky above the city – the gossamer web of dark cloud, the sallow purple light. Shyish was a cold and miserable place. Drear and unforgiving. Bleak, without mercy.

Better that none should live in such a realm.

He returned to the palace, where the Hekatoi awaited him.

Power was exercised through symbols as much as force, he had told Lycus. What he had not said was how easily those symbols could be torn down and cast aside. What seemed as impermeable as steel often proved to have no more depth or strength than a sheet of parchment, effortlessly torn. The symbols only worked as long as everyone agreed that they worked. Once doubt entered the mind, then they must be renewed…

They must be renewed by force.

'Ready my steed,' he said. 'Prepare the troops. *All* the troops. We march for Lament.'

25

A day passed in confusion and dread. The streets bore witness to the fighting after the rebels had seized power, but in truth the bloodshed wasn't as extensive as I'd feared when I stood on the other side of the walls. I saw bodies lying in the gutter as Selene and Dardus led me through the gate. There were scorch marks against the walls of the houses in the lower tier, but all was quickly put right. The rebels had no idea what else to do with the corpses and so had dragged them up to the platforms at the top of the Tower, exposed them there without funeral rites for the vultures to eat. The bodies would feed the sky and the Underworlds would take their souls.

The priesthood had been butchered, many of them knifed to death on Dardus' orders as they slept in their halls. Thanasis had been cornered trying to escape by the western wall. Some supposed he was intending to flee into the desert and seek refuge with the Bonereapers in Athrabis. This bought him little sympathy from his attackers and his death had not been easy. Other priests had made quick and no doubt insincere conversions to

Selene's faith and this had spared their lives. 'Hammer and throne!' they cried. 'Sigmar sees all!' Of the common citizens, most hid in their homes and waited for the storm to pass; there were few who would fight zealously on one side or the other. Like most people, they desired only peace. I was sorry that peace was the one thing I could not give them.

Selene took me to my mother's house, where she dressed my wounds. Dardus rallied his Failed to man the walls, to keep a keen eye on the Bonereapers as they withdrew across the scrubland.

'They'll be back,' I told Selene, as I sat on the couch in my mother's parlour. My eye strayed to the child who sat at her feet, playing clumsily with his wooden blocks, his set of coloured knucklebones. Her son, the boy she had had with Dardus.

He had blue eyes, I saw, as bright as his father's. Selene had said nothing about the boy to me when she appeared in my rooms in Athrabis. It was the sight of her son more than anything that made all my hope fade away. Selene was promised to another. If she knew of my love for her, she did not return it as I had thought.

My mother appeared in the doorway with a cup of water. I could not meet her eye, but I took the water and drank it down. Beside her was a squat, soft-faced man I vaguely recognised, guzzling eagerly at a cup of wine.

'If they return,' Selene said, wrapping the bandages, 'we will be ready for them.'

'It's not a question of if,' I protested. I turned to my mother. 'It's when, because they *will* return. Zothar will empty Athrabis to avenge this slight. None of you stand a chance.'

'And you didn't convince him to stay his hand?' my mother said. 'Did you even try?'

'Of course I tried! I'd have had better luck changing the direction of the wind by reasoning with it! Zothar believes I am the true Neophron, the final incarnation of his son. He has no more need of this city and would destroy it either way. I don't know what else I could do.'

My mother sat carefully on the edge of the couch by my side. Tentatively she reached out and smoothed back my hair.

'You did all you could, I'm sure,' she said quietly. Her voice sounded as if it came from far away. 'This is the month of the Games, did you know that? If everything progressed the way it had done for a thousand years, then in two weeks the Contest would have been run and I would have had to stand there in the agora and watch Zothar cut off your head. I would have had to pretend that this was all right and proper and according to our customs. I would have had to watch as another young boy or girl was snatched from their parents and taken into the desert by that thing, to face who knows what misery and torture.'

'Astraea...' said the soft-faced man.

'No, Haephastin,' she said, as she drew her hand away. 'If it has come to this and we are all going to die defending our homes from Zothar's army, then surely that is better than what came before? Better this blasphemy is scrubbed from the face of the realm than we collude in it any longer.'

'Praise Sigmar,' Selene said quietly.

'Praise Sigmar,' my mother said.

'And hail the Jackal Queen,' Haephastin said, with what I thought was a touch of irony. He raised his glass, but my mother flinched at his words.

'I am no queen,' she said. 'The Jackals of Lament and the vultures of Athrabis have brought nothing but misery to this city. Let them all die with it too.'

I heard the front door opening. Selene looked up as Dardus appeared in the parlour. He gave me a sour look as he saw me sitting there beside her, but his mood improved when he saw his son. The boy scurried over to him and Dardus lifted him up to kiss his forehead.

'Arius, my boy!' he cried. 'You'll be a brave soldier one day, won't you?' He looked at me. 'Like your uncle Lycus here… He's a brave soldier, did you know? He fights with the bone-men, he's seen many a battle in his time, I'm sure…'

Selene finished with my bandages, and I got to my feet.

'If you are set on fighting,' I said, 'then let me fight with you. Let me lead your troops, such as you have. We cannot hope to stop the Bonereapers.' I nodded at Arius in Dardus' arms. 'But we can perhaps delay them long enough for some of us to escape into the hills, or along the coast. The people of Lament could find new refuge, far from here.'

'You seemed to come off the worst in your duel by the gates,' Dardus laughed. He put the boy down and sent him off to his room. 'What makes you think you're the man to lead us? You're no son of Lament, you've made that quite clear already.'

'I know their tactics,' I said, 'their dispositions. I've fought alongside them for ten years. We can use the streets to our advantage, the gates that separate each tier. Make them fight their way up tier by tier, reinforce the Regent's Palace at the very top. If we can concentrate the Bonereapers there, then perhaps others could slip away over the southern walls and head into the hills while we delay them.'

'To be eaten by bone-gryphs?' Dardus scorned. 'To die of thirst and hunger and be picked off by Zothar's patrols?'

'The choice would be theirs,' I said. 'It's either that or die in their houses, for Zothar will not leave one stone on top of another when he takes this city. That I promise you.'

I tried not to think of my father then, the moments we had spent in the ruins of old Theres, when he had revealed to me what remained to him of his soul. I felt an ache inside me, a hollowness at my betrayal. Even then, as we waited for the avalanche to smother us, I couldn't bear the guilt of what I had done.

Dardus thought on this, his jaw tight. Haephastin, the former elder from the council, drained his glass and sat back heavily on the couch.

'Melissta is dead,' he said. 'Baeothis is dead, Kaitellin has returned to his home and a glass of hemlock... I'm not sure what is left for me, but neither death at the hands of the Bonereapers or death in the hills sounds appealing, I have to confess.' He sighed. 'Really, it's all too much.'

He sat there in silent dejection, Astraea's hand on his shoulder.

'For my mind,' she said, 'I think we should fight. Let everyone square the decision with their own conscience, but if you can help us last as long as we can, Lycus, then please do.'

'Agreed,' Selene said.

'Your son, your boy...'

Selene looked at me with such steely determination that I almost feared her.

'I will see that he is safe. When the storm passes over us, he shall be sheltered from it. I swear it.'

Dardus shook his head and gave a bitter laugh.

'Very well, I see I am outvoted.' He gave a derisive bow. 'Lycus – or is it Lord Neophron? Either way, your military assistance will be much appreciated, I'm sure.'

I picked up my helmet from the floor. My armour felt as if it were twice my weight.

'I will do what I can,' I said. 'Reinforce the gates. Place barricades on every avenue leading from tier to tier. Form your fighters into small, mobile bands, and do not let them get bogged down in combat. Keep torches to hand – fire may slow the Bonereapers down.'

'Fine tactics, I have no doubt, general, but I have plans of my own,' Dardus said. He stabbed a finger at me. 'Don't think I'll jump to your tune just because you're wearing that ornate armour and you have a decent sword on your hip.'

'Then let me hear them,' I said. I refused to be drawn. Even now, on the very edge of destruction, Dardus had not forgiven me. What I wouldn't give, I wanted to say, for him to be standing where I was now.

'I'll take a small force up the coast,' he said. He spoke confidently. 'We have skiffs and fishing boats hidden near the bluffs, I can take them around and harry the Bonereapers from the rear. I have no expectations of a mighty victory,' he grinned, 'but it may be enough to draw some of them aside. Depending on how it works, we can retreat and disperse and try to get back into the city by the southern wall.'

'Then all speed to you, and to your fighters,' I said. I placed the helmet on my head. 'And let us hope King Zothar still knows the meaning of mercy.'

26

Ten centuries. Decade after decade, year after year.

Neophron... each Games I see you anew. The old, accustomed face falls away and is replaced, again and again and again. Yet now, you will forever be Lycus, the boy from Lament. At the end of it all, you will be the last Neophron to die...

'Nagash,' Zothar muttered. 'Lord of Souls, hear me now. Our bargain is finally complete. When Lament falls, the Obsidian Coast is yours and I will have cast down every civilisation that stood against you. But my son will fade now and wander on the cold breeze of Shyish, ever seeking new harbour and none there to provide it. Such is the fate I have chosen...'

He raised his hand from the reins of his warhorse and drew his skeletal fingers across his skull. The ridge of his cheekbone, the cavity of his eye socket, the hinge of his jaw. A hundred times he had taken Neophron's head, staring into his son's eyes as he swung the blade. There was not a single part of him that hadn't been repaired with the bones of his son's corpse over the last thousand years. In many ways, he was closer to Neophron now than he ever had been in life.

He remembered the moment he had taken his son's body from Lament, after he had fallen. Neophron had been wrapped in grave shrouds and laid on an ornate bier, accompanied by his personal bodyguard of troops. Zothar had ridden beside the procession as they left the city, his head held up proudly for the honour of his name. He had not wept that day. The Jackal Kings had paid him insult, though, by not attending as he took his dead son from their Contest. Sated and fat in their palace above the city, the twin monarchs had been indifferent to Zothar's loss.

Such are the Games, they would have said. *It has ever been thus.*

And they would have laughed and returned to their feasting, for how many other people had lost sons and daughters to the rigours of the Contest that day?

Yet he was a prince of Theres, Zothar thought, *and due the respect of his station. And the Jackal Kings did not sit sated and fat in their palace for very much longer.*

He looked back at the line of the army as it followed him from Athrabis: the columns of troops so long he could not see the end of them, the Deathriders fanned out in an immense screen on either side, the Mortek Crawlers lumbering through the dust the rest of the army kicked up in its wake. Athrabis had been emptied. The entirety of the legion marched to war.

Ahead and to the east, the amethyst skies began to burn with light. Dawn was near.

Aye, Zothar thought. *Lament was arrogant in those days. Little did it realise that the days of its power were nearly at an end…*

I watched from the balustrade atop the gate to the second tier. I could see beyond the walls of Lament to the desert and the scrubland in the north. I saw King Zothar's army approach; it was as if the horizon itself, a blur of dust and sand, was rolling towards us.

I had seen that army invest the lines of barbarian tribes and orruk warbands alike. I had ridden in the vanguard as it smashed aside some of the hardiest and most brutal killers in Shyish, men and orruks and duardin who gave no quarter, nor asked any in return. I had fought in line and column and at the side of the king, in battles so violent and merciless that they would have turned the hair white of any bold rebel who stood on the walls and watched them now. I saw King Zothar come on towards Lament and I knew that we could only stand a moment against him.

My mother was standing on the street beneath me, her arms folded. She wore her diadem, the wreath of an elder on feast days and festivals. She wore the black mourning robes I imagined she had last worn when my father – Cleon, my true father – had died.

'You do not wear the mourning mask, Mother?' I said to her. 'Surely there is no better time than now. In a few hours, if we can, we will be mourning the death of a city.'

'I would not wear that now, even if I was mourning your loss, my son,' she said. 'For too long we've hidden our grief behind the face of our enemy.'

'You should take comfort in the thought that we'll soon be able to wear our grief openly,' I said, as I clambered down. 'Before the day is out, I shouldn't wonder.'

'I fear it will be the last luxury open to us,' she said. 'We snatched freedom for a moment, and it was only long enough to compose ourselves for death.'

I couldn't answer her. *What did you expect?* I wanted to say, but there would be no profit in it now.

'Fight well,' she said. She reached up to touch my face, leaned up to kiss my cheek. 'Be brave, and be safe. And if this is the end of everything, then know that I have always been proud of you,

Lycus. You have done what no one else has done, for a thousand years.'

I couldn't speak. All I could do was nod and mask my sorrow in action.

I drew my sword while she took herself towards the Regent's Palace, a hand-picked bodyguard with her. I looked to the band I had gathered, twenty fighters taken from amongst the Failed. They stood there lining the Keening Way, standing in the shade of the trees. I didn't even know their names. They were young men and women, bitter and full of rage, and they bore their scavenged weapons as if trained to it. They had been waiting for this moment for years, since they had first watched me being led away by King Zothar from the city gates. Ahead of them had only been their own miserable fates as those who had risked all in the Contest and lost.

I was sure I recognised some of them from those dreadful minutes when we had waited in the Tower of the Moon for the race to begin. Ten years had passed since then. It may as well have been a hundred for all the difference I saw between us. I had been raised in the palace of our conquerors, while they had scrabbled in the dirt of Lament, toting water buckets, cleaning drains, despised by those who had never had the courage to do what they had done.

What strange fate it was, I thought, to have brought us together like this.

I could hear the rumble of Zothar's army as it met the walls, the crash of marching feet and readied weapons. A cry went up from our ragged defenders and already I could hear the clash of blades. It felt like a stormfront had enveloped the city.

'They're here,' I said. 'The walls won't hold them and in moments they'll be into the streets. Remember what I told you – move fast, strike hard, and withdraw. Do not let yourself be drawn into a prolonged combat, for it will be the death of you.'

There was a screeching wail high above us. I glanced to the fading amethyst skies and saw a trail of spectral light streak across the city. Necrotic skulls fired by the Mortek Crawlers, I knew, the catapults of Zothar's war machines. Gnawing and biting, these dread skulls would not just shatter flesh and bone, their fell magics would drive people insane with terror as well. Soon, cursed stele would fall amongst the streets too, smashing stone and marble, unleashing their lethal hexes, and spreading dark flames wherever they landed.

What chance did we have against such horrors? Zothar could have held his army back and reduced us with this ammunition alone. He sent his troops in only to make an example of us.

Two of my warband collapsed to the ground as the skulls passed overhead, drained by fear. I did not admonish them, for the fighting would find them sooner or later as it was.

I rallied the rest of them, and we ran down the Keening Way towards the agora, sandals and bare feet slapping against the flagstones. There were ten other bands like this, spread out across the radial streets that led down to the third tier. Each had been given the same instructions – when the Bonereapers advanced into the marketplace, strike like arrows into their flanks. Slow them down, distract them, withdraw. And then do it all over again.

I had stacked a short barricade of broken wood, barrels, and bales of straw at the end of the Keening Way. We leapt over it and took cover against the walls on either side as the street opened up into the agora, hiding in doorways and crouching in the shadows. I could see the city walls ahead, on the other side of the marketplace, about two hundred yards away. Already the Bonereapers had set their scaling ladders to the stone and Mortek Guard were vaulting the balustrades. Dardus' fighters put up a brave defence, but there were no more than a hundred of them on the northern section. Zothar could afford to expend ten times that number as a mere distraction while he sent his main force to breach the gates. The Mortek Guard on the walls were relentless, stabbing in with their spears over the rims of their shields. I saw men and women cut down, the spray of blood, bodies falling from the wall into the streets below. Screams, people begging for mercy, although they received none. The city gates, at the far end of the Grand Avenue, began to shudder.

'This is it,' I said. I gripped my sword. I felt that liquid, hollow feeling in the pit of my stomach that always comes before combat. Who knew how my comrades felt, untrained as they were in the arts of war? 'Good luck. And do not falter.'

The gates burst asunder in a great rending crash. A flood of Mortek Guard poured into the Grand Avenue and began to cross the agora, hacking down all who stood against them. The defence on the walls had been swept away and more troops came scaling the ladders and dropping into the streets below. In moments, the defenders of Lament were outnumbered a hundred to one.

Tendrils of smoke drifted through the streets. The air was thick with dust and the stench of blood. I watched the Bonereapers charging across the mouth of the road ahead of us, while we cringed back into the shadows on either side, out of sight. When I judged that the flood had slowed, I held up my sword and screamed: 'Now!'

I ran, not even pausing to see if I was followed. Four quick steps from the mouth of the Keening Way to the agora and then I was swinging my sword in a great, cleaving arc to take the head from a Hekatos as he croaked orders to his regiment. His skull went sailing into the ranks of the troops behind him and before his bones had even fallen to the ground I was hacking in again. The edge of my sword sang as it met nadirite and bone, crushing ribcages, severing arms and smashing soul gems. I hacked the jaw from one Bonereaper even as he lunged in to fight back.

The others were with me, screaming their war cries. There was no art or finesse to their attack, but the sheer momentum of our charge caught the flank of the Bonereaper regiment off-guard. We punched into them like a spearhead, cutting left and right, giving them no quarter and no space to bring their spears to bear. The agora stretched away from us, packed with enemy troops. The Tower of the Moon loomed above everything like a sword-hilt plunged into the meat of the city.

I saw one of my band fall, a sword plunged into his throat and clean out the other side. Two more were surrounded and pierced in a dozen places, their hands slippery with blood as they tried to grab the shafts of the Bonereaper spears that pinned them, their faces wrought with agony.

'Fall back!' I cried. 'To the Keening Way!'

I parried a blow, sent my sword edge high and fast into a grim, skeletal face, slicing the cranium in two. I took a cut across the neck from a spear blade that passed over the curve of my pauldron, felt the blood drip down inside my armour. Slowly we managed to disengage, skipping back and sprinting for the barricade we had placed across the street behind us. Two more of my warband fell: a young woman whose name I had already forgotten, a spear thrust through her spine, and an older man, his beard frosted with bone dust, his berserker rage planting him immovably on the flagstones while he shattered his blade on the Bonereaper shields. Eventually he was brought down with a sword pushed up through his guts, another cutting down into the flesh of his shoulder.

Had we done enough? I had the sense of the Bonereaper regiment faltering, like a wave easing as it met the shore, unsure whether to press on across the agora or turn and meet this new and unexpected threat. As we ran back up the Keening Way, I wondered how the other bands were managing, whether any of them were left alive. The plan was to regroup up at the gates of the second tier, but I feared it would be a meagre force that was able to muster after these dreadful assaults.

We reached the barricade, the Bonereapers marching up the Keening Way to overwhelm us. I knocked a torch to the stacked wood and the quick flames smothered it, masking our withdrawal as we ran on deeper into the streets of the burning city.

The light banked wildly in the east, bleeding out into the dawn, tendrils of red and gold creeping into the amethyst skies. Such dawns were rare in Shyish; Dardus had known only a few in all his years. An omen, he hoped. The light of better things to come.

Twenty boats planed smoothly over the still waters, masked by a veil of morning mist. Skiffs, fishing vessels, their sails stowed. Oars dipped and pulled, the boats so near to shore they scuffed against the shale beneath them. Ten men and women in each skiff, two hundred in total. They clutched the hilts of their swords, the leather-wound bellies of their bows, wiped sweat from their faces though the morning was cool.

Docia sat beside Dardus, drawing her hand down the line of her jaw while she scanned the shore to their left. The curve of the beach, the rough spread of pebbles, the vacant land beyond it. She had crawled back to Lament a day after their skirmish with Zothar and Lycus in the desert, having run across the dead lands through the night until she made the safety of the city walls. Dardus had been impressed. He doubted he could have done the same. The empty lands of Shyish were no place to be after dark.

He remembered Markus hacking his horse forward, the sword that Lycus thrust through his jaw. He saw Zothar again, cutting through the others as easily as if they'd been unarmed. That had been a terrible thing. Lycus would pay for that, one way or another. He thought of him back in the city, watching over Selene and Arius. The thought was poison to him.

Let him fall, he thought. *Please, if nothing else, let that traitor fall before the end.*

He didn't pray. Praying was Selene's concern, not his. There were no gods. None worth worshipping, anyway.

Selene…

He closed his eyes and passed his hand over his face. Dardus doubted that he would ever see her again. Even now, he didn't know what their relationship really was. If he was capable of it, then he supposed that what he felt for her was a kind of love. He loved his son, he was certain of that, but with Selene it was different. They had been two lost people, damaged by the city they lived in, who had clung on to each other out of desperation as much as anything else. He was no fool – he knew perfectly well what Selene felt for Lycus. Perhaps if he had won the Contest and Lycus had become one of the Failed they could have found some way of making it work between them? Astraea could have intervened; the council could have been swayed to improve their conditions. They could have been happy.

But no, it was all no more than idle speculation, utterly pointless. The world was as it was. The die had been cast and there was no going back. Perhaps it was just something else to blame Lycus for. The way that he had snatched victory from Dardus' hands had cursed them all.

On his other side, Hesper fingered the edge of his sword. His rat-eyes quivered and there was a twitch in his jaw. Dardus didn't know how he had made it this far, but here he was all the same. Born survivor, he supposed. Lament could be razed to the ground and Hesper would go scuttling from the ruins with that same expression on his face.

'No sign of them,' Hesper whined now, peering at the coastline. He looked back at the other boats, strung out on the waters behind them. 'Think this is going to be enough?'

'We're not fighting a pitched battle,' Dardus said. 'We just have to draw enough of them away from the city to make a difference. Hit and run, like the great Lord Neophron said… And keep your damned voice down – even skulls can hear.'

Hit and run…

He had no illusions. The Bonereapers would do the hitting and they would do the running. But he couldn't stand the idea of sitting at Lycus' command back in the city, cowering behind the walls while they waited for the dead to overwhelm them. His whole life had been lived with a leash around his neck. He had chafed at it since he was a child, since Lycus had thrown him from the Tower. He might be running to his death, but at least they would take some of the bastards with them.

And if all goes well, and we actually make it back to the city…

He felt for the knife in his belt. One way or the other, he would see it in Lycus' throat before the day was done, he promised.

She rose from prayer, the light of Sigmar in her eyes. She closed the book, kissed the embossed seal on the cover – the Twin-Tailed Comet, Sigmar's sign. She looked from the window to see if its trail was even now painted across those dim, drear skies, but they were empty.

No matter, she thought. Sigmar sees all.

The pendant was heavy around her neck – but then she reached for it and remembered that it was no longer there. She smiled and thought of her grandfather. He had worn it every day of his life, since first it was given to him. She thought of his old bones under the floorboards of their home, the years he had spent there in peace and silence.

'Sigmar bless you, Grandfather,' she whispered. 'And bless Lycus and my son. And Sigmar bless Dardus too, and Astraea, and everyone who stands now on the edge of the chasm, with only your name to comfort them. Lend your strength to their arms, and your courage to their hearts, my lord.'

She left the book on the table in the little annexe room off the main hall of the Regent's Palace. When this day was done, there would be no one left to read it. She picked up her hammer and strode across the green-flecked marble flooring, the faded frescoes looking to her like tattered things not worthy of preservation. She remembered arguing with Lycus here, four years ago, as she had tried to convince him to murder King Zothar. The desperate midnight ride to Athrabis, the terror of her journey through the streets to Lycus' chambers. All these things she had done in her short time and now that time was coming to an end.

So be it. We are not given the means to understand our own place in creation and must trust in our gods to guide us. All we can do is what we deem to be right.

Her heart felt hot and swollen in her chest. There was something boundless in her, unquenchable. She felt the strength of her soul and knew it could level mountains.

Selene smiled as she left the palace and saw Astraea hurrying up towards the gates. Framing her, a backdrop to this last tragedy, was the ruin of Lament. Columns of smoke rose from the lower city, screams cut across the air, and from far across the streets came the endless rolling crash of steel and marching armies. Specks of black light came sailing in from the scrubland beyond the walls, the screaming skulls of Zothar's war machines. Selene felt no fear now. What was death in the end, but the reward for hard and loyal service in the name of one so much greater than you?

'They're at the gates to the first tier!' Astraea cried. Her face was streaked with tears, her black, lacquered hair in disarray. 'Sigmar save us now!'

'He already has,' Selene said. She lifted her hammer. 'Our souls are our own, free of any stain. All our bodies can do now, for a little while longer at least, is defy those who would harm us.'

She took a short sword from the scabbard at her hip and passed it to Astraea.

'Fight, until all your strength is gone. Fight, as long as you can. That is Sigmar's only commandment,' she said. 'If you follow it, you will die a pilgrim of the Comet and the Hammer, and your name will be blessed.'

Astraea nodded and took the sword, her face a mask of dread and confusion. She looked as if her mind was wandering through more peaceful times and each glimpse of the horrors before it made it recoil.

'Where is Arius?' she said at last. 'My grandson…' She looked to the palace, but Selene shook her head.

'He is safe,' she said. 'Trust me in this. When all is done, and Lament is but a memory, he will live still.'

She strode away, walking purposefully down the incline towards the palace gates. The sound of combat was loud and discordant beyond them, and she smiled to meet it.

'Where are you going?' Astraea called. 'For Sigmar's sake, Selene!'

'I am going to do his work,' she said. 'And I am going to save the man I love.'

The skiffs beached with a crunch of sand, the oars snapping with a clatter to the gunwales. Dardus was first out, bare feet into the slush of pebbles, sword drawn. He hiked fast, knees up, climbing the soft incline to the spread of rocks on the southern side. The water behind him lapped and gurgled, oily and dark, a horrible chuckling sound to it.

He heard the others clamber free, fanning left and right, breasting the rise and taking cover amongst the rocks. Whispers, a quiet groan as someone tripped and turned an ankle. A backwash of water feathered over the pebbles and withdrew with a hiss. He laid the flat of his blade against his bare arm, flinching at the kiss of cold steel.

The mist peeled away as the light strengthened. Day was on them now. Ahead, as the ground levelled out, there was a slight depression covered on both sides by the flanks of the rocks. A rise of dunes tailed away towards the south and masked them from the sight of the city, about two miles away. He could hear a faint percussion in the air, like a storm racketing in the far distance. The ground beneath him trembled slightly, a pulse, like a heartbeat. He looked to Docia, who looked back with her face drawn, her dark skin grey in the half-light. He nodded, lifted his sword horizontally above his head and ran up at a crouch into the depression. The others followed, two columns, one on either side, about twenty yards between them.

He crept through the dunes, the grey sand coarse under knees and elbows, hidden by the spiked tufts of saltgrass. The scrubland plains before the walls of Lament were strung out before them. He heard Hesper suck in a breath, choking as he tried to breathe it out.

Dardus took in the sight of Zothar's army. There were blocks of troops marching inexorably towards the city, each block at least a thousand strong. There were war machines strung out in line upon line at the rear of the Bonereaper force, their great catapults swinging and relinquishing their loads, again and again. A haze of dust rose up as the army marched forwards, as the cavalry wheeled around the flanks and waited for their turn to move through the splintered gates.

Smoke rose from the walls, oily and black. Flames licked and shivered. He could hear the cries from here, the jumbled cacophony of fighting. There was the best part of half a mile of open ground between the coastline and the edge of the Bonereaper force.

'We need to get back to the city,' Docia hissed at his side. She took his arm, but Dardus shook it off. 'Did you hear me? We can't do a thing here. We'll be cut to ribbons before we've gone more than a few yards across the scrub!'

'She's right,' Hesper whined. 'Two hundred of us against *that*? We don't stand a chance!'

Dardus turned on them. He jabbed the point of his sword towards the burning walls.

'And what do you think we could do in the city? Do you think they've got it any better than we do? Looks like we picked the safer spot out here if you ask me. We just need to draw them off, just a few of them…'

Docia's fingers dug into the meat of his arm. Fear wrenched her face into something wild.

'It's over, Dardus! Lament is done, there's nothing we can do for it now.'

She glanced back towards the skiffs on the beach and bit at her dry lips.

'We can still get away,' she said carefully. 'Take the boats, follow the coastline. Find somewhere away from Zothar's control.'

Dardus laughed, a grim sound on that dead coast.

'Run where? Zothar controls the Obsidian Coast as far as you could sail in a week. No,' he said. 'I would know if my wife and my son were dead, at the very least, and I would die with them if I could.' He pictured Lycus and his fingers strayed to his knife. 'And I would have my last chance at revenge…' he muttered.

The air quickened suddenly. The pulse in the earth began to run faster and faster and the tremble moved up Dardus' arm. He looked south, where the dunes sloped and tumbled into the scrub, where the walls of Lament in the distance poured with smoke and flame. He looked north – and then the Deathriders were on them.

They came down like a spear point, a wedge of horse hacking

into the depression. Three abreast at the tip, four more behind them, five behind that. The ground shuddered and the skulls of the riders were fixed in a pitiless leer. Nadirite swords flashed, armour glinted.

Someone screamed. A few of the rebels tried to run, breaking from the column and sprinting back for the boats, but the Deathriders pummelled them into the sand. The hooves of the warhorses clattered over them and in their wake was left nothing but bloody sand and tangled meat.

The riders wheeled as they met the shore. As they hammered back up the depression, they flicked their blades out and cut the rebel fighters down as they tried to parry. Then, reaching the cusp of the defile, the first wave passed over and split into two columns as the second wave came in down the centre, spears and lances spitting men and women to the sand.

The rebels broke. Some, baying with fear, fled into the plains and were hunted down with sword edge and spear point. Others scrambled into the rocks on either side of the depression, picked off as the Deathriders threw their short spears into them. Still others made a dash for the boats and were cut down in the surf. In moments, the white foam of the tide frothed red.

Some fought. They stood their ground, swords raised, swinging out as the riders hacked past them. Dardus saw heads tumble to the ground, severed arms. He saw Hesper hit by an underhand blow so powerful that it nearly split the little man in half, head to sternum. A sheet of blood flashed out onto the sand.

'Not a survivor after all then…' he murmured.

He threw himself to the ground as a sword whistled over his head, rolled out of the way of another rider, raised his blade, and felt it smashed from his hand. He scrambled up towards the dunes, flinched as a spear came slamming into the earth beside his head. He ran on, tripped, and fell badly onto his knee, howling with the pain. Kicking back, rolling down the other side of the dunes, Dardus looked to the line of the sea as it slopped against the beach.

The skiffs were scattered, but he could see one of them drifting away towards the south, bucking up against the shoreline as the hull caught against a spar of sand. As he clambered down the slope, he saw something moving in the water, a few yards from the shore. It was Docia, he realised. The back of her head was slick with blood, and she was swimming out towards the open sea. Arm over arm, legs kicking out behind her – and then she looked back towards the shore, her face blank and withdrawn. It was like she was lost in some dream and everything she looked on now had no more substance than a memory. She raised her hand and turned to swim on.

Dardus fell the last few feet down the slope and slammed onto the rocks, breath knocked from him. His legs were shaking as he waded out into the water, reaching for the skiff before the tide could pluck it away. There were still two oars tacked to the gunwales, he saw. The sail was still furled at the stern. He kicked the boat away and fell into it, face down, breath churning in his ears.

The sound of fighting on the beach seemed very far away all of a sudden. Slowly, his arms trembling, he raised himself up and looked towards the open water, but he couldn't see any sign of Docia. The waves had taken her, as they took the weight of the skiff and drew it slowly back towards Lament.

27

So unfolded the rest of that desperate morning. We fought and we struggled, and we died – and the Bonereapers did not stop.

Even for one who knew the army well, I was shocked at the scale of the forces Zothar had thrown against us. There was an immeasurable number of troops at his disposal. Each sally we made against them, no matter how many we managed to cut down or incapacitate, was like throwing stones into the sea. At the gates of the second tier, we managed to hold them for a bare half hour, fracturing skulls and crushing shields with blocks of marble that we prised from the walls of houses already streaked with flame and smoke, flinging them down from the balustrade. The Mortek Crawlers continued to send their dread ammunition sailing high across the roofs, smashing buildings to pieces, unleashing howling, spectral winds that tore down the streets and drove people mad with terror. I saw ordinary citizens throw themselves onto the Bonereaper spears, so deranged had they become with fear.

My own little warband dwindled as the day went on. Some of my fighters tripped and fell as we tried to retreat, speared mercilessly as they lay sprawled on the paving stones. Others lost themselves in battle-madness, charging the Bonereaper lines with inarticulate screams until they were hacked to pieces. Sprinting through one of the ornamental gardens against the walls of the second tier, we were almost caught up in a cavalry charge, the great barded warhorses of the Deathriders thundering across the cultivated lawns and flowerbeds. I made it to the gates of the first tier with only three of my original band remaining.

The other warbands had fared equally badly. Although our hit-and-run tactics had taken a toll of the Bonereapers as they moved up through the streets and tiers of the city, it was nowhere near enough to give them significant pause. Every soldier we cut down was taken by the Boneshapers and moulded to new purpose, set again to pick up its spear and shield and advance.

At the scorched gates of the first tier, I looked around at what little forces remained to me; no more than two dozen desperate fighters, Failed and citizen alike, their faces bloodied, smeared with dirt and soot, their swords still held in trembling hands. I saw in their faces a mix of emotions, from fear to defiance, to a cynical refusal to meet their deaths with anything other than disdain.

'This is the last defence,' I said, pointing with my sword at the gate. 'We have drawn their gaze ever upwards through the city, until they press us finally here. After this gate, there is only the Regent's Palace to hold them. We must hope as many of our people managed to escape by the southern walls as possible.'

In truth, I had no idea if anyone had managed to escape, but I held to the hope all the same. I pictured desperate families scrabbling over the walls or slinking through hidden breaches from cellars and tunnels beneath them, their scant possessions wrapped in cloths, their children borne on their backs as they scuttled off into the half-moon of hills that flanked the rear of the city. I remembered running through those hills during the Contest and I prayed that they would be safe from the bone-gryphs that haunted them. Perhaps one or two families would survive that awful journey, there to carry through all the ages that followed the tale of Lament and its people. How they defied a god and how they were punished for their hubris.

I could hear pockets of fighting elsewhere in the city, groups of rebels caught down in the second and third tier still, selling their lives as dearly as they could. I looked from this elevated perspective down into all the tiers of the city spread out below me. I could see the Bonereapers choking the streets as they marched towards us.

The serene marble walls of Lament were stained with battle. Here and there I could see companies of enemy troops methodically razing buildings to the ground, passing from doorway to doorway with lit torches. Down in the agora, the Tower of the Moon itself was aflame, like a candle guttering in the pale afternoon air. I saw the vultures riding the thermals high above it. I wondered if they were angry at the destruction of their home, or if all the death below them was recompense enough. They would feast well tonight. When every other living thing had been expunged, they would have their pick of the leavings.

I looked for my father, King Zothar mounted on his steed, but I couldn't see him anywhere. There was no need for him to lead from the front here, no need to be the rock around which his army swirled. This was no great battle for him to win; rather, it was a distasteful task, the sooner accomplished the better. He did not deign us with his presence, even as he crushed us under his heel.

We had barricaded the gate as best we could, dragging chairs and tables from the mansions that surrounded us, cutting down the woe trees that shaded the pathways and piling them up in front of it. Behind the gate I set a line of fighters across the width of the road, armed with scavenged spears and shields, a reserve line behind them with swords at the ready. Our right flank was anchored on a slope of broken ground, a decorative patch of rock garden that tumbled down towards the lower road that ran along the span of the first-tier walls. There were fine houses on the other side of this road, suitable for the wealthier residents of the city, but with their blackened empty windows they seemed to gaze up at us now like a line of beggars. Inwardly I gave a bitter laugh at the terms I was using. 'Fighters', 'flank', 'reserve'... These were military terms. No matter how brave they might have been, the troops I led were not soldiers.

'Will that hold them?' one of my comrades asked. A woman, one eye fused shut with a livid scar, her hair scorched on one side. She grimaced at me, gave her sword an experimental swing. 'To my remaining eye, it doesn't look like it'll be good for more than five minutes. And that's if we're lucky.'

'What's your name?' I asked. 'I would know it if we're going to fight together, here at the end.'

'Zylina,' she said. She gave me a sardonic smile. 'No need for introduction, Lord Neophron, I already know your name.'

'Lord Neophron...' I said. 'I have had that name for ten years now, and I don't think I've ever really understood what it means to him who gave it to me.'

'King Zothar?' Zylina said. 'What do you think it means to him?'

'Life,' I said. 'Purpose. And I have taken that away from him.'

'Well,' she said, drawing up her sword. 'It looks like he's here to take it back.'

I looked to where she pointed. Custom more than force kept the Failed from the different tiers of the city and these ironoak doors into the first tier were hardly substantial barriers. They were no more than ten feet high, with an arch of marbled stone passing above them, and were not built to withstand serious assault. Even as I watched, the gates began to shake against their hinges and the wrought-iron bar that passed across them began to bend and shiver. Scaling ladders appeared on either side of the archway. Our barricade seemed a feeble thing then, and as the gates crashed aside the piled wood fell too. I saw snarling skeletal faces press themselves to the gap, spears thrust through to try and lever it still wider.

Zylina stiffened beside me, her teeth bared, her sword up. I pulled her back to the second line of defence and called to those in front.

'Level spears! Meet the charge! Every second you win now is another second of life for your families!'

The gates broke; the barricade fell. The dead poured through.

The hammer felt as if it weighed nothing in her hand. Her robes felt like adamantine around her, like polished armour wrought in the greatest forges of the realm. The sounds of battle were sweet music playing in a shady bower and every step she took quickened her heart with joy.

She thought of her son, safe now, and gave thanks to Sigmar. All her life, it felt, had been leading to this moment. She had been given a great gift and she was thankful for it.

She pushed open the gates from the palace gardens into the wide and airy streets of the first tier. She began to run, pacing down the short marble pathway onto the avenue that ringed the frontage of the palace grounds, following it as it curved around to her left and passed through a grove of ornamental trees. Here the road widened and dropped in a gentle incline towards the gate, the grand mansions of the city's wealthier residents lining it on either side, each manse with an apron of courtyard before it, decorated with statuary and sunken gardens. Here was where the cares of the city were left behind and here was where the vanguard of Zothar's army had penetrated at last. There would be no peace for the citizens of Lament any more. Their last refuge was about to fall. The banners of King Zothar would fly from the pediments of the Regent's Palace. When all was tumbled stone and blackened ruin, all that would be left of the city was a whisper on the breeze of what once stood here – the remains of a city that had defied a god.

I will give all of what I am, unto this last... For many shall be called to the grace of Sigmar, but few chosen.

They crowded the brackets of the gate, pushing in with shield and spear, their faces as cold and pitiless as the mourning masks of Lament. Men fell from them and women cowered. Brave souls tried to fight and were brushed aside, their swords dead in their hands. Spears were shaken and the points came surging through the breasts of those who stood against them. Blood watered the pale marble flagstones and bodies lay in silent repose.

She ran and it was as if a golden light enveloped her. She saw Lycus fall back, blood against his face, his sword up. He was screaming to his comrades, but his voice was silent in her mind. The wind whipped at her robes. She felt joy and anger, love and hatred, gratitude, and bitter scorn. She ran and the dead were before her.

Lycus cried out. Their eyes met as she brought the hammer down. It was as though the golden light infused everything around her but was most radiant in the face of the man she loved.

She smiled, and the light burst apart, and the hordes of the dead were scoured and blackened from the gate, nothing but ash on the breeze – and then all she could see was the image of her grandfather growing closer and closer, smiling gently, his strong right hand reaching out for her.

There was a luminescence that covered all things in its celestial grace, and slowly it faded to a clean, pure point of light in the centre of all that she was and had ever been, burning brighter than any sun.

It was her soul, she realised. Her soul was free at last.

28

The afterburn of the light blinded me. I covered my eyes, but when I looked back Selene was gone.

Prisms and flashes of white burned in my eyes. My face felt as if it had been scorched and I found I was weeping. I stumbled and fell back, my sword so notched it was less than useless. I threw it aside and unstrapped the broken helmet from my head, staggering to the gutter at the side of the road. I fell down onto the cool grass of a mansion forecourt. I saw the road curve away ahead of me, leading up through a line of pavement trees towards the palace grounds. I looked back towards the gate.

The marble flagstones were charred black. The gates smouldered with flame. The Bonereapers that had besieged them were scattered lumps of charcoal and ash, just a twist of drifting smoke.

All the men and women who had fought with me were dead, cut down by the Bonereapers before they were immolated, their bodies lying broken on the ground. I saw Zylina, her fused eye crusted with blood, but I could not see Selene. It was as if she had simply stepped into that flash of light and vanished. Not a trace of her remained.

I looked to the heavens, where the mouldering skies of Shyish rippled and swam. Perhaps her god had taken her from here as payment for her faith, snatching her up in a flash of lightning? Perhaps even now she dwelled with Sigmar in sympathy and grace, and looked down on all that she had left behind?

'Selene…' I whispered to the sky. I wiped the tears from my face.

The Bonereapers who had breached the gate had been destroyed, but they were a mere fraction of Zothar's army. Already I could hear more of them surging up the avenue from the second tier towards me, clashing their weapons on their shields. There was only one last gate remaining and it was a mere ornament that barred the entrance to the palace grounds. Whatever Selene had done, she had bought me time at least. I got unsteadily to my feet and ran.

Necrotic skulls and cursed stele fell from above, cast high into the pinnacle of the city by the Mortek Crawlers down on the plains. The screams of this dread ordnance cut through me like knives, but I tried to block my ears against it. I saw missiles strike the portico of the palace as I burst through the gate, barring it behind me. A pillar cracked and fell, the mantled architrave tipping with it and scattering in fragments to the marble floor below. There was a great cloud of dust and smoke, a whisper of dread spirits, although after ten years in the bowels of Athrabis they did not frighten me. I ran on, up the short path towards the palace doors, which lay open onto the hallway beyond. The brands of the two torches on either side of the door were dull.

'Mother!' I called.

I ran across the marble floor of the hall, past the frescoes on the wall, the tapestries, and the sconces with their dormant lamps. The high windows cast a dull light onto the floor. I called for her again, heard her voice at the head of the staircase on the far side of the hall. She was sitting there on the top step, her arms wrapped around her knees. Her bodyguards were gone. Her face was a blank mask, her diadem thrown aside. I remembered the image I had had of that diadem on King Zothar's wall, along with all the other trophies of his conquests and victories. I hoped that in the final destruction of the city it would be lost forever. If all Zothar took from Lament was the memory of its defeat, then he would have to be content.

'Lycus,' she said. Her voice was dreamy and detached. For a moment I worried that she had taken poison. 'Lycus, you're alive…'

'It's over, Mother,' I said. 'The city has fallen. I do not even have a sword to defend you when they reach the palace, and we have only moments before they're here. Perhaps, from the gardens at the back, you could climb down to the second tier, take your chances at the southern wall. It is a long drop, but there is ivy that grows there, and its roots may be strong…'

'No, my child,' she said, again in that dreamy voice. Death was already near her, I saw. She had made her peace with it. 'There is no use in running, not now. Selene…?'

I swallowed, looked away. 'She is gone,' I said. 'The Bonereapers had breached the gate and she came running, her hammer held high. And then…'

There was a roar from the shadows on the other side of the hall. I spun around to see Dardus, knife in hand, bare feet slapping on the marble as he ran at me. The tangled hair streamed back from his head, his gap-toothed snarl like a rabid dog's. There was blood on his face, dust and mud on his feet, and his tunic was torn. I had time to wonder how many Bonereapers he had fought through, just so he could plant that knife in my chest.

'You killed her!' he screamed. 'All of this is your fault, Lycus, every piece of this disaster has been wrought by your hand!'

He swept in with the blade, low to high, the point skimming over the planes of my breastplate. I threw myself back and circled him warily. I was unarmed, exhausted, my eyes still dancing with the lights that Selene had called down from the heavens.

'Zothar is to blame,' I said. 'Not I. We live and die by his design.'

He lunged in, stabbing the blade at my throat. I caught his wrist in one hand, tried to snap an elbow onto the bridge of his nose, but he twisted his head, ducked, slammed his shoulder into my stomach. I fell back and without a pause the knife came in again to slice a cut across my cheek.

'And did any of us complain, all those years?' he said. 'If I had been Neophron, none of this would have happened. I would have served. I would have reigned over you and if I had ever had the temerity to rebel, it would have been with the army of Athrabis at my back!'

He thrust the knife underhand to stab up into my stomach, but I blocked his arm and kicked out, sweeping his feet from him. It was an old move Khetera had used on me innumerable times in the course of my training. I had learned it well.

Dardus landed heavily and rolled away, winded, the knife spinning off across the marble. I scooped it up, held it at guard, waited for him to come to me. There was so much anger in him, I knew he would not fight rationally, as a trained man. He didn't want to live. He only wanted me to die first.

'The prize was mine,' he wheezed as he regained his breath. 'On the Tower, you threw me to the ground and stole it from me. I would have won. And none of this would have happened.'

'I did not cheat,' I said. 'But if the prize still means so much to you, then come and take it. Give Zothar my head and see if he will let you reign in the ruins of Lament.'

He gave an inarticulate scream and charged. His eyes were deranged, and all the years of his hatred flowed through them into me. I almost felt sorry for him. But then I thrust the knife up and its blade was in his throat, and his blood was spilling out over my hand.

Gently I laid him to the ground as the life flowed out of him. His hands plucked at my arm. He gasped against the blood that poured from his mouth. I leaned down as he groaned his last words.

'Arius…!' he said. 'Selene…!' And then he could say nothing more.

I wiped the blood from my hand, turned to see my mother sobbing on the stairs, her face covered. I felt my heart would break.

The Jackal Queen, I thought. *The last queen of Lament.*

I threw down the knife, and then I walked from the palace to seek what terms I could with my father.

29

The legion was ranked up in the agora and the flames still burned in the lowest tier when Zothar deigned to enter the city. His Deathriders hunted those who had fled into the hills. Companies of Mortek Guard moved from house to house to put everyone who had survived the assault to the sword. Phaetor writhed at Zothar's side, appalled at this waste of bone.

'We have taken more casualties than I would have expected, my liege,' he said. 'Let us replenish our losses while we are here.'

'Leave it,' Zothar said. 'Let the vultures feast when we are done, but Lament will give nothing more to the Legion of Athrabis.'

He moved on his steed through the ranks of his troops, glancing at the smouldering ruin of the Tower of the Moon. It was no more than a ring of heat-cracked stone now, scattered across the flagstones from where it had fallen. The platforms for the dead had been burned away. The corpses of Lament would no longer feed the sky. He lived again in the depths of his memories, for the briefest moment; he saw Neophron's hand slipping on the stone, the poised and endless moment as he met the open air. More than anything, Zothar wished he could drag the Jackal Kings back here through all the dead centuries and show them what had finally become of their city.

This is what you made me do, he thought. *Even now, I take no pleasure in it, and it costs me more than you know.*

Eventually the screaming stopped, and the cries of the dying faded away across the rooftops. Houses gave a guttering crash as their walls collapsed. Trees were pillars of flame, bending to the course of the breeze. Smoke curled sinuously through what remained of the streets.

They brought Neophron from the palace at the pinnacle of the city. Zothar slipped from his saddle as the Mortek Guard marched him down what had been the Grand Avenue into the agora, flanking him on either side. He had shed his armour and his tunic was torn and bloodstained. He limped from a wound in his leg. His face was smeared with dirt and blood, his black hair lank with sweat, but his green eyes pierced as sharply as they ever had; they were proud and unbowed. They were the eyes of a man who had fought to his utmost and kept his honour.

'King Zothar,' he said, as he limped near. Zothar signed for the Mortek Guard to release him, although he thought the boy might fall, he was so exhausted.

'Do you surrender?' Zothar said. 'You note that I give you this choice, one which is ever denied to my enemies.'

'Am I your enemy, Father?' he said. His voice was hoarse. He tried to smile.

'You have raised arms against Athrabis. There can be no other outcome but enmity between us… my son.'

Neophron looked to the burning wreckage of the Tower – and beyond that, to the littered streets, the rubble smouldering under twists of smoke, the very walls of the city breached and ruined.

'The Games would have taken place this month,' he said, as if recalling lost and better days. He stared into the far distance. 'The Contest would have been run, and I would have given my life so that Neophron could live again. You have lost that, Father. When I die, you will never see your son again.'

Inwardly, Zothar recoiled, although he kept his outward composure. The boy's words wounded more deeply than any spear or sword. They were sharp with the truth, that thing which no shield can guard against.

'So be it,' he forced himself to say.

'You will lose that last connection to your humanity... to that thing which still kindles a flame of goodness in you. Lament was that connection...'

'And now Lament is no more.'

He turned the fierce yellow lights of his eyes onto the boy, as if he could scour him from the flagstones with the force of his gaze. But the boy only shook his head, weary beyond his years. He glanced back over his shoulder to the tiers of the city rising level upon level above him, to the palace at the very top, its roof punctured by artillery, its gardens filthy with dust and soot.

'My mother still lives,' he said. 'She takes refuge in the palace. I will surrender myself to your judgement if you only leave her alive. Please, let her depart from this place and find safety along the coast, in some trader's caravan perhaps.'

'And why would I do this? Is mercy a quality you associate with me, child?'

'You once held a sword above her head,' he said. 'Here, where we stand. With a gesture you would have had her cut down for offending you, but at my request you spared her life. I would ask that same indulgence now. Please. If the last ten years have meant anything, then grant this, I beg you.'

Zothar stood there, silent. He tried to imagine the life this woman would live in the wilds of Shyish. There were no traders' caravans who could offer her refuge – he had seen to that, after learning where the rebels had bought their weapons. There was nothing for her on the Obsidian Coast and no chance for her to pass beyond it to more accommodating shores. If she were to survive, he would need to give her escort to the borders of his kingdom. He would have to allow her to take the song of Lament with her, to pass word of its life and death to anyone who cared to listen. A way to burnish his legend, perhaps, to remind all who might think of standing against him what they could expect…?

He looked at Neophron, the boy leaning all his weight onto his good leg, his eyes heavy with fatigue. He knew he was going to die. But would it be willingly, or with a curse on his lips?

Zothar nodded to his Hekatoi. The call went up, passed from the agora to the Grand Avenue, to the scrubland outside the city. After a moment's pause the catapult arms of the Crawlers began to stretch and throw, their dread payload soaring over the ruins of Lament to strike the roof of the palace. They did not stop until it was no more than a pile of smoking rubble.

'Kneel,' Zothar said to his son.

The boy shook his head. When he spoke, his voice was thick, as if he struggled to emerge from a cloying sleep.

'I will stand to meet this. I will die on my feet, not on my knees.'

Zothar drew his sword. He held it against the boy's neck, and it was as if a touch of ice flowed along the length of the blade to chill his bones. He had not felt anything for a thousand years, but there was a dread in him now that he could not bear. It took every last exertion of his will to tamp it down.

'Did you kill Se'bak?' Zothar said.

'Yes. If I regret anything, it is that. He was always kind to me, and yet I could not risk him telling the truth of my soul's provenance while Lament still stood.'

'And did he tell you this truth before he died?'

'No,' Neophron said. 'I did not wish to hear it. I already know the truth.'

He looked at Zothar with those bold green eyes. There was no fear in them. There was only pity, and something like love.

'And what is that truth?' Zothar asked in a whisper, so that none but them could hear it. 'That you were... that you are Neophron, the First Prince of Athrabis?'

He willed it to be so. With every fibre of what remained of his soul, he wanted this to be the truth his son had guarded from him.

'No,' the boy said. 'That I am Lycus, son of Cleon and Astraea. And that I will die not as the First Prince of Athrabis, but as the last man of Lament.'

Zothar nodded. The blade faltered in his hand. He saw again the moment that seemed to last forever in his memory, of a hand slipping on the edge of the stone, a young man falling backwards into the open air. Falling, falling for eternity...

And then he swung the sword.

Phaetor came to him as they prepared to leave.

'My liege,' he said. 'The bones of... Shall they be incorporated into you, as is the custom?'

'No,' Zothar said. He gained his saddle. 'Lament is dead, its customs with it. Raze it all to the ground.'

Phaetor bowed and slipped away. Zothar spurred his steed. He did not look back at what was behind him now. Ahead was only the desert, and Athrabis, and all the lands beyond the Obsidian Coast yet to be conquered.

'The wake is over,' he said.

EPILOGUE

She didn't like the pictures on the walls. There was something sinister about them, especially that shadow with the ravenous grin. It made her shiver. She recognised Neophron falling from the Tower. She felt afraid and made the sign of the comet against her chest as her mistress had taught her.

The boy played with his pebbles in the flickering torchlight. He looked up at her with those bold blue eyes and grinned. She smiled back, but then she felt afraid again. The cave was dank and silent around her, cold and dry and miserable. She could hear the boom and clatter from the city, and she pretended to herself that it was just the waves smacking against the shore at the base of the cliffs. That's what she said to Arius when he asked, anyway. No use frightening the boy, although he was as bold as his father and not easily scared.

Kalista sat on the dry ground and hugged her knees. She was an old woman, and she wasn't used to this. She thought of her mistress and of Selene, the priestess. One small childish part of herself hoped they were safe, but the older, more cynical part, that had given three of her own children to the Tower when they didn't live past their first birthdays, knew that they were not. No one in Lament was safe now.

She drowsed and slept awhile on the stone floor and the boy slept too. When she woke, she fed him from the stores at the back of the cave. She realised that she couldn't hear that boom and clatter any more and so she crawled carefully to the mouth of the cave, out onto the little shelf of rock before it, and peered across at the city.

She felt she wanted to cry. She didn't though. She had to be strong for the boy.

'Arius,' she called as she crawled back into the cave. 'Gather your things, it's time to go.'

'Are we going to see Mother now?' the boy said, but Kalista shook her head.

'I'm sorry, my love, but we won't see her again. She had to go.' She gathered the boy into her arms and held him close. 'She had to go somewhere, to keep you safe.'

'Where?'

The boy seemed unperturbed. He was of an age when any explanation, no matter how strange, can make sense purely because it's the only one you've got.

'She's with Sigmar now,' Kalista said. She kissed him on the forehead. She tucked the hammer pendant under his shirt and helped him pack his bag.

The boy's father had carved steps into the side of the bluff, on the sea-facing side, and although it was a slippery and dangerous climb, it was easy enough to get down to the beach. The boat was tied there, more stores packed under an oilskin sheet. The sail was unfurled, and the boat reared up against the waves as if eager to go.

Sail, the priestess had said. *Sail as far south as you can go, and then keep sailing. Sail until the Obsidian Coast is no more than a memory that wakes you in the night, and, troubled, you turn over and push it from you mind. And Sigmar watch over you every moment of your journey, until my son is safe.*

Kalista felt the tears coming again, but she remembered those words and held them close. She remembered Sigmar and she felt strong.

Arius clambered aboard the boat and Kalista pushed it off, and then the sail was buckling in the breeze and carrying them away from the shore. She held the rudder, so they cut to the south. The boy turned to her and laughed as the salt spray kicked up around them.

Strange, Kalista thought. For a moment there, in the wan morning light, his eyes had looked almost green.

ABOUT THE AUTHOR

Richard Strachan is a writer and editor who lives with his partner and two children in Edinburgh, UK. Despite his best efforts, both children stubbornly refuse to be interested in tabletop wargaming. His first story for Black Library, 'The Widow Tide', appeared in the Warhammer Horror anthology *Maledictions*, and he has since written the Age of Sigmar novels *Blood of the Everchosen*, *The End of Enlightenment* and *Hallowed Ground*.

YOUR NEXT READ

PRINCE MAESA
by Guy Haley

Discover the tragic tale of Prince Maesa, a nomadic aelf willing to brave the terrible might of Nagash to find respite from his grief.

For these stories and more, go to blacklibrary.com, games-workshop.com, Games Workshop and Warhammer stores, all good book stores or visit one of the thousands of independent retailers worldwide, which can be found at games-workshop.com/storefinder

YOUR NEXT READ

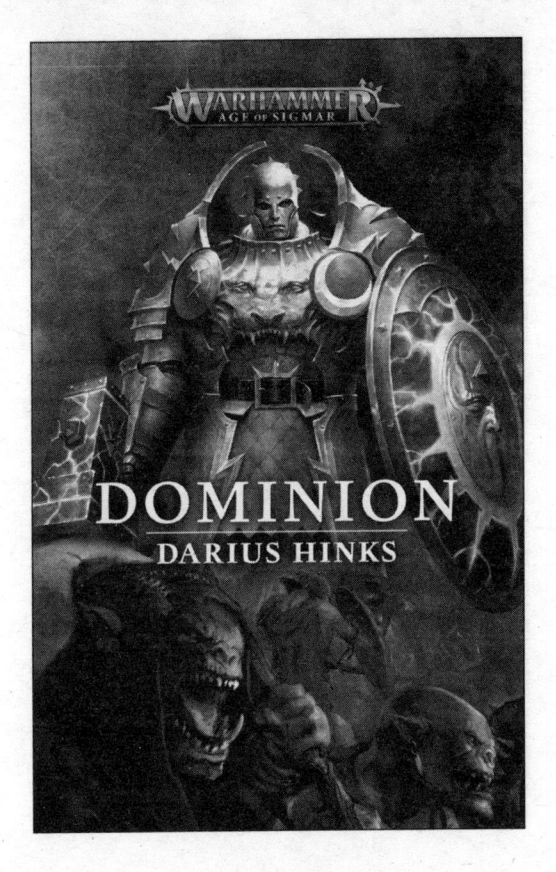

DOMINION
by Darius Hinks

Witness the destructive forces that are on the rise in the Realm of Beasts first-hand, and see the indomitable defences of Excelsis tested like never before.

For these stories and more, go to **blacklibrary.com**, **games-workshop.com**, Games Workshop and Warhammer stores, all good book stores or visit one of the thousands of independent retailers worldwide, which can be found at **games-workshop.com/storefinder**

YOUR NEXT READ

CURSED CITY
by C L Werner

When a series of vicious murders rock the vampire-ruled city of Ulfenkarn, an unlikely group of heroes – a vampire hunter, a vigilante, a wizard, and a soldier – must discover the truth even as the city's dread ruler takes to the streets and the bloodletting increases.

For these stories and more, go to blacklibrary.com, games-workshop.com, Games Workshop and Warhammer stores, all good book stores or visit one of the thousands of independent retailers worldwide, which can be found at games-workshop.com/storefinder